This book should be returned to any branch of the
Lancashire County Library on or before the date shown

Lancashire County Library
Bowran Street
Preston PR1 2UX

Lancashire
County Council

www.lancashire.gov.uk/libraries

LANCASHIR

30118

D0411634

THRICE *the* BRINDED CAT HATH MEW'D

"Bradley's heroine is one of the most delightful, and one of the sharpest, sleuths to come along in a long, long time."

—*Alfred Hitchcock Mystery Magazine*

"The preteen version of Miss Marple . . . In addition to the meticulous investigations, what makes these novels, including this eighth in the series, so enjoyable is the personality of the primary character who, while being a murder investigator savant, is also an emotionally vulnerable little girl. It is a very unusual combination . . . and it works."

—*Mystery Scene*

As **CHIMNEY SWEEPERS COME** *to* **DUST**

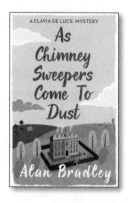

"Eleven-year-old Flavia de Luce, perhaps **contemporary crime fiction's most original character**—to say she is Pippi Longstocking with a Ph.D. in chemistry (speciality: poisons) barely begins to describe her—is finally coming home."

—*Maclean's*

"Plot twists come faster than Canadian snowfall. . . . Bradley's sense of observation is as keen as gung-ho scientist Flavia's. . . . The results so far are **seven sparkling Flavia de Luce mysteries**."

—LibraryReads

"Even after all these years, Flavia de Luce is still **the world's greatest adolescent British chemist/busybody/sleuth**."

—*The Seattle Times*

The DEAD *in* THEIR VAULTED ARCHES

"Bradley's latest Flavia de Luce novel reaches a new level of perfection. . . . These are **astounding, magical** books not to be missed."

—*RT Book Reviews* (Top Pick)

"It's **hard to resist** either the genre's pre-eminent preteen sleuth or the hushed revelations about her family."

—*Kirkus Reviews*

"Excellent . . . Flavia retains her droll wit. . . . The solution to the murder is typically neat, and the conclusion sets up future books nicely."

—*Publishers Weekly* (starred review)

SPEAKING FROM AMONG *the* BONES

"The precocious and irrepressible Flavia **continues to delight.** Portraying an eleven-year-old as a plausible sleuth and expert in poisons is no mean feat, but Bradley makes it look easy."

—*Publishers Weekly* (starred review)

"Bradley's Flavia cozies, set in the English countryside, have been **a hit** from the start, and this fifth in the series continues to charm and entertain."

—*Booklist*

I AM HALF-SICK *of* SHADOWS

"**Every Flavia de Luce novel is a reason to celebrate,** but Christmas with Flavia is a holiday wish come true for her fans."

—USA *Today* (four stars)

"This is a classic country house mystery in the tradition of Agatha Christie, and Poirot himself would approve of Flavia's skills in snooping and deduction. Flavia is everything a reader wants in a detective—she's smart, logical, intrepid and curious. . . . This is a **refreshingly engaging** read."

—RT *Book Reviews*

"This is a **delightful read through and through.** We find in Flavia an incorrigible and wholly lovable detective; from her chemical experiments in her sanctum sanctorum to her outrage at the idiocy of the adult world, she is unequaled. Charming as a stand-alone novel and a guaranteed smash with series followers."

—Library *Journal* (starred review)

A RED HERRING
Without MUSTARD

"Bradley's third book about tween sleuth Flavia de Luce will make readers forget Nancy Drew."

—*People*

"Think preteen Nancy Drew, only savvier and a lot richer, and you have Flavia de Luce. . . . Don't be fooled by Flavia's age or the 1950s setting: *A Red Herring* isn't a dainty tea-and-crumpets sort of mystery. It's shot through with real grit."

—*Entertainment Weekly*

"Bradley's characters, wonderful dialogue and plot twists are a most winning combination."

—*USA Today*

The WEED That STRINGS the HANGMAN'S BAG

"Flavia is incisive, cutting and hilarious . . . **one of the most remarkable creations in recent literature.**"
—*USA Today*

"Bradley takes everything you expect and subverts it, delivering **a smart, irreverent, unsappy mystery.**"
—*Entertainment Weekly*

"The real delight here is her droll voice and the eccentric cast. . . . **Utterly beguiling.**"
—*People* (four stars)

"**Endlessly entertaining** . . . The author deftly evokes the period, but Flavia's sparkling narration is the mystery's chief delight. Comic and irreverent, this entry is sure to build further momentum for the series."
—*Publishers Weekly* (starred review)

The SWEETNESS *at the* BOTTOM *of the* PIE

"**Impressive** as a sleuth and enchanting as a mad scientist . . . Flavia is most endearing as a little girl who has learned how to amuse herself in a big lonely house."
    —Marilyn Stasio, *The New York Times Book Review*

"Sophisticated, series-launching . . . It's **a rare pleasure** to follow Flavia as she investigates her limited but boundless-feeling world."
    —*Entertainment Weekly* (A–)

"**A delightful new sleuth.** A combination of Eloise and Sherlock Holmes . . . fearless, cheeky, wildly precocious."
    —*The Boston Globe*

By Alan Bradley

Flavia de Luce Novels

The Sweetness at the Bottom of the Pie

The Weed That Strings the Hangman's Bag

A Red Herring Without Mustard

I Am Half-Sick of Shadows

Speaking from Among the Bones

The Dead in Their Vaulted Arches

As Chimney Sweepers Come to Dust

Thrice the Brinded Cat Hath Mew'd

The Grave's a Fine and Private Place

Flavia de Luce Stories

The Curious Case of the Copper Corpse

The Grave's a Fine and Private Place

A Flavia de Luce Novel

ALAN BRADLEY

ORION

First published in Great Britain in 2018 by Orion Books
an imprint of The Orion Publishing Group Ltd,
Carmelite House, 50 Victoria Embankment,
London EC4Y 0DZ

An Hachette UK company

1 3 5 7 9 10 8 6 4 2

A CIP catalogue record for this book
is available from the British Library.

ISBN (Hardback) 978 1 4091 7288 8

Printed and bound by CPI Group (UK) Ltd, Croydon. CR0 4YY

To Shirley, my inspiration

The grave's a fine and private place,
But none, I think, do there embrace.

—Andrew Marvell, *To His Coy Mistress* (1681)

The GRAVE'S *a* FINE
and PRIVATE PLACE

·ONE·

I AM ON MY deathbed.

Again.

Although I have done everything in my power to survive, it has not been enough. A human being can only bear so much.

I turn my face to the wall in bitter remembrance.

Father had died suddenly at Christmas, leaving a colossal vacuum which we quickly realized would never—*could* never—be filled. In some strange way, he had been the secret glue which held us all together, and with his passing my sisters and I, never friends at the best of times, had now—and quite inexplicably—become the most deadly of mortal enemies. Each of us, wanting desperately to be in charge—to gain some control over her shattered life—found herself at odds with the others at every turn.

Words and crockery were thrown with equal carelessness. It didn't seem to matter much who was hit.

With our family on the verge of breaking up, Aunt Felicity had come down from London to sort us out.

Or so she claimed.

In case we had forgotten it, we were quickly reminded of the fact that our dear auntie was—as *The Book of Common Prayer* so charitably puts it—a woman who followed the devices and desires of her own heart.

In short, she was at best a stubborn old woman and at worst a bully and a tyrant.

Buckshaw was to be sold at once, Aunt Felicity insisted, even though in law it was mine to do with as I pleased. Feely was to be married off to her fiancé, Dieter Schrantz, with all haste—or at least as quickly as possible—as soon as a respectable period of mourning had been observed.

Daffy would be sent up to Oxford to read English.

"Who knows but that, given time, you might even become a gifted teacher," Aunt Felicity had said, upon which Daffy had thrown her teacup and saucer into the fireplace and stormed out of the room.

Tantrums were useless, Aunt Felicity had told us icily. Tantrums solve no problems, but only create new ones.

As for me, I was to be taken up to London, along with my cousin Undine, to live with Aunt Felicity until she could decide what to do with us. In my case, I knew that meant sending me somewhere to continue those studies which had been interrupted when I was chucked out of Miss Bodycote's Female Academy, in Canada.

But what of Dogger and Mrs. Mullet? What would become of *them*?

"They shall be paid off and each given a small pension in proportion to their years of service," Aunt Felicity had decreed. "And I'm sure they will both be very grateful."

Dogger fobbed off with a pension? It was unthinkable. Dogger had given us almost his entire life: first to my father, then to my mother, and later to my sisters and myself.

I pictured him sitting on a quaint wooden bench by a river somewhere, dressed in a rough-spun pensioner's jacket, forced to beg bread from the passing tourists, who took occasional snapshots of him to send home to their cretinous relatives.

Dogger deserved better than that.

And Mrs. Mullet?

Left to cook for total strangers, she would languish and die, and we would be responsible.

Our lives were looking exceedingly grim.

Then, at the beginning of February, to make matters worse, King George had died: King George VI, that lovely man who once sat and chatted so happily with me in our drawing room as if I were his own daughter; and with his passing, the entire nation—indeed all of the Commonwealth countries, perhaps even the whole world—joined in the shock and sadness of our own recent bereavement.

And what of me? What of Flavia de Luce?

I would perish, I decided.

Rather than submit to a lifetime locked in some dismal pigeon-infested London square with an aunt who valued the Union Jack more than her own blood, I would simply do away with myself.

And as an authority on poisons, I knew precisely how to accomplish it.

No cyanide for me, thank you!

I knew the symptoms all too well: the vertigo, the dizziness, the burning in the throat and stomach and, as the vagus nerve becomes paralyzed, the difficulty in breathing, the cold sweat, the feeble pulse, the muscular paralysis, the crushing heaviness of the heart, the slobbering . . .

I think it was the slobbering, more than anything, that put me off the cyanide. What self-respecting young woman would want to be found dead in her bedroom drowned in her own drool?

There were easier ways of joining the Heavenly Choir.

And so, here I am on my deathbed, all warm and cozy, my half-closed eyes moving slowly for the last time across that ghastly red-clotted mustard-yellow wallpaper.

I shall simply fall asleep and they will never find so much as a trace of what it was that did me in. How clever of me to have hit upon it!

They'll be sorry, I thought. *They'll all be sorry.*

But no! I mustn't let it end like that. Mustn't let it end with such a commonplace expression. That was the kind of platitude milkmaids died with—or match girls.

The death of Flavia de Luce demanded something greater: some great and noble words to hold in my mind as I stepped across the threshold of the universe.

But what were they to be?

Religion had been done to death.

Perhaps I could conjure up some great insight into the peculiar electron bonding of diborane (B_2H_6), for instance, or the as yet unsolved atomic valences of Zeise's salt.

Yes, that was it!

Paradise would welcome me. "Well done, de Luce," the vast crystal angels would say, flickering with frozen fire as I set foot upon their doorstep.

I hugged myself, cuddling in my own warmth.

How comfortable death was when properly done.

"Miss Flavia," Dogger said, breaking in upon my pleasant thoughts. He had stopped rowing the skiff for a few moments and was pointing.

I snapped out of my reverie in a split second. If it had been anyone but Dogger, I'd have taken my sweet time about it.

"That's Volesthorpe over there," he said, pointing. "St. Mildred's is just to the left of the tallest elm."

He knew I wouldn't want to miss it: St.-Mildred's-in-the-Marsh, where Canon Whitbread, the notorious "Poisoning Parson," had just two years ago dispatched several of his female parishioners by lacing their Communion wine with cyanide.

It had been done for love, of course. Poison and Passion, I have discovered, are as closely connected as Laurel and Hardy.

"Looks a harmless enough place," I said. "Like something from the pages of *Picturesque England*."

"Yes," Dogger said. "Such places often do. Horrific crimes can sometimes bleed a location of all feeling."

He fell into silence as he gazed across the water and I knew he was thinking of the Japanese prisoner-of-war camp in which he and Father had been so badly abused.

As I have said, Father's death, six months ago, was the reason we were now adrift on the river: my sisters, Ophelia and Daphne, and, of course, me, Flavia.

Undine, as originally planned, had already gone up to London with Aunt Felicity.

In the bow, her face damp with mosquito repellent, Feely lay languishing on a couple of striped pillows, staring down at her own reflection in the still water just ahead of our punt. She had not spoken since we set out this morning. The fingers of her right hand hammered out a tune on the gunwales—one of Mendelssohn's *Songs Without Words:* I recognized it by the rhythm—but her face was a perfect blank.

On the raised wicker seat, Daffy sat hunched over a book—Robert Burton's *Anatomy of Melancholy*—oblivious to the glorious English landscape sliding slowly by on either side.

Father's sudden and unexpected death had knocked our family into a kind of coma, brought on, I believe, by the fact that we de Luces are constitutionally incapable of expressing our grief.

Only Dogger had broken down, howling like a dog in the night, then silent and impassive in the long and tortured days that followed.

It was pitiful.

The funeral had been a shambles. Denwyn Richardson, the vicar and one of Father's oldest and dearest friends, had been seized at the outset by uncontrollable sobbing, unable to continue, and the service had to be halted until a stopgap clergyman could be found. In the end, poor old Canon Walpole was located in the next village, dragged from his sickbed, and rushed to St. Tancred's, where he finished what his colleague had begun, barking from a rattling chest cold at the graveside like a hundred hounds.

It was a nightmare.

Bent on taking charge, Aunt Felicity had (as I have said) swooped down from London, the death of her only—and younger—brother having driven her into a frenzy, during which she treated us all like particularly dim-witted galley slaves, slinging orders about like a grill cook:

"Straighten those magazines, Flavia. Put them in alphabetical and then in chronological order, right side up, in the cupboard. This is a drawing room, not a jackdaw's nest. Ophelia, fetch a mop and pull down those spider's webs. The place is like a tomb."

Then, realizing what she had said, she went all fretful with suppressed shame, and made even more hurtful remarks, which I will not report here for fear of her reading them someday and taking revenge.

Am I overdramatizing the situation? Not entirely.

"You look like a school of slugs," Aunt Felicity had told us. "You need something to burn away the slime."

And so it was decided—I'm still not entirely sure by

whom—that we all of us needed a holiday: something with charabancs and gaily striped deck chairs by the sea, or at least exposure to the great outdoors.

It was Dogger, I think, who had come up with the idea of a boat trip: of lazy days on the river, of cold-meat hampers with flasks of lemonade and ginger beer from Fortnum & Mason, of goose-down mattresses at night and hot beef roasts in an ever-changing string of country hotels.

"Think of *Huckleberry Finn*," Daffy had said. "Who knows, Flavia? You might even be fortunate enough to find a dead body in a floating house."

It seemed unlikely, but anything was better than staying at Buckshaw, which now seemed likely to remain in mourning until the last day of the last month of the end of time.

There now seemed to be a sudden damp dustiness about the house that I had never noticed before: a certain staleness of the air, as if the ashes of generations of de Luces had been shaken from the bag of a hoover and allowed to settle wherever they wished. In fact, it was Daffy who had pointed this out to me:

"It's like the moldy little church in the park in *Bleak House*," she had said with a shiver, pulling her cardigan closer about her shoulders, and referring to the book which she claimed to have been reading obsessively again and again since she was in a pram, beginning anew each time she finished. "'There is a general smell and taste as of the ancient Dedlocks in their graves.' Gaak!"

The "Gaak!" was Daffy's, not in Dickens's original.

Feely's marriage to Dieter Schrantz, which had been planned for June, was postponed out of respect to Father. There had been scenes of dinnerware thrown, wallpaper ripped, upholstery gutted, and so forth, but all of it had been in vain.

"For the death of a parent, a heavy mourning period of six months is laid on," Aunt Felicity said, betraying her military attachments, no matter how top secret they were supposed to have been. "And not a day less. And all your shrieking cuts no ice with me."

And that was that.

What should have been a time of bliss now became a nightmare as Feely's nerves, fear, and anger seized reason by the throat and shook it dead. The result was a spectacular series of split-ups and reconciliations with Dieter, followed by suddenly renewed outbreaks of hostility that would have put even Genghis Khan to shame.

Through it all, Dieter had been a brick, but had at last, as all heroes must sooner or later do, retired to lick his wounds.

And so it came to pass that we had packed up with little ado—except on the part of Dogger, who was never ill-prepared—and set out on what was hoped would be a time of healing.

But things didn't turn out that way.

By the time we were finally able to make our first escape from Buckshaw, Father had been dead for nearly six months, during which it had seemed, at least in the beginning, as if Dogger had lost some essential part of his soul. But as the days went on, it became ever more apparent—to me, anyway—that he was gaining something greater.

In the past several weeks especially, Dogger had been acquiring a glow. It's hard to describe, but I'll do my best.

It was not a superficial effect, as if he had just shaved and patted his face with a bay rum lotion, for Dogger would never stoop to such artifice.

No, it was as if he had begun to grow a nimbus: that pale radiance which, in paintings of the medieval saints, is portrayed as a gold halo about the head, as if the saint in question were wearing an inverted brass kettle.

There are, in fact, no halos in the Bible—just as there are no cats or accordions. If it's halos you're after, you'll have to look them up in the *Encyclopaedia Britannica*, where they come between "Hallucination" and "Halogens." Physical halos, such as those observed around the moon or sun, are caused, as everybody knows, by the reflection and refraction of light by ice crystals suspended in the atmosphere. But for the halos of saints, no cause is given—although one can easily imagine. At least, I can.

In Dogger's case, it was a kind of glow, or glory, which was coming upon him only gradually. I had made a point of going into the kitchen first thing every morning to observe him closely, although I was, of course, discreet about it.

There was a rather growing pinkness of the cheeks, and I had worried at first about stramonium poisoning, or plague. But since Dogger knew better than to handle the potted Datura plant (*Datura stramonium*) that grew in my chemical laboratory, and because the Black Death had been extinct in England since a last reported case near Ipswich had taken the life of a Mrs. Bugg in 1918, I decided that Dogger's growing radiance could be only for the good.

And so it was. On this particular morning in June, sitting dead center in the skiff, digging the blades of the sculls firmly into the warm muddy river water, Dogger was as handsome and as healthy as I had ever seen him: like a cinema star, in fact. If this were a film, rather than real life, he would be played perhaps by John Mills, squinting knowingly with a slight smile into the morning sunshine as if he saw already what lay just round the next bend. And perhaps he did.

"Have you ever been here before, Dogger?" I asked. "On this particular stretch of the river, I mean?"

"Many years ago, Miss Flavia," he answered, "but that was in another life."

And I knew enough to leave it at that.

I gazed across the water at the rich and comforting shades of the churchyard.

Most people probably never stop to think about why our burial places are so green. But if they ever did, their faces might turn the very shade of that graveyard grass, for underneath the picturesque moss and lichen, and beneath all those weathered stones, is a slowly simmering chemical stew, bubbling and burbling away in the dark earth as our ancestors and neighbors, with the help of a little chemistry, are returned to their Maker.

"For dust thou art, and unto dust shalt thou return," the Bible tells us.

"Ashes to ashes, dust to dust," says *The Book of Common Prayer*.

But both of these books, having been written mostly in good taste, fail to mention either the stinking jelly or the oozing liquids and the gaseous phases through which each of us must pass on our way to the Great Beyond.

The average churchyard is a first-rate meat tenderizer.

Shocking, perhaps, but true.

In an issue of *The Illustrated London News* from several years ago—which I found abandoned under a sofa in the drawing room at Buckshaw—it was reported that an extract of the humble papaya fruit was now being marketed to soften the squire's steak.

What a colossal waste! I had thought. *A faster and much more powerful and effective product could be easily manufactured simply by bottling—*

By now, we were drifting along just feet from the edge of the churchyard, and St.-Mildred's-in-the-Marsh loomed above us, the shadow of its square tower blocking the morning sun. A sudden chill came into the air, and it wasn't just from the light wind which had suddenly sprung up, signaling a change in the weather.

"It was just there by the old dock, wasn't it, Dogger, that Canon Whitbread chucked the poisoned chalice into the river?"

I knew perfectly well that it was. I had pored for ages over the photographs in *News of the World*, memorizing the details: the path, the dock, the sloping riverbank, the reeds . . . all helpfully labeled, with arrows, for the convenience of the bloodthirsty reader.

He had thrown the vessel into the river in the belief that it would sink to the bottom and remain there in the mud until Judgment Day. He hadn't counted, however, upon the villainy of some earlier churchwarden who had replaced the original silver with a thinly plated alloy replica which, unfortunately, floated and remained bobbing among the reeds for a farmer's boy to find.

"He oughtn't to have dumped it on a moonless night," I said aloud.

"Just so, Miss Flavia," Dogger said, easily able to read my thoughts. "He might have seen that it hadn't sunk."

"It might have, though," I said excitedly. "It could have been brought back up by some punter's pole or a heavy oar."

"Could have," Dogger said. "But not likely. I believe the police rejected that theory on the grounds of fragility. The rather frail replica would almost certainly have been dented by such an instrument, but it was not."

"Odd, then," I said, "that Canon Whitbread had never noticed the lightness of the substitute chalice."

"Unless it was he himself who swapped it," Dogger said.

I slapped the surface of the water in excitement, my heart thrilling at the idea that it was here, at this very spot, that the traces of cyanide and strychnine had been washed away. Perhaps some of the molecules still remained—vastly diluted, of course, but still, if the homeopathic theories of Samuel Hahnemann were to be believed, deadly effective.

"Flavia!" Daffy shouted. "You flaming idiot! You've soaked my book!"

Daffy's magnificent vocabulary always failed her when she was genuinely angry.

She slammed the volume shut and jammed it into the wicker picnic basket.

There was a blessed—but slightly tense—silence along the river now as we drifted beneath the arches of the willows. Now and then the glassy surface would be broken by a fish's bubbles. (*Do fish break wind?* I idly wondered.)

We were not far from one of the great universities. Surely someone there would know: some famous scientist—some ichthyologist, to be precise. Some young up-and-coming ichthyologist with a square jaw and curly blond hair, a pipe and blue eyes. I could drop in to consult with him about some rarefied chemical question . . . one that would make him realize instantly that I was no rank amateur . . . *The Dispersal of Cyanide and Strychnine in Riverine Fish Habitats*. Yes! That was it!

Roger, his name would be. Roger de something-or-other, to suit my own . . . from an ancient Norman family with enough arms, crests, flags, banners, and blazons to shame a secondhand automobile mart.

"Roger," I would say—

No, wait. *Roger* was too commonplace. Something you might call a dog. His name needed to be Llewellyn, pronounced the proper way: Thew-ETH-lyn, the way they do in Wales.

Yes, Llewellyn.

"Llewellyn," I would say, "if ever you have a case of piscine poisoning to solve, I should be happy to help."

Or was that too forward?

I had never actually performed an autopsy on a fish, but it couldn't be all that different from dissecting bloaters at the breakfast table.

I sighed with pleasure and let my hand dangle languidly over the side.

Something touched it. Something grazed against my fingers and I instinctively made a grab.

Was it a fish? Could I possibly have caught a fish by hand?

Had some dim-witted chub or stupid pike mistaken my trailing fingers for a bit of floating food?

Not wanting to lose the opportunity to go down in history as "Fishhook Flavia," I hung on for dear life, hooking my fingertips firmly behind the hard ridge of bone I could now so easily feel. I planted my thumb for a firmer grip. This catch was not going to become "the one that got away."

"Hold on, Dogger," I said, trying to keep my voice level and matter-of-fact. This story was going to be handed down for generations, and I wanted to make sure that my coolheadedness was properly noted. "I believe I've caught something."

Dogger stopped rowing and let the skiff drift. I could feel the dead weight of the thing dragging at my arm. It must be one of those gigantic fish—famous in local lore— that lives for centuries at the bottom of a pool. "Old Moldy," or some such name, the villagers would call it. Would they be outraged to hear that I had caught their beloved monster with my bare hands?

I smiled at the thought.

Whatever it was, it wasn't putting up much of a fight.

Although Daffy and Feely were pretending to be disinterested, both had turned toward me.

Holding on with all my strength, I gave my extended arm a good shake, taking care not to let go of my prey—whatever it might be.

I had seen photographs in the picture magazines of the American author Mr. Hemingway battling a giant marlin on the end of a ridiculously slender pole. Even *he*, I'll bet, had never landed such a fish by hand.

Flavia, I thought, *you're about to become famous.*

As the boat slowed and the water cleared, a shadow—and then a brighter patch—appeared just beneath the surface. *A fish's belly?* It was certainly light enough.

I hauled it in for closer inspection.

Although the object was upside down, it was now easily recognizable.

It was a human head—and attached to it was a human body.

My fingers were inserted firmly in the corpse's open mouth, locked behind its upper teeth.

"We'd best make for the pier, Dogger," I said.

·TWO·

BRINGING THE SKIFF ALONGSIDE the pier behind the church was not so easy a task as it might have been.

For one thing, Daffy was busily disposing, over the gunwales, of every bite she had eaten since last Thursday fortnight. If you've ever seen those cinema newsreels in which a trawler dumps its nets, you'll know what I'm talking about. To say that her gorge was rising would be a gross understatement. Hurling her guts out was more like it. To be honest, it was awe-inspiring.

If it hadn't been for the seriousness of the situation, it might even have been amusing.

Dogger, to his great credit, said not a word. A single glance over his shoulder told him all he needed to know, and he reacted accordingly. Slowly, but steadily, we edged in silence—except for Daffy's retching, of course—toward the riverbank.

Nearby boaters, of whom there were several, would assume that a young lady had been taken ill. Paste sandwiches that had gone over, perhaps, or a bit of bad tongue. It would not do to stare, and no one did. None of them could see, of course, what I was dragging by its open mouth.

As the skiff bumped against the wooden dock, Dogger handed me the tartan picnic blanket we had intended to sit upon for tea. I knew at once what he wanted me to do, and I did it.

Without attracting attention, I took the blanket with my left hand, unfolded it, and spread it casually over the floating corpse. Having made fast the skiff, Dogger stepped out into the shallow water, took hold of the shrouded figure, lifted it gently in his arms, and waded to the grassy bank beside the pier.

In another moment he had laid the body in the grass at the edge of the churchyard.

I couldn't help noticing the bruise on the back of the neck, as if the man had somehow stumbled, banged his head, and fallen into the water. Dead men don't bruise, I remembered.

"Artificial respiration?" I asked, trying to think logically.

Dogger had once told me of his studies in the Kanō system of Jiu-Jitsu, in which drowning victims had been restored to life by a sharp blow across the soles of the feet.

"I'm afraid not, miss," Dogger said, lifting a corner of the blanket. "It's too late for that. The fish have already been at this poor fellow."

And he was right: The earlobes and the nose had certainly been nibbled.

As for the rest of the face, the dead man had been handsome enough. Those long, lank red locks, now plastered down by the wet, must once have curled fetchingly enough about the lace collar of his ruffled silk shirt.

I am not making this up: It really *was* silk, as were the blue trousers, which were fastened by buttons and silken ribbons at the knee.

I had the strange impression that I was looking at someone from the eighteenth century: some time traveler who had slipped playfully beneath the surface of the water in the days of King George III, perhaps, and decided just now that enough was enough.

My next thought was this: Had anyone gone missing from a masquerade? Or from the cast of a cinema film?

Surely such a thing would have been widely reported, and yet here was this healthy young specimen (aside from being dead, of course) laid out like a trout on the riverbank as if it were the most natural thing in all the world.

He was almost too beautiful: like the *Blue Boy* of Gainsborough's famous painting, but rather more pale.

But wait! It *was* a painting he reminded me of—yet it certainly wasn't a Gainsborough. No, it was a work by a much less well-known artist named Henry Wallis.

The Death of Chatterton, it was called, and it depicted the body of that sad young poet who had poisoned himself in 1770 at the age of seventeen, having been exposed as a literary forger.

I ought to have realized this at once, but I didn't, even

though a large framed reproduction of the original had been hanging for years in a place of honor on my bed-room wall.

It is one of my favorite works of art, I must admit.

In the painting, Chatterton, his flesh an awful fish-belly white, lies stretched upon a shabby couch in his rented garret, the fingers of his left hand seeming to bare the breast in which his heart had quite recently been beating.

His right hand lies stiffly clutched on the floor, near the empty arsenic bottle.

All art ought to be this fascinating.

"Please remain where you are, Miss Ophelia and Miss Daphne," Dogger said, pulling me out of my thoughts. "Keep a sharp eye out, both up and down the river."

What a clever man, I thought. He meant to keep them occupied; keep them from going into hysterics; keep them from trampling the evidence.

It is a remarkable fact that orders given in a firm voice at the scene of a tragedy are invariably obeyed.

"If you'd be good enough to stay here, Miss Flavia," he said, "I shall go for the police."

I gave him a brisk nod and he was off, scrambling up the grassy riverbank toward the church, the wet turn-ups of his trousers sloshing round his ankles, but still dignified in spite of it.

As soon as he was gone, I lifted the corner of the blan-ket.

The pale blue eyes, which were half open, the pupils

dilated, gazed up at me in surprise—as if I had suddenly snatched a coverlet from the face of a light sleeper. The irises matched the color of his lips and the silk ribbons at his knees.

I sniffed the lips—actually touched them with the tip of my nose—but could detect nothing but the brackish smell of river water.

I leaned low over the corpse and drew up into my nostrils the smell of his eyeballs.

I was already half expecting it: the odor of apples.

Potassium cyanide, I recalled, is quite odorless until mixed with water, in which it freely dissolves to form an alkaline solution, from which prussic acid is abundantly evolved, which, when exposed to air, volatilizes to produce the smell of apples.

The tissue of the eyes, being the thinnest and softest in the body, not only are more absorbent of chemical odors than are other parts of the body, but retain them longer. If you don't believe me, take a whiff of your own tears an hour after you've eaten onions.

Also, the eyes, having been fixed in a half-closed position, would have been better protected from the diluting effect of the water than the nose and lips.

His complexion was—well, let's just say that it was interesting. Although the features were somewhat bloated, there was remarkably little lividity: a sure sign, I remembered, either that the body had not been in the water for long, or that it had been sunken in the cooler depths for several days. The fact that it had now floated up to the surface, though, was a likely indication of gaseous putre-faction. There were other possibilities, of course, but that was the most likely sequence of events.

Further physical signs (which I could have checked) might also be present, but examining these would have involved stripping the body, which, I decided, would not be decent. Besides, there wasn't time: Dogger would be returning with the police at any moment.

In drowning, it is sometimes the internal evidence which turns out to be most crucial. Obviously, I couldn't conduct a full-scale postmortem here on the riverbank. I would have to settle for the next best thing.

Placing both hands in an overlapping position on the dead man's chest, I threw all my weight into a powerful straight-armed push.

I was amply rewarded: A surprisingly rich flow of frothy broth, followed by what I took to be water, streamed out from between his blueish lips.

Reaching for my handkerchief, I blotted up the mess, folded it inward in a ball to avoid contamination, and returned it to my pocket.

Certain people—such as Mrs. Mullet, for instance—kept going on about the importance of always carrying a clean handkerchief about one's person, and for once they were right.

A quick look round told me that I had not been ob-served.

Returning to my physical examination of the corpse, I felt the palms of the dead man's hands for looseness of skin, the "glove effect" which would indicate a longer immersion in the water, but they were remarkably firm.

Almost without thinking, I raised my fingertips to my nose.

It's remarkable, really, how much we ignore our sense of smell: until, that is, we detect one extreme or another, fragrant or foul—either roses or rot. The human olfactory system has trained itself to ignore anything that doesn't matter.

I sniffed my fingers.

Aha! I hadn't really expected anything out of the ordinary, but my nose was picking up an unmistakable smell.

Paraldehyde, by all that's holy! Good old, jolly old $(CH_3CHO)_3$—a foul-smelling, foul-tasting, but colorless liquid which can be easily produced by treating aldehyde with sulfuric or hydrochloric acid. The stuff was first synthesized in 1829, and had once been combined with extract of vanilla, syrup of raspberries, and chloroform to treat insomnia. It had also been used, mixed with equal parts of cherry-laurel water, to administer subcutaneous injections to the insane.

But because of the lingering reek of the breath it produced in the patient, paraldehyde had generally been abandoned a hundred years ago. Although I had overheard someone remark that there were still those—particularly among the aristocracy—who had gone beyond alcohol and become addicted to the stuff.

I sniffed my fingertips again to reinforce my memory of the facts.

Paraldehyde poisoning, if I recalled correctly, *contracted* the pupils, whereas this poor man's were dilated. It didn't quite add up. There wasn't that sudden "click" of certainty.

It would have to wait until later. There was no time now.

I returned my attention to the lower parts of the body.

On one of the feet, which stuck out slightly beyond the far end of the blanket, was what I can only describe as a red ballet slipper. The other foot was bare. He was not a tall man, I judged: somewhat less than five and a half feet, perhaps, although it was difficult to estimate with him lying on his back and partly covered.

Yes! That was it: The man was a ballet dancer, which would account for his costume.

I was proud of myself. He had come down to the river-bank in the night, perhaps to practice his pirouettes away from prying eyes. *Swan Lake*, probably.

What a sight that must have been beneath the weep-ing willows and the sleepily flowing river—until he had misjudged—or tripped—and fallen into the dark water.

Or been pushed.

Had he become entangled in reeds or duckweed? I folded back more of the blanket. There was no vegetation clinging to his body.

Perhaps some of it had become caught up in his cloth-ing. I decided to search him.

Have you ever stuck your hands into the pockets of a corpse? Perhaps not. I myself have done it on only a cou-ple of occasions, and I can tell you that it's not always the most pleasant of occupations.

Who knows what may be lurking in the crevices of the clothing? With a drowning victim, you're at risk of eels, water snakes, crabs, and so forth, and I tried to recall quickly which species of these—such as the Chinese Mitten Crab—had been known to make their way upstream from the tidal waters of the Thames. When it comes to crabs you can never be too cautious.

I needn't have worried. Except for a wad of wet lint and a folded bit of soggy blue-lined paper from his trousers, the corpse's pockets were empty. I fished out the paper between my first and second fingers, noting as I did so that I would need to give my hands a jolly good scrubbing later because of the slime.

Smoothing it carefully with my thumb to avoid disintegration, I slowly unfolded the scrap. Something had been written upon it in pencil: a series of numbers.

54, 6, 7, 8, 9

A date perhaps? The year 1954—with 6, 7, 8, and 9 representing the months of June, July, August, and September? If so, it was still some two years in the future, since we were now in June of 1952.

People don't usually make appointments *that* far in advance.

Or could it be the combination to a safety lock? That seemed unlikely, since a series of four small numbers in strict numerical sequence would be extremely difficult to dial accurately—if it could be done at all. As Dogger had taught me, during one of our sessions devoted to the art of lock-picking, combinations generally contain at least two widely spaced numerals.

Or was it a telephone number? I couldn't be sure which exchange was represented by the first two digits, but one could always ring the number and see who picked it up on the other end.

The possibilities seemed endless, which made it all the more exciting, since possibilities are so much more thrilling than certainties—or so I've always thought.

I was about to stuff the wadded paper back into the corpse's pocket when a sudden shadow blocked the sun and fell upon the body. An electric chill shot through my bones.

I twisted round and put my hand up to block the light, but could see only a black silhouette hovering over my shoulder.

"What are you doing to Orlando?" demanded a voice, and I nearly leapt out of my liver. The speaker was seated in an antique wicker bath chair, and had rolled up in such silence that I hadn't heard her coming.

"What are you playing at? Is this a game? Another one of your larks? Get up at once, Orlando—you're soiling your silks."

"I'm sorry," I said, scrambling to my feet. "I'm afraid—"

"And well you might be, you shameless girl. What are you playing at? Answer me at once!"

My first impression of the woman was that she had a beak like a battleship: forward-jutting and powerful enough to slice through the most fearsome Atlantic breakers as if they were runny cheese.

Her snow-white hair was tied up so tightly into a large

bun at the back of her head that it gave her face the appearance of a squeezed pimple in the instant before it bursts.

The toe of a riding boot peeked out from under a lap robe, and an old school tie flopped out of a Norfolk jacket onto her ample chest. The woman seemed all odds and ends.

"What are you staring at?" she asked. "Didn't your parents teach you not to gawk?"

That did it. My parents—both of them now deceased, God rest their dear departed souls—had taught me the most important thing of all, which was to show some spine in the face of bullying.

I know that I ought to have been a fountain of condolences, a rock of sympathy in a sea of sadness, but this woman had stepped across my line of decency. I couldn't bring myself to touch her, let alone hug her.

"Orlando is dead," I informed her. "He drowned. We found the body."

I could tell she was not listening to me.

"Orlando, get up at once," she commanded. "The Hawthorne-Wests will be arriving in an hour, and you know how Parthia hates to be kept waiting."

Orlando's already pallid complexion was tinted an even more awful green by the closeness of the grass, and I couldn't help noticing that a couple of dandelions beside his ears were reflecting little yellow bruises onto his cheeks, like dabs of rancid butter.

"That's enough, Orlando," the woman said, releasing a foot from its stirrup beneath the lap robe and giving his shoulder a prod. "Get up now and come along."

I seized her arm.

"Better not touch him," I said. "He's dead. The police have been called."

The woman looked up at me—then back at the corpse—then back at me again. Her eyes widened and her vast and lightly whiskered upper lip curled back as a horrible wail shattered the quiet air—rising and falling like a demented air-raid siren.

Her ear-splitting screech caused Feely and Daffy to swivel their heads in our direction—but only for a quick glance, returning at once to scouting the river as Dogger had instructed them to do.

"See no evil, hear no evil" was their motto, and some small part of me didn't blame them. Being embroiled with bodies is not so simple as some people seem to think it is.

Looking away is easy, but staring Death in the face takes more than a strong stomach.

Dogger, I saw, was now returning through the church-yard, accompanied by two other persons. One, it was obvious by his uniform, was the village constable; the other, by his dog collar, the vicar, a roly-poly, jolly-looking gen-tleman.

Thank heavens, I thought. I would no longer have to deal with this howling harpy on my own.

"Stand back, please," the constable said, as I knew he would. I was happy to obey by getting to my feet and shuf-fling backward to a point where I could watch without being watched. Of such small tools from one's bag of tricks are great investigators made.

I know how stuffy that must sound, but it's true.

Dogger and I stood looking on as the constable—gingerly, I thought—peered under the corner of the blanket. Having satisfied himself that he was dealing with a dead body, he tugged at his jacket, straightened his tie, turned to us, and said, "Yes. Well, then . . ."

He jabbed his thumb vaguely toward the church and, presumably, the high street.

"I'd be obliged if you'd all step across to the Oak and Pheasant. The landlord lays on a good spread of pickled hocks and cheese, if you feel up to it, that is. I shall be along in due course."

If we felt up to it? I suppose he meant to sound solicitous. Or was it supposed to be humorous? Whose leg did this village idiot think he was pulling?

I had half a mind to tell him that there was nothing I loved more than gorging on cold ham while examining a particularly juicy corpse.

I caught Dogger's eye before I replied.

"That's very thoughtful of you, Constable," I said. "I think I could stand a whiff of smelling salts about now."

Because it was expected of a girl my age, I flashed him a quick but slightly sickly grin, leaving him to work out what I meant.

"Have we seen everything that we need to?" I asked Dogger from the corner of my mouth, as we walked to fetch Feely and Daffy from the punt.

"We have, indeed, Miss Flavia," he said. "More than enough."

·THREE·

"How perfectly icky!" Daffy whined when we were seated round a table in the saloon bar of the Oak and Pheasant.

I hadn't the faintest idea whether she was referring to the pub, the corpse, or the wailing woman in the bath chair we had left to the tender mercies of the constable on the riverbank.

Nor did I particularly care.

Feely shifted uneasily in her chair, giving quick, darting glances round the room. I knew at once that she was unable to hide her discomfort at being seated with a servant.

I don't know what she was worried about. The only other patrons in the pub were a group of rather shabby men of assorted sizes, all wearing colored kerchiefs round their necks, all busily poking one another in the chest and laughing loudly at the others' jokes.

Not that Dogger would have minded. We were on holiday, and so was he. Rank and station were forgotten—or were supposed to be. Things were different since the war. Feely had been brought up in a different world, and it showed.

I pitied my sister. Her life had not been an easy one—especially recently. She was mourning Father and moping over her postponed marriage. To someone used to getting her own way, it must have seemed like the Apocalypse.

"What'll it be?" the landlord asked, his pencil poised. "Ploughman's lunch all round?" In his apron and shirt-sleeves he was the very picture of an innkeeper in a cartoon from *Punch*.

"A pint of Guinness, please," Feely said, and I nearly fell out of my chair. It was the first time she had spoken since breakfast.

"Are you over eighteen?" the landlord asked. "Sorry, miss, but I'm obliged to inquire."

"I can vouch for her," Dogger said.

"I'll have the same," Daffy blurted, and the man was too taken aback to repeat his question. She was evidently even more shaken than I had thought.

"Ginger beer for me," I said. "And if it's not too much trouble, I'd like it warmed on the back of the cooker for three minutes."

It's always a good idea to demand some quirky service, to let them know that you're not just anybody.

I knew that with an investigation getting under way over against the churchyard wall, we were bound to be in this village for quite some time, and it was essential to establish priorities at the outset. You can't command respect after the starting whistle's been blown—especially among strangers.

The landlord gave me a squinty eye, but he wrote down my order.

"And you, sir?" he asked, turning to Dogger.

"Milk," Dogger replied. "A small glass of milk. It's pasteurized, I presume?"

"Pasteur-*ized* and past your ears, sir!" The landlord laughed, slapping his knee. I could have slapped his face. "You've never seen milk so pasteurized as our own. Why, just yesterday I was saying to Mr. Clemm, our vicar, 'You'll get no trade from *our* kitchen!'—meaning, of course, in the funeral department. He wasn't amused—like Queen whatsername."

I stopped listening. I knew all too well the dangers of unpasteurized milk.

The chemist Louis Pasteur was, after all, one of my great heroes. I had eagerly memorized the symptoms of tuberculosis—also known as consumption, or phthisis—and how the bacillus responsible caused the victim's lungs to turn into a kind of weeping cheese: the features becoming livid and darkening as the blood retains excessive carbon, the hectic fevers, the racking cough, the racing pulse, the wasting muscles, the night sweats, and the agitated delirium—the mind, however, remaining cruelly clear and focused almost until the very end.

There had been a time when, after first reading up on these horrors, I had refused to drink so much as a drop of milk without first taking it to my chemical laboratory and pasteurizing it personally, then examining it closely under the microscope for rogue bacilli.

Nowadays, of course, since the discovery of penicillin in 1928 by Alexander Fleming, no one dies of consumption except in the cinema, where its onset is invariably signaled by tragic glances, sprayed-on perspiration, soot rubbed below the eyes, dramatic coughing, and spitting of fake blood always—conveniently—into spotlessly white handkerchiefs.

My fascinating train of thought was interrupted by the arrival of our drinks.

"Cheers!" Daffy said quietly, raising her glass to each of us in turn. She was showing off—not giving a thought to the seriousness of the situation. Even if taste and decency are chucked out the window, there is one rule that remains: keeping a long face in the presence of death.

I shot her a wet-blanket look.

"Sorry," she said, surprisingly humbled.

In the silence that followed, I let my mind drift across the room, out the door, across the road, and through the churchyard to the riverbank.

Who was the dead man, and how had he come to drown? Had it been an accident, or—

"I want to go home," Feely said suddenly. "I'm not feeling well. I've had enough."

Oddly enough, I knew exactly what she meant. It wasn't just the finding of a corpse on the river. As I have said, Father's death had told terribly upon her, and the continued postponements of her wedding date, and the resulting battles, even more.

Poor Feely, I thought. Her life had been a will-o'-the-wisp, with true happiness always just beyond her grasp.

I had an idea, but it would keep until after we had eaten. I touched her arm as a kind of "message received" signal.

Was the look that she returned a grateful one? With Feely, one could never know.

Dogger, as I knew he would, ordered the ploughman's lunch, Feely a small salad, and Daffy a small dish of steamed carrots.

"I'm sorry," she said, "but I simply can't face meat."

I plumped for plain old chutney, cheese, and pickled onions, a favorite dish, which I had secretly named "The Embalmer's Breakfast." It was as like a chemical lab as you could get when away from home.

We ate in silence. The things that Dogger and I might have talked about were not suitable for my sisters' ears, while the topics I might have discussed with them were unfit for his.

As we were finishing our meal, the door of the public bar next door burst open, and a loud, breathless voice announced: "Somebody's drowned! They've fished a dead 'un out of the river!"

A general hubbub arose at once as chairs and boots grated noisily on the floor. Before you could say "Ninepins!" the place had emptied, and the only sound was that of a few retreating voices.

"Come," I said, tugging at Feely's arm. It was time to put my plan into execution.

"I'm not going back there," she said. "I don't feel well. I want to go home."

"I know," I told her, not loosening my grip. "But think—what's across the road?"

"A drowned body," she answered, shuddering.

"Besides that." She looked up at me dumbly.

"A church!" I said. "And where there's a church, there's an organ. No smoke without fire, and so forth. Come on, let's go. My ears are parched. I need a bit of Bach."

Something dawned on Feely's face. It wasn't exactly happiness, but it would do.

As she got to her feet, I took her forefinger and led her toward the door. It was the first time I had willingly touched my sister's hand since I was nine months old and learning to walk.

Outside, the June weather was glorious, and we both had to shield our eyes against the summer sun.

We crossed the road and approached the church along the gravel path.

ST.-MILDRED'S-IN-THE-MARSH, it said on the weathered signboard, and I gave a shiver of pleasure. The ghost of Canon Whitbread might, even at this moment, be peeping round one of those old, weather-blasted tombstones, looking over my shoulder.

As I stared up at the square tower, I had the distinct feeling that someone was watching us, but in a moment it had passed. Churches can do that to you.

In the porch, Feely made a beeline up the curving stone steps to the organ loft, and I took a pew at the front on the center aisle.

There is nowhere you can feel the presence of the dead more than in the damp dimness of an empty church. If you listen, you can hear them breathing. I know that makes no sense, because the dead don't breathe—at least in an earthly way. But you can hear them nonetheless.

I turned up the volume on my almost supernatural hearing. This was a trait I had inherited from my dead mother, Harriet, which, although generally a pain in the ear, sometimes came in handy.

But if the dead were whispering today, they were not addressing me. Perhaps the lady victims of Canon Whitbread were gathering round the Communion rail for a jolly good chin-wag. Wasn't it, after all, the very spot where they had been poisoned?

I stared at the altar with new interest. Was there a slight shimmering of the air? If so, it was nothing you could put your finger on. A thermal of warm air, perhaps, set into motion by the outside temperature: a silent gust from one of the underfloor heating ducts.

It was either moving air or ancient holiness, and if I had to make a bet, I'd put my money on a cold draft.

After a few hollow knocks and the rustle of paper somewhere at the back of the church, the organ began to speak. I recognized the melody at once: Johann Sebastian Bach's *The Art of Fugue*.

It began with the note of a single pipe, which sounded

at first like a dry bone singing itself to sleep in a crypt somewhere in the night. But it wasn't long before the other bones joined in—Bach's playful organ notes rising and flitting about high up among the rafters and hammer beams like a squadron of deliriously happy bats. An apt comparison, if I do say so myself, since the word *fugue* means *flight*.

Oh, it was delicious!

I sighed, took a deep breath, and closed my eyes.

Old Johann Sebastian, I decided, must have had a mind like mine, capable of being everywhere at once.

I have always found organ music to be great fertilizer for thoughts. With Bach in my ears and no distractions, my mind accelerated like a greyhound let off the leash.

Who was the dead Orlando, and who was the woman in the bath chair? What was the relationship between them? Why had she reacted so vigorously when I told her he was dead?

More important, what was the meaning of the numbers I had found in the corpse's pocket?

My eyes popped open at the thought, and were drawn immediately to the numbers posted on the hymn boards above the pulpit and the lectern. These were, of course, the hymns which were to be sung at the next service—or *had* already been sung at the last one.

Three only were listed: Hymns 289, 172, and 584.

I swiveled round and plucked a copy of *Hymns Ancient and Modern* (*Ancient and Laundered*, as Daffy calls it) from the rack on the back of my pew.

I thumbed my way to Hymn 289:

Days and moments quickly flying
Blend the living with the dead;
Soon will you and I be lying
Each within his narrow bed.

How I adore hymns! They have a sense of perspective that's all too often missing in everyday life.

Not much correspondence, though, with the numbers in the corpse's pocket. I called to mind the wrinkled bit of paper: 54, 6, 7, 8, 9, it had said.

Well, the 8 and the 9 of the first hymn number were the same but it wasn't enough. Two numbers out of six wins nothing on the lottery, and it didn't here, either.

I turned to Hymn 172:

Praise to the Holiest in the height
And in the depths be praise

This was more like it. I couldn't help but think of the dead Orlando, whom I had dredged from the depths, although I doubt if he was doing much praising about his predicament.

But for this hymn, only the 7 tallied. Worse odds than the previous one.

What if the numbers referred to Hymns 54, 67, and 89? My thumbs became a blur.

Hymn 54 seemed promising:

When shades of night around us close
And weary limbs in sleep repose . . .

But from there, it quickly wandered off into pity, guilt, and misery.

I flipped to Hymn 67.

The third verse had blood and water, and the fourth something about landing on the eternal shore.

I sighed and went on to 89.

Which was about Moses, fasting. Not particularly promising.

But then I remembered: *Hymns Ancient and Modern* wasn't the only flounder in the sea. No, indeed! The church, for as long as I could remember, had been tinkering with the hymnal and the prayer book so much as to make your head spin. Sunday morning services were like a steeplechase as we fanned pages in the next jump to get to the proper place.

And then, of course, there was *The English Hymnal.* That in itself was an entirely *different* kettle of fish.

Were all these fishy thoughts a kind of blasphemy? I decided not: Wasn't the fish, after all, as much a symbol of Christianity as the cross?

I twisted round again in my seat—actually got onto my knees on the pew—so that, facing backward, I could dig more deeply—I was going to say "fish," but I won't—in the book rack behind me.

And yes, as I somehow knew it would be, not far from my searching fingertips was a rather tattered copy of *The English Hymnal.*

This was larger—fatter—than *Hymns A & M,* due of course to the fact that it contained not only the words of the hymns with their titles in Greek and Latin, but also the music, as well as footnotes.

This was an industrial-sized hymnbook, intended for experts.

I turned to Hymn 54:

Ye clouds of darkness, hosts of night,
That breed confusion and affright
Begone!

Et cetera.

Could it have been a warning? That seemed unlikely.

I paged ahead to number 67:

Now is the healing time decreed.

Healing, perhaps, but disappointing.

Now only Hymn 89 was left.

My fingers were already feeling defeated.

But wait—here it was:

Soul of Jesus, make me whole,
Meek and contrite make my soul;
Thou most stainless Soul Divine,
Cleanse this sordid soul of mine.

I gave an involuntary shiver. Could this be a personal message from the universe to Flavia de Luce?

Was it like one of those oracles where you stuck your finger into the pages of the Bible at random and read out the text from wherever it landed?

I had seen Feely do this once—but only once.

"What shall I wear when Dieter takes me to the cinema on Saturday night?" she had asked, but when the Bible had replied: "My flesh is clothed with worms and clods" (Job 7:5), she had let out an unearthly shriek and canceled her date.

The hymn went on to talk about curses and ransoms, but not until the later verses. In my opinion, no one sending an encrypted threat would make use of any but the opening words. Otherwise, it would be too obscure. The intended victim would become bored and give it up before getting to the message.

I could see that the hymnbook idea was a washout, and I returned it to its rack.

Beside the two hymnals was a third book, thick and black, loose and battered from much use.

Not expecting much, I picked it up.

The Holy Bible—King James Version. It was as heavy as a brick.

Acting upon a sudden impulse, I shoved my forefinger in among its pages.

Her princes within her are roaring lions; her judges are evening wolves; they gnaw not the bones till the morrow.

Zephaniah, chapter 3, verse 3.

So much for oracles, I thought.

But, believe it or not, at that very instant, an idea came flying out of nowhere and landed on my head, like a pigeon on Lord Nelson's statue.

I turned to the front of the Bible, praying desperately for a table of contents.

Yes! Here it was—just as you would expect—at the beginning.

Genesis . . . Exodus . . . Leviticus . . .

A cold hand touched my bare arm. I leapt at least two feet into the air, and my pounding heart cowered behind my kidneys.

"I thought I'd find you here," said a voice at my ear, and I spun round in a state that was close to terror.

It was the woman from the riverbank. Once again, she had rolled up behind me in utter silence.

With my back turned to the altar, and the music from the organ, I had not seen or heard her bath chair coming. She must have entered the church through the transept.

"We got off on the wrong foot out there," she said, jerking a thumb toward the churchyard. "My fault entirely. You were only trying to help poor Orlando. I should have realized that at once."

She must have seen my astonishment. Could this be the same person who, not all that long ago, had been tearing out her hair on the riverbank?

"You must have been longing to slap my face, mustn't you? Oh, go ahead, admit it. I shouldn't have blamed you if you had."

I gave her one of those grim fishhooks-in-the-corners-of-the-mouth smiles, and turned my attention back to the open Bible.

Genesis . . . Exodus . . . Leviticus . . .

"Tell me you forgive me," she said, giving my arm a

tug. "The vicar and the constable advised me to come into the church and compose myself. Which is what I am attempting to do. But you must help me."

I tried to ignore her, but it was not easy.

"Here," she said, shoving a hand in my face. "Shake. I'm Poppy Mandrill. And who, pray tell, are you?"

"Titania Bottom," I replied, as I sometimes do when I'm annoyed.

The woman threw back her head and laughed—a surprisingly rich, warm, throaty laugh that flew up and joined the flitting notes of the organ.

"Come off it," she said. "I've directed enough Shakespeare in my time to know when my leg's being pulled."

She tapped her right knee—or at least, where her right knee ought to have been, but wasn't. I noticed for the first time that she was lacking a leg. Until now, the blanket in her lap had hidden the missing member.

"I—I'm sorry," I said, feeling like a chump.

"Don't be," she replied. "*I'm* not. It's curiously liberating, in a way. Oh, don't give me that look of pitying skepticism. I'm sick and tired of people looking at me like that. They don't know what to make of me. I may be lacking a leg but there's nothing wrong with my brain."

I had to admit to myself, grudgingly, that there was something in this woman I admired. I made a sudden decision and thrust out my hand.

"Flavia de Luce," I said, looking her in the eye as I gave her a firm old handshake to make up for my insolence.

"Tell me about Orlando," I went on, while our palms were still touching. "I feel so sorry for him."

She studied my face closely.

"And besides, I'm curious," I added.

"Fair enough," she said. "I believe you. Orlando was my . . . protégé."

An interesting word, that. I knew that it came from a French word meaning *to protect*. Feely's organ teacher, Mr. Collicutt, always referred to her as his protégé. At least, he always did before he was murdered.

But if Mr. Collicutt ever fancied he was protecting Feely from *anything,* he must have had the brains of a trilobite. My sister was born with the defensive instincts of a tiger shark.

No, there was another sense to the word, meaning a student, or pupil. That must be it.

"You were his teacher?" I asked.

Miss Mandrill sized me up before answering.

"In a sense, yes," she said at last.

I had learned some years ago by observing my friend Inspector Hewitt, of the Hinley Constabulary, that the best way to elicit further information is by keeping one's mouth firmly shut.

I said nothing—and by Jehoshaphat, it worked!

"Orlando was a very talented actor," she explained. "He might have become the greatest of our age—or of any other—had he lived. Another Gielgud—who knows? Perhaps even greater than Gielgud. He had the sensitivity and the steel combined: that precious alloy so lacking in so many of today's footlight trotters.

"All he lacked was opportunity, and now even that seems to have been snatched away from him."

By whom? I wondered grammatically. *By Fate?*

Or was Miss Mandrill suggesting that something much more sinister had taken place?

I thrust my face slightly forward to indicate intense interest.

"Well," she continued, giving her head a shake, "wherever he is now, he will be laughing at his own tragedy. That's how it's done, you know. *That* is the secret of true greatness."

She's right, I thought. I don't know how many times I've laughed aloud at the very thought of my own not inconsiderable talents.

I smiled modestly.

"And where do *you* suppose he is?" I asked, sneaking the question in under the wire, so to speak.

"Orlando?" She spoke his name with a little laugh. "Oh, he'll be perching on the edge of some mauve-tinged cloud, wiggling his toes, sipping a glass of absinthe, and chummying up to one of our more outré dead novelists. Ronald Firbank, or one of that lot."

"Not Shakespeare?" I asked, surprised.

"Shakespeare?" Miss Mandrill repeated, making a prune mouth. "Good lord, no! Orlando detested Shakespeare. 'High-blown muck,' he used to say. 'The lot of it. Like an explosion in a pigsty.'"

I couldn't help sucking in my breath. *Good thing Daffy isn't here,* I thought. She would have pulverized the woman for even repeating such sacrilege.

"I detect your disagreement," said Miss Mandrill. "It's written all over your face. Oh, well. I suppose there are people you can talk sense with, and others whom you can't."

How was I going to deal with this woman? One moment she was confiding in me like an old pal, and the next she was shooting at me with flaming arrows.

I couldn't afford to stalk off in "high dungeon," as Mrs. Mullet once put it, nor could I waste time playing on-again-off-again with such a wandering mind. It was like playing at bowls on a teeter-totter. Of course the woman was upset. Who wouldn't be to find their protégé dragged drowned from the drink and spread-eagled on a patch of grass?

"Had he any relatives?" I asked. "Anyone who ought to be informed?"

"Ha!" she barked.

And left it at that.

Feely by now had reached one of the quieter parts of *The Art of Fugue*, and the organ's notes, rather than flying and fluttering about, now roosted, whispering, up among the ancient timbers. In the near-silence, I heard the sound of approaching footsteps on the wooden floor.

And it wasn't the sidesmen bringing the collection plate to the altar rail.

It was the police.

"Constable Otter, miss," said an onion-scented voice at my ear. "A word outside, if you please."

I gave an eye-shrug to Miss Mandrill, crossed myself ostentatiously (you never knew), got to my feet, and followed the constable up the aisle and out into the sunshine, blinking madly at the glare.

I noted at once that the constable had had the good sense to come for me alone.

"Now then . . ." Constable Otter said, flipping open the pages of his notebook and licking the end of an indelible pencil, and I knew that I was, so to speak, home free.

·FOUR·

I CANNOT PRETEND THAT it was unpleasant to be questioned by the police. I had in the past become quite accustomed to occasional quiet chats with Inspector Hewitt: chats during which, as often as not, I was able to set the inspector straight on some of the finer points of chemistry and even, on one or two occasions, certain other matters as well.

Although I would have preferred to be grilled by the Detective Branch, I was nevertheless quite gracious to the uniformed Constable Otter. I put him at his ease at once.

"Ah! You've tracked me down at last," I said in an admiring voice. "Nothing like a mysterious death to liven up a lazy summer day, eh, Constable?"

I'd show him that I was an old hand at this sort of thing.

He gave me rather an odd squint. *Is it the sun?* I wondered. *Or have I misjudged the man?*

"Mysterious, miss?" the Constable asked.

Careful, Flavia! I thought. This man was quicker on the uptake than I had given him credit for.

"Well, you know what I mean," I improvised. "Drowned but not reported missing."

"And how do you know that?"

I could tell at once that Constable Otter was far from being the dullest blade in the drawer. In fact, I was already foreseeing great things for him in the future.

"By deduction," I said. "One would expect to find searchers on the banks, the river being dragged, and so forth."

Constable Otter scratched the tip of his chin with the point of his pencil. It left a small indigo mark, but I didn't point it out to him.

"Well, miss," he said, "I expect we ought to leave such deductions, as you call them, to the professionals: the chaps with the brains and the microscopes."

The constable was being witty, but I pretended not to notice.

He must have misread the look on my face, because he added: "A microscope, miss, in case you didn't know, is a device for magnifying small or minuscule objects. It makes a flea's eye look as broad as a barn."

Obviously, he did not realize that he was speaking to a person who had at home, in her own personal chemical laboratory, one of the finest binocular microscopes ever crafted by Ernst Leitz of Wetzlar, and that she bloody well knew how to use it! *Idiot!*

"No! *Really?*" I asked, letting the words writhe out of my mouth like a snake from a basket, and letting my jaw fall open the regulation three inches.

"Hmmm," he said, giving me that narrow look of his again. "Are *you* a professional, miss?"

His unexpectedly perceptive question caught me off guard.

"Well . . . yes," I said. "In a way, I suppose, you could say I am."

My reply was greeted with silence. This man had all the makings of a chief inspector. I'd better watch my step.

More important, I'd better get on the right side of him.

"You're very good at what you do, you know," I said.

Better not butter him up too much, though, I thought, *otherwise I might slip and fall on my face.*

He was giving me *that* look again, but I was saved from embarrassment by a cry from the water's edge.

"Constable! Constable Otter!"

It was the vicar and he was waving his arms in rather an unholy manner: more like a railway guard, I thought.

With great deliberation, Constable Otter returned his notebook and pencil to the breast pocket of his uniform. He was not a man to be stampeded.

With one last quizzing look at me, he turned and strode off purposefully along the path, his police boots crunching without mercy on the gravel.

Naturally, I followed. He had not instructed me to stay where I was.

Although our skiff was still at the riverbank, Dogger and Daffy were nowhere in sight. They must be still at the Oak and Pheasant, where Dogger would be doing his best to distract Daffy: to keep her mind—and eyes—away from the corpse. In spite of her steel-hard exterior, my sister was the tenderest of us all. She simply hated to show it.

When the cards were down, Daffy was always the first to fold. Anything truly gruesome, such as an arm or a leg broken in a tumble from a tree, or a toad speared on the tines of a garden fork, would reduce Daffy to a quivering, helpless jelly. The sight—or even the smell—of blood caused her to drop her dinner on the spot: as if her brain and belly were connected by a string.

But books were another matter. As long as it was only described in print, with no pictures, my sister could stomach anything.

Hadn't she read aloud to me with great enthusiasm, when I was still a child, the scene from *Crime and Punishment* in which Raskolnikov hacks two women to death with an ax? And she had positively burbled with delight at the death by pistol of Vladimir, in *Eugene Onegin*, in which his blood gushed, smoking, from the wound.

Books served Daffy as an insulation between the real world and her tender heart.

As for me, I was not like that at all. No, not in the least.

To me, an unexamined corpse was a tale untold: a knotted ball of a tale that was simply crying out to be unraveled until the last strand had been picked free. The fact that it was also a study in progressively putrid chem-

istry simply made it all that much more lively and interesting.

My point is that although there were obviously certain
similarities between Daffy and myself, there were also
insurmountable—in this life, at least—differences.

The vicar was still making wigwag signals with his
arms as I approached, just a few steps behind Constable
Otter.

"I thought you ought to see this," he was saying, holding out a sodden slipper.

It was red: a perfect match for the single one the corpse
was wearing.

"Where did you get this, then?" the constable demanded in rather a gruff voice. It had been my experience that the police do not like evidence to be discovered
by anyone but themselves.

"There," said the vicar, pointing a semi-accusing finger
at a rather ragamuffin lad who stood nearby beside the
wreckage of a sodden kite. I hadn't even noticed him.

"Hob Nightingale," the vicar said.

I turned my attention to this grubby child who was
staring attentively down at his oversized boots. Just a
couple of years younger than me, he might well have
been a porter at Covent Garden market; an orphan waif
from one of Daffy's Dickens novels. From his peaked cap
and baggy rumpled trousers, I knew at once that he almost certainly had an older brother—and no mother.

"What you starin' at, then?" he asked, looking up and
meeting my eye aggressively.

"Sorry," I said, and I meant it. I have a tendency to gawk when I'm fascinated.

He tossed his head and looked away. People who have been offended are entitled to a short sulk, as long as it doesn't drag on too long. I would have to wait a while to see if my apology had been accepted.

"Young Hob, here, was flying his kite," the vicar said. "A little gust brought it down among those reeds."

He pointed to a brackish bit of riverbank where a stretch of reeds and pondweed lined an indent in the river's course.

"Just over there," the vicar said, pointing.

"Floating, was it, the slipper?" Constable Otter asked. "In the water, like?"

The vicar nodded.

"And who fished it out, then?" the constable asked slyly.

"Why, I did," the vicar replied sheepishly, and I noticed for the first time that his trouser legs were rolled up to reveal a stretch of white ecclesiastical legs and a pair of fish-white feet. "Hob pointed it out. I waded in to retrieve it.

"He's just a child," he added. "I didn't want him to tumble in."

"I see," Constable Otter said, weighing the dripping slipper in his hand. "So you fished it out yourself? With your own hands?"

The vicar nodded meekly, and the constable, producing pad and pencil with the flourish of a stage magician, made a note in his book. There would be no catching out this stickler for detail at the inquest.

"Now then," the constable said, turning to the scowling Hob Nightingale. "What were you up to? No fibs, mind, else I'll tell your dad. He'll know what to do with you."

I blanched on the boy's behalf. I knew all too well what it felt like to be on the receiving end of a naked threat.

But I needn't have bothered.

"Go ahead and tell him. I don't care," Hob said, staring Constable Otter in the eye. "I wasn't doing anything wrong. Since when is it a crime to fly a kite?"

The constable was as taken aback as I was. He removed his helmet and scratched the back of his head with his pencil. I wondered idly if he'd placed an indelible mark up there, as well.

"Since when?" Hob persisted, his voice rising slightly: just enough to threaten a full-scale tantrum.

"Now then, little laddie," the constable said. "No need to get your nappies in a knot."

He turned to the vicar, expecting a smile at such rapier wit, but his little joke died on the vine. The vicar stared at him as blankly as if he were one of Einstein's equations on a blackboard.

"Well, then," Otter said. "Run along home now. If I need anything else, I know where to find you."

And suddenly I saw the way. As if the sun had popped out from behind a black cloud and lighted a path through the woods.

"I'll take him home," I said. "I can help carry his broken kite."

I almost stressed the word *broken*, but was able to suppress the urge before it passed my lips. I had spotted a shape beneath the rumpled paper that was certainly not part of the flying apparatus.

"You don't even know where I *live*," Hob protested.

"Never mind, sweetie," I said, hating myself as I said it. "You can show me the way. I'm a wizard with broken kites."

I bent and gathered up the soggy bundle of balsa wood, paper, and string (of which there seemed to be an exceptional mess), taking care to keep the object beneath it out of sight. As a safeguard, I wrapped the long tail of paper bows around my forearm to seal the bundle shut.

"Lead on, then, Hob," I said, in a mock dramatic voice.

Tossing his head up and his shoulders back, as if he were leading an army out of captivity in one of those stirring war films, Hob strode off through the churchyard, and I, with the shattered kite bundled awkwardly in my arms, followed him humbly.

No one would ever suspect me of removing evidence from the scene of a crime.

Hob did not so much as glance back at me. I might have been a mere servant carrying the train of his robe.

We made our way past the church, into the high street, and then into a narrow passageway that ran between a greengrocer's and an undertaker's. On the right was a brick wall and on the left a tall wooden fence.

"In here," Hob said, speaking for the first time since leaving the churchyard.

I stopped in my tracks, staring up at the painted sign on a weathered board above an open gate.

F. T. NIGHTINGALE, it read. FUNERALS ETC.

"Wait—" I said, but Hob shushed me with a finger raised to his lips.

"Keep it down," he whispered. "I don't want Da to hear us."

"Da?" I whispered back.

"My father," he said, pointing up to the sign. "The undertaker."

You could have knocked me over with an ostrich feather. It's not often that Fate deals you a winning hand, but I'd just been given four aces and a joker up my sleeve.

"The undertaker," I murmured. "Fancy that!"

"Nothing to be afraid of," Hob said, miming the words in an exaggerated manner with his lips.

"Are you sure?" I mimed back.

He did not reply, but, beckoning me with a curled forefinger, led the way into the fenced area.

Inside was a broad cobbled courtyard and I found myself in another century. From the gas lamp above the back door of the premises to the cast-iron hitching posts, it was clearly a place where funerals had been marshaled before their procession to the graveyard.

I could imagine the black horses standing patiently as they were harnessed for the hearse, which would have been a shellacked and solemn thing on slender wooden wheels, with unnerving slabs of glass all the way round, so that those fortunate enough to be still alive could have a jolly good gawk at the coffin as they envisioned its grisly contents.

There would have been cockades attached, of black-dyed ostrich feathers, designed to ruffle in the breeze like the feathers of dead birds—which they were—to generate a primitive shudder in the spectators and remind them of their own mortality; there would have been mutes in tall black hats to pace numbly alongside the hearse and catch the eye of anyone they could, as if to say, "You! You there! Yes, you—You Who Might Be Next."

Oh, for the good old days, I thought, *when Death was an everyday equal and not to be padlocked away like some dim-witted relative whom nobody wanted to see or spend time with.*

Today, at the door where once the horses were persuaded not to prance, stood a rather elderly and down-at-the-heels motor hearse. An Austin, I noted, which had apparently served in a former life as a London taxicab.

Looking round, it was obvious to me that this courtyard was the rear of the undertaking premises and not meant for public viewing. Wooden coffin cases leaned heavily against the fence, and boxes full of empty bottles were stacked in every corner. *Embalming liquids,* I noted appreciatively.

I leaned over for a closer look at one of the weathered labels.

Aha! Just as I suspected: formaldehyde, mercury chloride, arsenious acid, with a pinch of good old sodium chloride (table salt) plus a couple of drops of thymol, oil of cinnamon, and oil of cloves, to mask the stink.

I recalled with a delicious shiver that arsenious acid, in the form of arsenic trioxide, is one of the deadliest of poisons, and is often used to dispatch rats.

"Hurry up!" Hob hissed.

He was standing in an open doorway fanning frantically with his hands. I followed eagerly.

I let out a low whistle. We were in a large workshop, at the far end of which was a raised loft or gallery. Coffins and parts of coffins in various stages of construction were everywhere: resting on wooden trestles, leaning against walls, piled in corners. Planes, hammers, saws, and chisels covered every level surface, and the air was sweet with the smell of sawdust and wood shavings.

To a girl of my interests, the place seemed like Heaven.

It was like being in on the Creation!

Hob was already halfway up the ladder that led to the loft.

"Up here," he said. "Hurry up. Hustle your bustle."

I obeyed, dragging myself unsteadily up, rung by rung, with the crumpled kite pressed against my bosom. I must have looked like an apprentice paperhanger.

Hob reached out a hand to help me up onto the platform.

Without any further ado, he took the crashed kite from my clutches and threw it into a corner, revealing a black and boxy object, which he placed carefully atop a highly polished coffin.

I gave the hard finish a couple of sharp taps with my fingernail. Shellac, dissolved in methylated spirits: a coffin of the highest quality. Certainly not one of the cheaper finishes of linseed oil and lampblack to which a bit of gold size in turpentine has been added.

This box was meant for someone important.

From my own personal experience I knew a thing or two about the various varnishes and their qualities. An emergency repair of a seventeenth-century refectory tabletop at Buckshaw—ruined by my roller-skating on its polished surface—had once needed to be completed and invisible before Father got home from London.

At the thought, a twinge touched my heart.

"I hope this camera's not busted," Hob said, "or Pippin's going to slaughter me when he comes home."

Pippin? Who was this Pippin? I wondered. I raised my eyebrows.

"My brother," he said. "He's a pilot. Photo reconnaissance. He's mapping northern Canada for the Geological Survey. He used to fly a Spitfire. It's *his* camera. I nicked it for an experiment."

I could see the pride in Hob's eyes as the words came bubbling out of his mouth.

Reflected in the polished gloss of the coffin, the camera had rather an unearthly look: a strange scientific instrument from another planet sent, perhaps, to spy with its single, ever-open, all-seeing eye upon our backward world.

And yet at the same time it was a perfectly ordinary Kodak Brownie Six-20. There were plenty of them about. Every tourist in every English village had one strapped around his or her neck, clicking away madly here and there at every quaint cottage, every tithe barn, and every duck on every village green.

But this camera was different. A tiny hole had been drilled in the shutter release lever, to which had been fastened a length of fishing line that passed through a couple of small brass rings attached to the side of the camera.

"Have you got it worked out yet?" Hob demanded, hopping from one foot to the other with excitement.

"It's a cable release," I said. "A kind of remote control."

"Aerial photography!" he exploded, unable to contain himself any longer. "I knocked it together myself. Do you like it?"

"Extraordinary," I said, feeling much older than my actual years.

"Altogether ripping!" I added, more for my own benefit than for Hob's.

Hob fairly basked in the glow of my approval and I knew in that moment that he hadn't many friends.

"I have an idea," I said. "Let's take the film to the chemist's to be developed. I'll put it in my name and you can put your brother's camera back wherever you found it. That way, he'll never know you even pinched it."

"You're brilliant!" Hob said, and I had to agree.

A few moments later, the roll was in my pocket, along with my handkerchief and whatever remained of the fluids from the lungs of the late Orlando.

As I was giving myself a mental pat on the back, a door at the end of the loft swung silently open and a man dressed entirely in black came into the room. He must have moved on oiled castors, I thought. Even my keen hearing had not detected his approach.

He seemed almost as surprised to see us as we were to see him.

"Hob!" he said. "What are you doing here? I thought you were out playing. And who's this you've brought home?"

I saved Hob the trouble of explaining. Stepping forward in the most ladylike manner I could summon up, I offered him my hand and gave him a firm shake.

Remarkably strong, I thought, *for an undertaker.* And yet an undertaker had to be capable—when you got right down to it—of manhandling bodies as if they were so many sacks of potatoes.

His suit was clean but shabby, the cuffs slightly frayed. *From rubbing against so many coffins*, I thought. An honest workingman.

"I'm Flavia de Luce, sir," I said. "Hob had a bit of a prang with his kite and I helped him get it home."

"I'm much obliged to you, Miss de Luce," he said. "Most grateful."

He extracted an old-fashioned pocket watch from his waistcoat, glanced at it, and said: "But now you must excuse me. I'm afraid I have some rather urgent business to attend to, and—"

I knew what he was referring to even before he finished speaking.

Orlando! It had to be Orlando!

What else could be so urgent in a small town on a lazy summer afternoon? How many deaths were likely to come to light within the space of a single hour?

I fancied myself something of an expert on that topic. I knew, for instance, that most deaths in quiet country towns were due to old age, and that most of the elderly, when their time was up, tended to die quietly in the night and be discovered before breakfast.

Deaths in the afternoon, on the other hand, were much more likely to be due to causes such as heart attacks among hardworking farmers, or road accidents involving young drivers with an appetite for alcohol and speed.

There were other factors, of course, but these were the most likely.

"Of course, sir," I said, offering another shake. "It's been most pleasant to meet you."

Pleasant! You genius, Flavia! Even old Peter Mark Roget, the thesaurus boffin, couldn't have come up with a better word himself. Not in a hundred years. Not in an eon!

Mr. Nightingale adjusted his widower's cuffs, and I knew I'd been approved.

But just to make sure, I added: "I know you're extremely busy, sir, but I wanted to compliment you on your French polishing."

I touched the gleaming coffin lid with appreciative fingertips.

"I noticed by the bottles in the courtyard that you use shellac and methylated spirits. I love the luster it gives."

I caressed the highly polished wood.

Mr. Nightingale straightened his tie.

"Sometime, when you have a minute, sir, you must give me your views on the use of bullens as an ornamental device. I realize there's a great deal of controversy—especially in Dissenting parishes—but . . ."

I allowed my words to trail off.

Bullens were the square-headed brass nails beloved of undertakers who wished to make a bit of easy profit at little expense. I had read up on them with great interest in *Coffins and Coffin Making,* a well-thumbed copy of which was kept on a high shelf in the Bishop's Lacey Free Library.

I excused my boldness by forcing a slight but pretty blush, which isn't as easy as it sounds. It's a matter of holding one's breath while forcing air from the lungs toward the head without appearing to do so.

"I am flattered, Miss de Luce," the undertaker said. "Perhaps another time."

I inclined my head graciously and gave him a coy smile. It was jolly good luck I didn't have a fan in my hand!

Had he clicked his heels together, or was it my imagination?

At any rate, he was suddenly, smoothly, and gracefully gone, just as you would expect from someone of his standing.

"What a lovely man your father is, Hob," I remarked. He was grinning from ear to ear.

"Now then," I told him, dropping my duchess pose. "Let's go find out what's on that film."

·FIVE·

FORTUNATELY, THE CHEMIST'S SHOP was in the opposite direction from the church, so we were at little risk of running into anyone I knew. It simply wouldn't do to be stopped and ordered about by the police, although even that would have been better than coming face-to-face with Feely or Daffy.

Feely! I had completely forgotten about her. I had walked out of the church with Constable Otter, and left my sister producing a Niagara of notes on the church organ. For all I knew, she might still be at it. Old Johann's *Art of Fugue*, uninterrupted, could run on for as long as an hour and a quarter, especially if my sister was upset and had recently eaten.

"Musick has charms to sooth a savage breast," William Congreve had once written, in his play *The Mourning Bride*.

"'Musick *and* chicken sandwiches,' he ought to have said," Daffy once remarked as Feely had stormed away from the dinner table and taken refuge in one of the most beautiful and heart-wrenching of the piano sonatas by Beethoven.

"Did you say you were going to pay for this?" Hob asked, interrupting my thoughts.

"Yes," I told him. "But let's hurry before I change my mind."

If we cracked on with the film processing, I might be able to get back to the church and slip into a pew before Feely even noticed I was gone.

"What's the hurry?" Hob asked, shooting me a most penetrating look.

"Nothing really," I told him, biting my tongue. "It's just that I'm awfully keen on aerial photos. I haven't laid eyes on a good old aerophoto in simply ages. They used to print tons of them in *The Illustrated London News*, but that was before the war. Nobody gives a tinker's curse about them nowadays. Except you, of course—and me."

I shot him a beaming smile and he beamed back.

The chemist's was next door to a butcher's shop in the high street. WANLESS & SONS DISPENSING CHEMISTS, it said in peeling black and gold above the door and on the little bow window, in which were displayed two glass globes of tired-looking colored water.

A bell tinkled brightly as we stepped into a dim, cramped Aladdin's cave of bottles, flasks, tins, bags, and boxes. There was barely enough space in the place to turn around, and it smelled of sulfur; of lavender and mint; of bath salts and smelling salts; of licorice and aloes and *nux vomica*; of castor oil and oil of cloves (for toothache).

The atmosphere, I realized with a sudden start, was that of a sickroom—but the sickroom of a patient who had quite recently departed this life.

I didn't want to think about it.

Behind an arched wire wicket, the chemist, tall, thin, and white-jacketed like a London tearoom attendant, didn't bat an eye as I handed over the film.

"Prints?" he asked, his pencil poised.

"One of each," I told him.

"Name?"

"Flavia de Luce," I said. There was no point in lying about it.

"Are you from our neighborhood, Miss de Luce?" he asked.

"We're staying at the Oak and Pheasant," I said, "but we're expecting to leave tomorrow. Do you think they'll be ready by then?"

This was pure invention. I had no idea when we were leaving, but I wanted the prints as soon as possible.

The chemist frowned.

"I can't promise anything. We process every day except Sundays, of course. But this is our busiest time of year . . ."

He didn't say "because of the tourists" but I knew that's what he meant.

I formed my mouth into a little pout to indicate that I might take my business elsewhere.

"Sometimes," the chemist added reluctantly, "they're ready the same day, but only rarely. We're rushed off our feet this time of year, you know."

I put on a guilty look, as if it were all my fault.

He stared at me intently for a moment and then, as if having come to some momentous decision, turned away and began to paw with his right foot at the wooden floor-boards, as if he were a maddened bull who had just spotted the matador in the ring.

"Howland!" he shouted in a new and alarmingly loud voice, quite unlike the one in which he had been speaking to me. "When can you do a roll of six-twenty?"

Howland, whoever he was, must be remarkably hard of hearing.

From under the floor there came an angry subterranean grumble, as if the gods of the underworld were suffering badly from indigestion.

I could not make out any of the words.

I peered round the edge of the wicket at which I was standing. Sure enough, there was a trapdoor beneath the chemist's feet. The invisible Howland must have his photo darkroom in the cellar.

"In due course," the chemist said, turning back to me.

"Thank you," I replied, baring my teeth and rewarding him with a full-on but well-chosen grin from my inner grab bag of smiles.

"I know you'll do your best," I said, and somehow I knew that he would.

Outside in the high street I said my goodbyes to Hob.

"I must get back," I said, "otherwise my sister will be frantic. She worries about me too much. You know how it is."

A little untruth never hurt a casual acquaintance.

Hob nodded and made off along the high street.

Only after he was gone did I realize how few words he had spoken.

As I walked back toward the church I heard the unmistakable sound of a hurdy-gurdy. Was it a wandering organ grinder with his monkey? I wondered. A "peripatetic pest," as Daffy would call him?

My question was quickly answered as I came to a short passageway on the left side of the street. Through a brick archway was a cobbled lane that led to an open space beyond which were fields. I knew by the ancient stone cross and cattle troughs that this was the town marketplace, now taken over by a small traveling fair.

A canvas banner announced that this was SHADRACH'S CIRCUS & MENAGERIE: THE GRANDEST LITTLE SHOW ON EARTH.

The music was coming from a small merry-go-round, its gaudy horses, pigs, griffins, and a single (but fierce) fire-breathing dragon spinning endlessly in the warm summer sunshine. There were no more than a handful of small riders astride these handsome beasts, and one of those, a red-faced little chap, was holding on for dear life and wailing for his mother.

Nearby, a bored-looking elephant, shackled at the leg, munched half-heartedly on a mound of hay.

Arranged round the four sides of the market square

were the usual stalls: a coconut pitch and a pieman, a ring-toss, and an Aunt Sally. Directly across from these was a shooting gallery, with flying mechanical ducks, grouse, partridges, and a leftover portrait of Neville Chamberlain flying jerkily across a crudely painted landscape. Someone had painted a happy grin on Chamberlain's exhausted-looking face with lipstick.

Beyond, in a row of side stalls, were games of Crown and Anchor, Under and Over, and, in spite of the ban on casino games at village fairs, a surprisingly large illuminated roulette wheel. A hand-lettered sign on a stick said No CHILDREN PLEASE.

For the little ones, there was a fishpond with magnetic hooks to pull worthless trinkets from a cellophane "pool."

"Hello there!" someone said behind me, and I spun round to find myself face-to-face with one of the men I had seen in the pub. The largest one. I recognized him by his polka-dot kerchief.

"Haven't we met before?" he asked. "Your face is familiar."

I knew better than to fall for a line like that. Daffy had coached me in dealing with strange men who claim that you have a familiar face. Her instructions ranged from the sharp retort and rapid departure all the way up to a swift kick in the colonies.

"You have to show them you mean business," Daffy had said.

I shook my head and turned away. But the man was not so easily discouraged. He shuffled round in front of me, blocked my way, and held out a roll of colored tickets.

"Take a chance on the Lucky Draw," he coaxed. "Six-pence each, six for a shilling. What could be fairer than that?"

"Go away," I said quite loudly. That was Step A.

"Come on," he persisted. "You look like a sport—a girl who likes to take a chance."

"Go away," I repeated. That was Step B.

"Can't win if you don't enter," he said, going into a faint whine.

Step C was not to be executed unless the man physically laid hands upon you, but if he did—even so much as a finger—he was fair game.

"I'm warning you—" I said.

A hand touched my upper arm. I swung round, spotted my target, and—

"Let's go, Flavia," Hob said, tugging at my sleeve. "You can buy me a candy floss."

I had come within an ace of flattening him. Had the little dickens been following me?

I gave him a raised eyebrow.

"You know as well as I do that sweets are still rationed."

"I *do* know that as well as you do"—Hob grinned—"but I have a ration book."

And so it was that the two of us, our faces covered with cobwebs of pink sugar, strolled back into the high street, licking our chops like butcher shop cats, and wiping our sticky fingers on the leaves of overhanging trees.

Gorging on sweets together creates as strong a bond between two people as being in love. Or so it seems to

me, although I've never been in love. Nor am I much accustomed to sugar. The war had seen to that.

And yet, walking along with Hob, both of us inhaling
spun sucrose like a pair of jet engines, we became, almost
instantly, old pals.

"How does it feel to have an undertaker for a father?" I
asked.

It was a question I had been dying to ask him since the
moment we met; a question to which, for some strange
reason, I desperately required an answer.

"Do you really want to know?"

"Of course I do," I said, picking strands of pink fiber off
my chin. "It's the kind of thing that interests me. I wish
my father had been in the trade."

"Wasn't he?" Hob asked.

"No. At least not directly."

I was thinking of Father's wartime service, when he
and Dogger had been shipped out to the Far East in order
to dispatch foreigners to an early grave.

"Anyway," I said, pulling myself back into the moment, "you haven't answered my question."

Hob shrugged.

"Well," he said, "they tease me about it at school."

"I'd rip their hearts out," I said, suddenly fiercely defensive of this tiny creature.

"Oh, I don't mind," Hob said. "Da says that life is full
of death, and that it's better to make friends with it than
fight it."

Oh! The wisdom of the man!

It was as if the heavens had suddenly opened and a disembodied arm had handed down to me the Secret of the Universe, scribbled on a slip of wrinkled paper.

A weight had been lifted from my shoulders: a weight of which I hadn't been aware until it was gone.

I wanted to hug someone. I wanted to burst into glorious song.

"Hmmm," I said. "Yes. I suppose that's one way of looking at it."

I hadn't noticed until now that Hob had stopped strolling and begun cantering. Yes, *cantering*!

It seemed as if a little of my elation had rubbed off on him.

"What do you know about Poppy Mandrill?" I asked suddenly.

In my experience, it is often a bolt from the blue that shakes loose the biggest avalanche.

"Everyone's afraid of her," Hob replied, without batting an eye.

"Everyone?"

"Well, I'm not, of course," Hob said, jutting his chin out. "But I only know her to see her."

I couldn't resist.

"Then how do you know everyone's afraid of her?"

"Because I keep my ears open," Hob said. "At funerals."

I realized at once, of course, that I had, almost accidentally, tapped into a vast reservoir. If there's one place where people speak with unguarded tongues, it's at a funeral. Emotion—and especially grief—loosens tongues even more than alcohol.

I'll bet there have been more truths told over an open coffin than in all the confession boxes in Christendom.

"Do you really?" I asked admiringly.

Hob fairly preened.

"Mrs. Perry said that to Mrs. Belaney at old Mr. Ark-wright's funeral. As soon as Poppy Mandrill came into the room, everybody moved away from her—as if she had the Black Plague or something."

"Perhaps it was respect?" I suggested.

"Phah!" Hob said. "They were afraid of her. Mrs. Perry leaned over and whispered to Mrs. Belaney: 'They're all afraid of that—'

"I'm not allowed to say the next word, but you must know the one I mean. I heard it with my own ears."

"You're a very clever lad, Hob," I said, and he nearly burst into flames.

"I knew it!" he said, hugging himself. "I knew it!"

"Well, you are," I assured him. "What else have you heard? About Poppy Mandrill, I mean. We can get to the others later."

"She's with the Puddle Lane Little Theatre." Hob rolled his eyes as if I would understand. "They put on plays in the Town Hall. Pantomimes at Christmas. You know."

I did indeed. We suffered in much the same way at Bishop's Lacey with the same kind of dreary and awkward—but compulsory—comedies.

But why on earth would the dead Orlando be dressed for a Christmas pantomime? It was June, for goodness' sake! Rehearsals wouldn't even begin for months, and as for *dress rehearsals*—well, they were simply out of the question at this time of year.

"Is anyone holding a masquerade?" I asked.

"I don't know that word," Hob said.

"A masquerade? A dress-up party. Costumes. Highwaymen, for instance. Gents in powdered wigs, ladies in silk dresses like tents at the fête, and black beauty spots stuck on their cheeks."

"Ugh," Hob said. "Doesn't sound very beautiful to me. I've never heard of such a thing."

"Why are they afraid of Poppy Mandrill?" I asked, trying to get my line of questioning back onto the track.

"She's bossy," Hob said. "Always giving people orders."

"Isn't that what a theater director is supposed to do?" I asked, only half seriously.

"Not in church!" Hob exclaimed, his eyes widening and his hackles rising visibly.

"Did you actually see that happen?" I asked.

Hob nodded several times to make his point. "Only once," he said. "She shouted out at the vicar, right in the middle of his sermon."

"Good lord!" I blurted. Even *I* wouldn't have dared such sacrilege. "Do you remember what she said?"

"She said 'Cut the cackle, Vicar. I've a train to catch.'"

"Was this on Palm Sunday, by any chance?" I asked. "About three months ago?"

"How did you know that?" Hob asked. "We all had our

palm fronds in our hands. Lizzy Pleasance tried to strangle me with hers. I took mine home and made a straw soldier out of it."

I couldn't help wondering idly what Hob would have thought if I'd told him I usually twisted my own annual palm frond into a hangman's noose.

Actually, naming the date was a brilliant bit of deduction on my part. I knew by bitter experience that the Palm Sunday morning service was the longest in *The Book of Common Prayer*. The Gospel was taken from Matthew, chapter 27.

Which, as I recalled, ran more than a thousand words. I knew this because I had counted them, one by one, following with my index finger, as our own vicar, Denwyn Richardson, had read them aloud on several Palm Sundays, back home in Bishop's Lacey.

"You lot are getting off easily," he had told us at Confirmation class. "Had you been unfortunate enough to have lived in about 1550, in the time of King Edward the Sixth—who died at the age of fifteen . . . younger than you, there, Ted Pullymore . . . yes, you, Ted . . . and who died coughing up green, black, and pink matter, leading some to believe he had been poisoned—you'd have had to sit still three times longer than we do nowadays. In those days, the Gospel reading for Palm Sunday combined Matthew chapters 26 *and* 27, and would have lasted somewhere between twenty minutes and half an hour. Fortunately, the many editors of *The Book of Common Prayer*, in their wisdom, took mercy upon our poor, aching sitters and slashed the reading substantially."

That's what I loved about Denwyn Richardson: He simply oozed history.

"And what about the dead man?" I asked Hob. "Orlando. Did you know him?"

"Orlando?" Hob snorted noisily. "Everybody knew Orlando."

"Everybody except me," I said. "I don't even know his last name."

"Whitbread," Hob said. "Orlando Whitbread. His father used to be the rector of St.-Mildred's-in-the-Marsh."

Whitbread?

You could have knocked me over with a bit of goose down.

"Canon Whitbread?" I asked. "Not *Canon* Whitbread? Not the one who—"

"Choked on a rope?" Hob said. "Yes, that's the one. I helped Daddy embalm him."

· S I X ·

WHAT CAN YOU POSSIBLY say to a child who has helped his father pump preservatives into the carotid artery of a hanged murderer?

Precious little, I discovered. There are no words suitable for the occasion; no words to convey my shock, my awe, my admiration, or my jealousy.

"Are you surprised?" Hob asked. "You seem surprised."

"Not at all," I said, leaping madly aboard the opportunity. "Tell me about it."

"You look surprised," Hob persisted.

"All right, then. I'm surprised. Astonished. Flabbergasted, in fact. Tell me about it."

"Perhaps when I know you better," Hob said.

Where did this little lad get his spunkiness from? What crazy corner of the universe animated his mind?

"All right," I said. "I don't mind. I'm really not all that interested anyway."

Hob said nothing, but gave me a look that suggested I'd just been caught poaching his father's chickens.

If undertakers, in fact, *had* chickens. I could think of various reasons why they might and might not keep poultry, none of them suitable for discussion with anyone other than the most confidential friends. And even then . . .

But before I could stop him, Hob was loping off toward home.

"Farewell," he called back over his shoulder.

Had I scared him off by being too familiar?

Well, no matter.

But I didn't think of the obvious question until he had already disappeared round a corner.

"Hob! Wait!" I called, but he didn't hear me. Or pretended not to.

I could have run after him, but there was no time. *Never mind*, I decided, *there will be other opportunities*.

Meanwhile, Feely, Daffy, and Dogger would already be worrying about me. Or would they? I could never quite be sure.

In any case, I needn't have bothered. By the time I got back to the church, Feely was still lost in *The Art of Fugue*, which was now nearing its end—or what passed as its end, since J. S. Bach had never finished the thing. At the point where he had abruptly given it up, Bach had noted on the manuscript that, at this point, the composer had died. Which was, Daffy said, a colossal joke that no one had yet spotted: that somewhere up among the stars, Bach was still waiting for someone to laugh.

I gave a quiet chuckle at the thought, and old Johann Sebastian, from somewhere beyond Pluto, raised two fingers and gave me the "V for Victory" sign.

Dogger and Daffy were sitting side by side in a back pew, eyes closed, hands folded on tummies like a pair of well-fed pigeons on a ledge at Westminster Abbey, listening contentedly to the music.

I slid in quietly beside them, and although Dogger opened the corner of one eye, Daffy may as well have been somewhere in the far-off Fiji Islands.

I walked my fingers slowly and quietly across the pew as if they were a hump-backed spider.

With my forefinger, I tapped out a message in code on the back of Dogger's hand: a quick touch for a dot and a long touch for a dash. Jolly good thing I had been forced to learn the Morse system at Miss Bodycote's, in Canada.

Dot-dash-dash-dot, dot-dash-dot, dash-dash-dash, and so forth, until I had spelled out the letters *P-R-O-G-R-E-S-S.*

For just a fraction of a moment I thought he hadn't got it, but then I saw his head incline by about a sixty-fourth of an inch. If you hadn't known Dogger, you'd have sworn he hadn't budged.

Now his hand was lightly touching mine: *E-X-C-E-L-L-E-N-T,* his fingers tapped.

A warm glow came over me, and I hoped I wasn't flushing. I sneaked a glance at Dogger, but his eyes were still closed. How noble he looked! How like a god.

The Art of Fugue ended abruptly as I knew it would: cut off in mid-flight—just like Orlando Whitbread.

And, come to think of it, just like his father, late of St.-Mildred's-in-the-Marsh.

As the music came to a stop, the organ made the usual little dying noises as the air left its lungs. Somewhere behind the tall ornamental pipes, leather bellows collapsed, and all the tiny tin and wooden arteries, deprived of wind, wheezed into a restless silence.

For a moment, the three of us, Daffy, Dogger, and I, sat in that uneasy vacuum that always comes into existence when the music ends, each one of us reluctant to be the first to speak.

In the end, it was me.

"We'd better get back to the Oak and Pheasant," I said. "We'll need to book rooms. I don't expect we'll be going home until further notice."

"Those arrangements are already seen to, Miss Flavia," Dogger said. "I shall go fetch the car."

We had left the Rolls parked a short distance up the river at the boat rental establishment.

"Good old Dogger," I said, patting his hand. "You are the one fixed point in a changing age."

He smiled and vanished.

"Sherlock Holmes," Daffy said, her eyes popping open. "'His Last Bow.' 'There's an east wind coming all the same, such a wind as never blew on England yet. It will be cold and bitter, Watson, and a good many of us may wither before its blast.'"

Even though she was quoting from memory, Daffy's

words shook me to the core. I was seized with a sudden crawling chill. Instead of the word "England," she might have said "such a wind as never blew on *us*," *us* meaning the de Luce family.

With Father's death, the blight had already begun. This happy holiday was no more than the gentle and deceiving slope at the lip of the pit.

There was a clatter behind us on the stone steps, and Feely appeared.

"Come along, slugs," she said, meaning Daffy and me. "I'm famished."

Feely was like that. She could switch her attention from Gregorian chant to the state of her own gut in half of a horsefly's heartbeat.

I had come to realize that I simply didn't understand my older sister, and I never would.

As we came out of the church, I noticed that Orlando's body had been removed from the riverbank. Constable Otter was nowhere in sight. Nor was Miss Mandrill.

A cluster of women in housedresses stood on—or close to—the spot where Orlando had until lately lain leaking into the grass. Even at this distance, and against the wind, I could hear the sound of their magpie chatter.

Back at the inn, we found that our rooms had already been assigned. Feely was to be given the best bedroom: a low-timbered chamber at the front of the building, which faced the church and in which, or so it was said, Queen Elizabeth I had slept on one of her many Progresses round her kingdom.

"Is there a single bedroom in all of England in which

she didn't?" Daffy asked sourly, but the landlord, who was accustomed to such impertinence, shot back:

"Yes. Mine."

Daffy had the good grace to laugh, although I knew her well enough to recognize that it was insincere.

Daffy had been given a cozy little chamber, up one step on the west side of the building, which, in the days of Good Queen Bess, had been a small country house.

"Longer daylight for reading," she said.

Although she had spotted a small library, which was little more than a couple of shelves banged together half-way up the stairs, she had written it off at a glance.

"Anthony Hopeless," she said. "Ouida . . . Sabatini . . . Michael Arlen . . . Rider Haggard . . . and not so much as a single scribble by the Divine Charles."

Meaning Dickens, of course, to whom she had constructed a small shrine in her bedroom at Buckshaw. Before coming away on our holiday, I had suggested she have the whole setup mounted on an oxcart as they did with their portable altars in the Middle Ages.

"We can tow it behind the Rolls," I told her. "Think how handy it would be to have the whole lot of it: portrait of the Divine Charles, candles, snuffers, incense, first editions of *Bleak House* and *The Pickwick Papers* all right there at your fingertips in case you suffer withdrawal symptoms."

Whereupon I had been driven from the breakfast table in a hail of bath buns, which, considering that they had been baked by Mrs. Mullet, was a good deal more life-threatening than it sounds.

As for me, I was to be quartered in a tiny room at the rear of the inn, which had once, the landlord assured me, been a small minstrel's gallery.

"Don't worry if you hear strange voices singing in the night," he told me in a confidential tone. "They're mostly harmless—even though the last lady wot heard 'em went stark mad," he added, dropping into a dialect stage whisper, "an' 'ad to be put in a straitjacket!"

I ignored him.

A glance out of the narrow single window told me that the only voices I was likely to hear would be those of the old gaffers sitting round the trestle tables in the sunken garden with their tankards of ale.

I raised the flyblown Holland blind to let more light into this murky chamber.

The furnishings were sparse, to say the least: a small bed complete with a chamber pot, a cheap wooden table with ewer and pitcher, a safety lamp with candle and glass chimney—presumably for emergencies in the night—a chair that was straight out of a painting by Vincent van Gogh, a sink that had seen goodness-knows-what, a hot plate and tin kettle, and an oval mirror with yellowed glass.

Dogger was already back, bringing with him my small traveling case from the Rolls. Unlike Daffy, who had insisted on dragging along a wooden packing case containing *The Works of Charles Dickens*, complete in twenty-six fat, red, heavy leather-bound volumes, I had brought only the bare necessities: a toothbrush, and Taylor's *Principles and Practice of Medical Jurisprudence*. In order to keep down the weight, I had selected only the second volume of that great work: the one containing the poisons.

I waited until the landlord, with his hand-rubbing ghost stories, was out of earshot, and even then, I closed the door.

"Dogger," I asked, "where do they bury executed murderers?"

"Well, Miss Flavia," he said, "that depends upon the times. In the eighteenth century, they were sometimes left hanging on the gibbet. The birds took care of the rest."

I gave a delicious shiver at the thought.

"Some were buried at a crossroads," Dogger went on, "as were suicides, until the practice was abolished by an Act of Parliament in the 1820s."

"Why a crossroads?" I asked.

"It was believed that the meeting of four ways would reduce the chance of the ghost finding its way back home."

"And nowadays?" In my excitement, I could hardly get the question out.

"Nowadays," Dogger replied, "the bodies of executed murderers are the property of the Crown. They are buried in perforated coffins in unmarked graves within the precincts of the prison in which their sentence was carried out."

"Not handed over to the family? Not turned over to the undertaker?"

"Not unless directed otherwise by the sheriff of the

county," Dogger answered. "Once buried, exhumation requires a formal license from the Home Office, which must
be signed personally by the Home Secretary. Although I
understand that this is frowned upon, and would be
granted in only the most extraordinary circumstances."

My mind was floundering to stay afloat.

Unless Hob was a downright liar, it was simply not possible for him to have been present at the embalming of
Canon Whitbread.

In the first place, if the canon had been hanged at one
of His Majesty's prisons, the body would not have been
embalmed. A perforated coffin could mean only one
thing: that the speediest possible decomposition was desired. Embalming would only prolong it.

Which left only a handful of possibilities: that the
body of the hanged canon had been turned over to the
family after execution but before burial, upon receipt of a
direct order from the sheriff; that the body on Mr. Nightingale's slab had not been Canon Whitbread; or that
Canon Whitbread had not, in fact, been executed.

I couldn't contain my excitement.

"Where was Canon Whitbread buried?" I asked.

"Ah," said Dogger. "That is the question, is it not? We
shall have to find that out."

We! Dogger and me. The two of us, on the case together.

My heart began to glow like a potbellied woodstove in
a logger's cabin.

"Where shall . . . we . . . begin?" I managed to say.

"With the parishioners of St. Mildred's," Dogger answered. "It is a fact often overlooked by the law that when it comes to murder, the parishioners know all the answers."

"Did you say *murder*, Dogger?"

"I did indeed."

Now, suddenly, I was glowing like the midsummer sun. Dogger had—independently—come to the same conclusion I had.

"We mustn't discuss specific details," I whispered. "In order not to contaminate each other's evidence."

"Of course," Dogger agreed. "I was about to say the same thing myself, Miss Flavia."

I let out a long, noisy breath—a hiss of almost serpent pleasure.

The murderer of Orlando Whitbread was doomed. From that very moment, he hadn't the chance of a snowman in Hades to escape the team of Dogger and De Luce.

I desperately wanted to rub noses with my new partner but I didn't dare. Eskimo kisses would have to wait until we were more firmly established.

"And now, miss," Dogger said, turning to my single piece of luggage, "shall we unpack the poisons?"

·SEVEN·

THE "POISONS" TO WHICH Dogger referred were those discussed in the fat blue volume of Taylor's *Medical Jurisprudence*, in its Ninth Edition, which I believe I have already mentioned.

"Sorry for the weight," I said, as Dogger hoisted my suitcase onto the bed. I knew perfectly well that mine was nothing compared with the oxcart of books dear Daffy had dragged along. I trusted that, in Dogger's mind, I would seem thoughtful by comparison.

"'A good book,'" he said, squaring up the heavy volume reverently on the bedside table, "'is the precious life-blood of a master spirit, embalmed and treasured up on purpose to a life beyond life.'

"Or so, at least, says Mr. Milton in his *Areopagitica*," he added.

I nodded wisely in agreement, even though I wasn't

quite sure who Mr. Milton was, what he meant by the remark, or what his *Areopagitica* might happen to be.

Still, any quotation with the word *embalmed* in it can never be a bore.

"Dogger," I said, "what do you think—"

But Dogger stuck up a warning hand, palm toward me: the universal symbol for "Hush!"—or perhaps "Shut up!"

I shut up.

Incredibly, I had not heard the footsteps on the stairs outside. Fortunately, Dogger had.

"I shall find a tackle shop, Miss Flavia," he said, keeping his hand in the air, "and some suitable rods. If we are to be detained for a day or two in order to assist Constable Otter, I am quite confident there can be no harm in a bit of fishing."

On the last word, he gave me a broad wink, and I had to clap a hand over my mouth to keep from giggling.

"Oh, must we?" I said, falling into the role as Jean Simmons might have done. "I *detest* fishing."

"I daresay," Dogger replied with a poker-straight face, "that you will feel quite differently when you catch something."

I hugged myself with delight. *This* was living! The shadows of the past six months—at least most of them—vanished at the prospect of . . .

Well, I wasn't quite sure what, but reeling in a murderer would certainly keep our minds occupied.

"I suppose you're right," I said, trying to inject unwillingness into my voice, but even as I spoke, Dogger was moving slowly and silently toward the door. When he reached it, he seized the knob and gave it an easy, fluid twist.

"Oh, Mrs. Palmer!" he said. "You startled me. I didn't realize you were here."

You old fox, I thought. *You clever old fox!*

"Oh, Mr. Dogger," the landlord's wife said. "I was just about to say the same. We've gone and startled one *another*, haven't we? I was just coming up to see if anything was required."

Another old fox, I thought. Or, rather, *Another old vixen.*

I was keenly aware that I was watching two Old Masters at work.

"Nothing, thank you," Dogger said, pretending to brush a fleck of dust from the suitcase.

"And you, dearie?" Mrs. Palmer asked, fixing me with the most awful, leering counterfeit grin. "Anything to make you comfy?"

I had once made a solemn pledge to flay alive and use their skin for a horse blanket the next person who dared to call me "dearie."

Her awful word hung in the stale bedroom air. And then:

"Just a bit of quiet, thank you," I heard my mouth saying. "I have the most awful headache."

It was the first time in my life I had ever used this Neanderthal excuse but I knew, even as I said it, why at least two thousand generations of females have employed those very words—or, at least, their equivalent—in whatever language they may have spoken.

As an argument, the phrase was unassailable: a conversational stone wall. Who, for instance, could ever prove you hadn't one?

As a sword shrouded in velvet—a gentle weapon—it was probably unequaled.

Six simple words, of which all but two were of a single syllable, and yet which fairly oozed accusation: "*I have the most awful headache.*"

I knew that it was unfair: a cheat, a deceit, and—well, why not put it plainly?—a lie.

At the same time, I rejoiced in knowing that it had wandered in from some distant room in my brain.

"I shall be all right," I said. "It's just . . . just . . . the . . . shock of . . ."

I let my voice trail off into nothingness.

Flavia! You fibber!

"There, there, dearie," Mrs. Palmer said. "I understand. I've been taken that way myself on many an occasion."

There was that word again.

I had somehow to restrain myself.

In my mind, I pulled from my pocket a needle and a reel of fishing line. I imagined popping the end of the tough black fiber into my mouth to moisten it, then squinting as I pushed it through the eye of the needle, which I shoved in through my lower lip, out through my upper lip, pulled it tight, followed with another loop—and another—and another. When I was finished, my mouth looked like one of those stitched-up shrunken heads that are brought back by explorers from the Amazonian jungle.

I was proud of my handiwork. Against all odds, I had managed to keep my mouth shut.

Mrs. Palmer was giving me what I believe is called a quizzical look.

Shoo! I told her with my mind. *Buzz off! Go away! Vanish! Vamoose! Get lost! Take a powder!*

And, by the jawbone of Jupiter, it worked!

Mrs. Palmer blinked.

"I'd best be getting back, then, if there's nothing I can do," she said, dusting her hands as if to signal she was finished with me.

"Thank you, Mrs. Palmer," Dogger said, and I thought I heard a muffled "humph" as she clumped noisily down the stairs.

"Back to the poisons," I said when she was gone and the door was firmly shut.

"Back to the poisons," Dogger echoed.

I have to admit that I was reluctant to tell him what I'd done, but after only a couple of false starts, I found myself explaining in detail how I had used my handkerchief to swab a sample of liquid from the corpse's lips.

I needn't have worried.

"Excellent," Dogger said. "You were thinking of the diatoms, no doubt?"

"No," I admitted. "I was thinking of potassium cyanide, prussic acid, and paraldehyde."

Dogger nodded.

"Quite right," he said. "The three P's. Very proper. We shall test for those also."

"Tell me about the diatoms," I said.

When the speaker was Dogger, I was more than willing to be instructed.

"The diatoms," Dogger explained—and I could see that he was enjoying this—"are a vast species of microscopic algae belonging to the class *Bacillariophyceae*, which are notable for secreting a hard outer skeleton of siliceous matter—"

"Hold on," I said. "Are you telling me they secrete a shell of sand?"

"Well, virtually—in its hydrated form, of course. Their cell walls are of the same material."

"Like tiny army tanks!"

"Precisely."

"The point being?" I could hardly contain myself.

"The point being that, in cases of drowning, the presence or absence of diatoms in the lungs may well indicate whether or not the victim was breathing when he or she went into the water."

I wrinkled my brow.

"I don't quite follow you," I said.

Dogger reached into an inner pocket and pulled out a small black notebook. After flipping through a great many pages upon which were written a great many notes in his tiny, meticulous hand—O! How I wish I could have read it all!—he came at last to a blank page.

Unscrewing the cap of his fountain pen, he began to draw a series of small triangles, ellipses, and circles, then filled them in with elaborate but regular patterns of cells and chambers: some like snowflakes—or miniature honeycombs—or snooker balls in their triangular racks—or the hugely magnified fly's eyes in one of those endless instructional films we were made to watch in St. Tancred's parish hall.

"Diatoms are abundant in both fresh and salt water," Dogger said. "If we analyze the residue on your handkerchief—"

And suddenly the light went on!

"We can tell if he was breathing. We can tell if he was murdered!"

"Perhaps," Dogger said. "Putting aside the bruise on the neck for a moment, there were no marks of restraint on the visible parts of his body. It is remarkably difficult to hold an unwilling victim under water. Ropes are usually required."

"Or handcuffs," I added.

"Or handcuffs," Dogger agreed. "Although it's the extremities of the limbs that flail about, so that abrasions generally tend to be found on the wrists and ankles."

"That makes sense," I said, and it did. How did Dogger know all these things?

"All that remains," said Dogger, "is a proper chemical analysis."

"We'd better get on with it," I said, "before the evidence evaporates."

"Possibly, with reference to the cyanide, the prussic acid, and the paraldehyde, but as for the diatoms, there is no urgency whatever. The frustules for which we are searching consist virtually of glass, which will last for millions of years. I suggest we have time for tea."

"But I don't want tea," I protested. "I want to roll up my sleeves and get to work."

It took me a moment to see what Dogger was smiling at. In my light summer dress, I had no sleeves worth speaking of to *roll* up.

"And so do I, Miss Flavia," he said, "but first we shall have to assemble certain . . . ah, philosophical instruments."

Because "philosophical instruments" was the phrase used by Dr. Watson to describe certain of Sherlock Holmes's chemical apparatuses, I knew what Dogger meant.

"Of course," I said. "We must assemble our philosophical instruments."

Not yet having the faintest idea what these might be.

"Well, we can boil our own water, anyway," I said, pointing to the electric hot plate and tired-looking tin kettle that sat on a table in front of the window.

"An excellent start," Dogger said, rubbing his hands together. "I shall be back in a jiff."

Back in a jiff? What was the world coming to? That Dogger should use such slang was unthinkable. But before I could remark upon it he was gone.

I went to the window and peered down through the curtain. A few seconds later, Dogger appeared in the inn yard, walked casually to the parked Rolls, removed a couple of items from the boot, and retraced his steps.

"You're very cheerful, Dogger," I twitted him as he came back into the room. "Did you win something on the dogs or the horses?"

"I am not a betting man, Miss Flavia—except upon

the great game of Life and Death. In my own turns at the table, I have been most fortunate to date."

I ought to have known better.

"I'm sorry, Dogger," I said. "I didn't mean to—"

"Nor did I," said Dogger. "It is time, I think, to make our first move."

And with that he placed two objects on the bed. The first was a man's black leather travel case; the other I recognized as the first-aid kit from the boot of the Rolls.

From his pocket he produced the powerful torch normally kept in the car's glove box.

"Now then," he said, "one thing more . . ."

He opened the door and, after looking both ways, stepped into the hall and vanished to the left, which direction, I knew, led only to the WC. Otherwise, it was a blind corridor.

There was a silence, and then came the gush of a flushing toilet.

There are times when it isn't polite to listen, but the proximity of the water closet to my bedroom at the Oak and Pheasant made such niceties difficult to observe.

A moment later Dogger was back.

"Always flush when you are up to no good," he said with a solemn face. "It puts them off the scent."

I couldn't believe my ears. Was Dogger making a joke? He was talking to me almost as if I were an equal.

From behind his back he produced a yellow metal tin.

"There is no good landlord—or landlady, for that matter—from Land's End to John o' Groats who doesn't lay in a good supply of drain cleaner."

He held out the tin for my inspection.

"Drain Bane," I read aloud. "Is that really the name of it?"

"Unhappily, yes," Dogger said. "But fortunately for us, it is nothing more than sodium hydroxide putting on airs."

Sodium hydroxide! I clapped my hands together. Caustic soda to the masses, but good old NaOH to those of us who are lucky enough to be chemists.

As if I were home again in my lab at Buckshaw, a great calm came over me.

"Where do we begin?" I asked, suddenly breathless at the prospect.

"I suggest we prepare the diatoms," Dogger replied.

I dug into my pocket and extracted the handkerchief, taking great care to keep it balled up to protect the evidence.

I handed it over to Dogger, realizing, even as I did so, that this frail bit of linen might well become the noose round the neck of some person or persons as yet unknown.

It was an eerie feeling—but a pleasant one. It would be nice to believe that Justice plays no favorites.

To my surprise, Dogger set the handkerchief aside. Well, not exactly aside, but he pushed it gently into a glass drinking tumbler which he took from the black travel case.

"First things first," he said. "First things, in this case, being distilled water."

He half-filled the kettle with water from the small sink in the corner, and placed it on the hot plate. Setting aside the lid, he replaced it with the glass chimney from the candle holder, capping this with a second tumbler from the travel case.

"Almost a perfect fit," he said, switching on the hot plate. "It will do."

"You've done this before," I observed.

"No," Dogger said. "I'm afraid I am improvising."

"Improvising is half the fun," I said. "If it works."

"It is, indeed," Dogger agreed.

·EIGHT·

IT WASN'T LONG BEFORE the kettle's steam began rising into the lamp chimney and condensing on the colder glass. Dogger let it boil for two and a half minutes before switching off the hot plate, by which time the inside of the chimney was completely filled with steam, its inner surfaces streaming water droplets like a rain-lashed window.

With a swift movement, Dogger seized the makeshift apparatus and, removing it from atop the kettle, flipped it over and placed it gently on the table. The drinking glass was now on the bottom, the inverted chimney on the top. Already the condensation was forming beads, running down the inside of the glass, dripping into the tumbler.

"That's our distilled water," I said, ticking it off on my fingers.

"We shall set aside a bit of it for our cyanide and paraldehyde experiments," he said, tipping a couple of ounces into a drinking glass from the bedside table.

"Do we have enough?" I asked.

"We shan't require a great deal," Dogger said, decanting the remaining water carefully into the glass containing my handkerchief, and tamping it down with the end of his fountain pen until the whole wad was thoroughly wetted. "The evidence is microscopic."

"What's next?"

"We shall leave it to percolate for a while," Dogger said.

Time becomes glacial when you're impatient, and after just a few minutes I found myself sitting on my hands to keep from fidgeting.

"Shall we get on with our cyanide and paraldehyde testing?" Dogger suggested with a gentle smile, as he took down a white stoneware soap dish from a shelf above the sink.

I hugged myself with joy.

Because potassium cyanide (KCN) would have been converted by Orlando's stomach acids to prussic acid (HCN), these tests were simple. We could, of course, have produced the required picric acid with a handful of aspirin tablets in sulfuric acid, but we quickly decided upon an easier method: A couple of grams of sodium bicarbonate and a few drops of picric acid antiseptic, both from the first-aid kit Dogger had brought from the Rolls, would do the trick nicely.

I watched as Dogger carefully washed and dried the

soap dish, tipped into it an ounce or so of the solution in which my handkerchief was soaking, then added a few drops of the antiseptic to the sample.

As I was half expecting it would, the fluid, due to the formation of potassium iso-purpurate, quickly took on a faint reddish brick color.

"Interesting," I said, trying to contain my excitement. "Cyanide. The presence of which would, in itself, suggest accidental poisoning, suicide, or murder."

Dogger nodded.

"And now for the paraldehyde. I've also taken the liberty of siphoning a small quantity of battery acid— sulfuric, of course—from the Rolls," he said, producing a small glass bottle which I recognized at once as having formerly contained smelling salts in the car's glove box.

"You are amazing, Dogger!" I clapped my hands together.

"Thank you, Miss Flavia," he said. "'*Amazing*' is a word for wizards. I prefer to think of myself as merely practical."

Because Dogger's gentle rebukes were always as warm as honey, I treasured them. I vowed never to use the word again.

"Would you care to do the honors?" he asked, and I knew that I was forgiven my momentary indiscretion.

After heating the bottle gently in the steam from the kettle, I removed—with great care—the stopper of the salts bottle and decanted a few drops of the sulfuric acid into the soap dish, which contained the small sample of what I now thought of as my handkerchief water.

Just as the picric acid signaled the presence of cyanide by turning red in the first sample, so did the sulfuric acid tell us we were in the presence of paraldehyde by going yellow with a greenish tinge.

Dogger and I looked at each other: snug as two bugs in a rug.

"Cyanide," I said again. "*And* paraldehyde."

"It certainly seems so," Dogger agreed. "And now for our friends the diatoms. If you will be so good as to prepare a solution of the sodium hydroxide—a couple of cubic centimeters ought to be sufficient."

Taking the now-empty drinking tumbler from our makeshift distilling apparatus, I placed it in the bottom of the sink and poured into it some of the remaining hot water from the kettle.

One needed to be extremely careful at this game. Dogger nodded approvingly as I raised the window sash.

Sodium hydroxide crystals, upon contact with water, generate sudden tremendous heat—the so-called exothermic reaction—resulting in a furious foaming, which explains why they are so highly regarded in the unclogging of stubborn drains.

Because of the caustic nature of the stuff, it is necessary to protect the skin and clothing from unexpected splashes. I loved it that Dogger didn't tell me to be careful.

"May I borrow your driving gloves?" I asked.

Did Dogger raise an eyebrow?

Perhaps by the width of a hair, but he hid it well.

"Of course you may, Miss Flavia," he replied, and fished them from his jacket pocket.

As I slipped them onto my hands, I marveled at the soft luxury of the gloves, which Dogger had once told me were stitched from the skins of young hornless goats from the Cape of Good Hope.

Poor babies! I thought as I wiggled my fingers into position. *I'd better be careful not to damage them.*

Uncapping the tin of Drain Bane, I tipped a few crystals of the stuff into the glass of water from the kettle. They sank to the bottom. A few more crystals and they began to fizz. A few more and—

I stopped abruptly. Like a dose of stomach salts, the stuff was suddenly foaming fiercely up the sides of the glass, but fortunately it stopped just before reaching the lip.

"Perfect," Dogger said. Until that moment I hadn't realized he was watching me.

"As for the required glassware, I have taken the liberty of bringing up the bud vase from Miss Harriet's Rolls-Royce."

How I longed to hug him! Not just for thinking of how to provide a makeshift test-tube, but for still thinking of the Rolls as belonging to my late mother.

In the days when she was still alive, this small glass trumpet from Liberty's had been one of two in the car, which my father had kept perpetually supplied with roses from the garden at Buckshaw.

The thought of it tugged at something inside me, but I didn't want to give in to emotion in front of Dogger.

"Brilliant!" was all I could manage. "What shall we use for a stopper?"

But Dogger had already thought of that. "Candle wax,"

he said, reaching for the hand lamp whose glass shade we had already put to such good use.

He plucked the candle from its socket, held its butt end over the hot plate, and turned on the switch. Rotating it as it warmed, he soon had a teardrop of wax the size of a penny ready to drop.

"If you'll be so kind as to hold this for a moment," he said, and taking the glass containing the submerged handkerchief, he gave it a final stir and a good poke with his pen.

Having done so, he poured some of the liquid contents into the bud vase and handed it to me.

With thumbs and first two fingers, I worked the wax to form a perfect plug, then pressed it into the top of the vase.

"Watertight!" I said, and Dogger nodded.

"Now for a centrifuge," he said quietly, almost as if to himself.

Centrifuge?

At home, in my laboratory at Buckshaw, I had the lovely professional centrifuge that had been brought from Germany by my late uncle Tarquin. With an electrical motor powerful enough to swing an ox until Doomsday at 2000 revolutions per minute, or until the electrical power was cut off, whichever came first.

But here in a miserable bedroom at the Oak and Pheasant? What were we to do?

A small light dawned in my brain. I was already grinning from ear to ear.

"The blind cord!" I blurted. Then gaining control of

myself, I said in softer tones—and with considerably less volume: "I think the cord from the blind will serve admirably."

The look on Dogger's face was worth a sultan's ransom, as if his horse had won the Derby. If this wasn't pride, it was something very much like it.

"Quite right," he said. "I'm sure the good Mrs. Palmer won't mind, as long as we leave everything as we found it."

He stepped to the window, lowered the blind, brought out his penknife, selected the smallest blade, and before you could say "I name this racehorse Jack Robinson," had detached the flaxen cord.

With a firm reef knot—left over right, right over left; granny knots begone—he fastened the cord firmly to the tapered neck of the bud vase.

"Now for the acrobatics." He took up a position at the foot of the bed. "Please sit in the corner and mind your head."

As I retreated to the chair in the corner, Dogger seized the cord in its center and, like an American cowboy about to lasso a calf, began swinging it—and the bud vase with its precious cargo—in a circle round his head.

As the speed accelerated, Dogger let out more and more cord until the glass was coming within a foot of each of the walls.

I watched for a while until—as always happens when you're watching someone swing a rope—I began to grow bored.

"How long will it take?" I asked.

"Fifteen minutes, I reckon," he said.

"I reckon"? Was this meant to be a joke? And a cowboy joke, at that? Was I supposed to laugh?

I smiled to cover all the possibilities and returned to my watching.

I understood perfectly what was taking place, of course. Inside the bud vase, the diatoms (if there were any), because of their relatively heavy siliceous composition, were overcoming both buoyant and frictional forces of the liquid solution as centrifugal force rammed them relentlessly and tightly into the very bottom of the bud vase.

"Shall I spell you for a while?" I asked Dogger, and he nodded with a look of what I guessed was gratitude.

I ducked in under the rope and synchronized my motions with his. Like a country stationmaster handing off the right-of-way token to the engine driver of the Flying Scotsman at speed, the transfer was perfection.

Dogger stepped neatly out of the way and perched on the edge of the chair.

"This is harder than it looks," I said after a couple of minutes. My arm was already beginning to ache.

"Sustained muscular action often is," Dogger said. "Without prior training, that is. Such fatigue is due largely to a surplus of chloride, potassium, lactic acid, and magnesium, caused by muscular contraction, and a simultaneous insufficiency of creatine phosphate, glycogen, and adenosine triphosphate."

Why had no one ever put it so plainly? It suddenly made such perfect sense.

Muscle power needed to be chemically provided and, at the same time, muscular waste products efficiently removed, to allow Harry Plunkett to lift his father's Clydesdale horse, Colossus, clear off the ground for charity every August at the Hinley Goose and Gooseberry Show.

My arms were feeling suddenly less heavy.

Round and round the bud vase flew on the end of its cord, producing an audible humming noise.

I was an angel and the glass container my oversized halo. But wait! I was now being transformed into a helicopter on the verge of lifting off!

If I could, I would fly out the window, across the road to the church, and hover there, an eye in the sky, getting a firsthand view of the landscape in which Orlando Whitbread had met his bitter end. There would be no need to wait for Hob's aerial snapshots from the chemist's.

"That ought to be sufficient," Dogger said, snapping me abruptly out of my daydream.

I slowed the high-speed missile, letting it descend gently, little by little, until it came almost to rest, rotating slowly and idly, at the end of the cord.

"Now then," Dogger said. "The sodium hydroxide ought to have digested any organic matter which was present in your sample—"

By my "sample," he was referring to the slimy liquid I had wiped from Orlando's mouth.

"—leaving only the siliceous cell walls and outer skeletons of the diatoms—presuming, of course, that diatoms *were* present."

As he spoke, he poured off into the sink the excess

liquid—which was quite clear—leaving only the slightest trace of a foggy residue in the bottom of the bud vase.

"And if they weren't present?" I asked, knowing the answer perfectly well, but wanting to hear it again from Dogger's lips.

"If they weren't present, then we can certainly make the case that our deceased friend was already dead when he entered the water. All that remains for us now is to improvise a microscope."

Improvise a microscope? I think my heart stopped. Was all this to be for nothing?

"Which is quite easily done," Dogger said, ignoring my open mouth.

Taking the torch, he switched it on and stood it on the table so that its beam was striking the ceiling.

Then, slipping two fingers into his waistcoat pocket, he removed a tiny object and held it up for my inspection.

"A paper clip?" I asked.

"Indeed. The humble paper clip, in certain circumstances, can be of more practical use than a magic wand."

And without another word, he opened out one end of the metal clip and, with fingers as deft as any surgeon's, twisted it into a tiny loop. From the first-aid kit he removed a small jar of petroleum jelly, into which he dipped the wire circle.

"Now," he said, taking a deep breath, "shall we rake out the contents of our vase—whatever they may be— onto the bottom of . . . this?"

"This" was a small graduated measuring glass, which

he was removing from the first-aid kit. He turned it upside down and placed it on the table beside the torch.

With a wooden tongue depressor—also from the first-aid kit—I scraped out the residue from the vase and spread it thinly on the bottom of the glass.

Dogger picked up the glass and slipped it, inverted, over the glowing lens of the torch. Drawing the loop of his paper clip along the inside of the glass lamp chimney, which still contained a small puddle of distilled water, he pulled it out and held it up for my inspection. Suspended in the loop of the clip was a single drop of water, which sparkled like a diamond in the light from the window.

"Wonderful," I said, and I meant it.

It was the petroleum jelly, of course, which held the water drop in place. How clever of Dogger to have thought of it!

"Our objective lens," Dogger said, moving it into position just above our smudge of residue on the bottom of the glass.

"What do you see?" he asked.

I bent at the waist until I was directly above the drop of water, which was illuminated from below by the torch. Several tiny grains, fringed with many colors, shimmered before my eyes.

"Are those diatoms?" I asked. "They're quite tiny."

Dogger reached into the pocket of his resourceful waistcoat and pulled out his reading glasses. "Use these as a magnifying eyepiece."

I slipped them onto my nose and ears.

Gently, so as not to dislodge the drop of water, I took

the paper clip from Dogger's fingers, moving it up and down until the image in the water drop was clear.

Success! The reading glasses more than doubled the magnification of our homemade microscope.

I drew in a breath.

"What do you see?" Dogger asked.

"Stars," I told him. "Triangles . . . circles . . . rods . . . strings . . . tiny seashells. It's like a kaleidoscope."

Dogger leaned in for a look.

"Diatoms," he said in a quiet voice. "Definitely diatoms."

"Meaning?" I asked.

"Death by drowning."

Drat! I had been counting on cyanide to be the killer.

"Oh, well," I said, trying to hide my disappointment. "At least it was an interesting chemical experiment."

"Indeed it was, Miss Flavia. How is your headache now?"

I had completely forgotten my fib.

"It's gone away," I said.

Dogger nodded wisely.

"Yes," he said. "Chemistry has that effect, has it not?"

·NINE·

THERE WENT ALL MY theories: shot down in flames.

So much for death by prussic acid. So much for the paraldehyde.

Death by drowning, Dogger had said.

Orlando, the idiot, had probably caught his foot on a plank while practicing his dance on the dock behind the church. He might easily have suffered a dizzy spell, fallen, and banged his head, or had a heart attack, or, suddenly tired of life, had sipped a bit of cyanide and hurled himself into the water and, by sheer determination, had kept his head beneath the surface until it was too late to be rescued.

That was easy enough to do. Virginia Woolf, Daffy had told me, loaded the pockets of her overcoat with stones and waded into the River Ouse.

I had a sudden sinking feeling. Had I checked Orlando's pockets?

I had, and had found nothing but wet lint and that mysterious bit of paper.

Perhaps I had overlooked something.

"Dogger," I asked, "did you by any chance check the pockets?"

There was no need to explain whose pockets I was talking about. That was the great thing about Dogger: He could follow my train of thought as easily as if he owned the railway.

"I could feel them, Miss Flavia, as I carried him ashore. No stones. And now, if you'll excuse me—"

He needn't have asked, as both of us knew perfectly well. His sense of duty was calling him to check up on my sisters. He had spent enough time with me.

Not that they needed him, of course. My two sisters were as tough as a pair of old blacksmith's boots, but still, they enjoyed going through the motions of helplessness.

I knew that in a matter of minutes, Daffy would be sending Dogger off on a search of the local library for the second volume of John Forster's *The Life of Charles Dickens*, the only book missing from the deluxe morocco-bound set in our library at Buckshaw.

Or should I say *my library*?

Because Buckshaw was now legally mine, lock, stock, and barrel, so, supposedly, were all the books in that vast mountain range of printed matter, *including* the missing Forster—wherever it might be.

Perhaps upon our return I would gift wrap the two surviving volumes and present them to Daffy with my compliments. I might even go so far as to inscribe them on their flyleaves.

But no—that might be a bit presumptuous: as if my name deserved to be displayed beside Dickens's. Besides, an incomplete set of anything was hardly a decent gift, was it? That would be like presenting an avid golfer with a set of antique clubs that were missing the niblick, or the mashie, or whatever those iron bludgeons were called.

I would bide my time.

As for Feely, she would be sending Dogger trotting off to the chemists with instructions to replenish her stock of Dekur Bonne Nuit Turtle Oil Cream, Rubinstein's Valaze Blackhead and Open Pore Paste, oatmeal cream, and a couple of Crinofricto Depilatory Stones.

The fact that she continued to medicate her hide indicated—to me, at least—that despite their most recent crockery-tossing split-up, she still had plans of making it up with Dieter.

As I made my way down the narrow creaking stairs, I heard piano music. Someone was singing:

"I'm the girl that makes the thing that drills the hole
that holds the ring that drives the rod that turns the knob
that works the thing-ummy-bob . . ."

I looked in through the glass door of the saloon bar and saw that it was Feely. She was seated at a rather battered piano, surrounded by three men in kerchiefs: the same three men we had seen when we first arrived at the pub. I had seen the one with the polka-dot handkerchief again at the fair.

"I'm the girl that makes the thing that holds the oil
that oils the ring that takes the shank that moves the crank
that works the thing-ummy-bob."

I couldn't believe my eyes. Feely was evidently having the time of her life and never had she had a more appreciative audience.

The three men hung on her every word, nodding along, tapping their feet and fingers and occasionally joining in to roar with her, as they raised their glasses of ale, the words at the end of each line:

". . . that works the thing-ummy-bob!"

I recognized the song, of course. It was one of Gracie Fields's wartime classics: the one about the girl in the munitions factory making the parts for some top-secret but important machine whose function is a mystery.

Feely's voice was high and clear, rising like a skylark above the coarse, rumbling voices of the three men who hemmed her in. Could this possibly be the same person who had, less than two hours ago, sat at the organ and summoned up the mathematical ghost of Johann S. Bach?

In spite of living with her all my life, there were still sides of my sister I had never seen before. She had as many facets as an icosahedron, that twenty-faceted form

into which Plato believed—wrongly, as it turned out—
the water in our human bodies decayed when we were
dead.

There were faces of Feely which, like the far side of the
moon, were always turned away. Perhaps this came of
looking at herself in mirrors so much. Perhaps parts of her
had, like Alice, slipped through to the other side of the
looking-glass.

The song came to a sudden end:

". . . that works the thing-ummy-bob!"

Feely looked around the room as if she had just awak-
ened from a long trance and found herself on another
planet. She got up from the piano, clasped her arms, and
hugged herself in the way that she always does when she's
ashamed.

"You're a corker, gal!" said one of the men. "Gi' us another!"

"'Kiss Me Goodnight, Sergeant Major,'" demanded
the tallest one, leering and wiggling his ginger mustache
at her as he spoke. "Do you know that one?"

Feely looked from one of the men to another with startled eyes.

"No, she doesn't," I interrupted, flinging open the glass
door and stepping into the saloon bar.

Six eyes—eight counting Feely's—swung round and
fixed me in their glare.

"Come along, Ophelia," I said, putting on a pretentious

voice. "You're wanted at Miss Wilberforce's bedside. She's taken rather a nasty turn and you're needed at once."

Who Miss Wilberforce was, or from what horrid malady she was suffering, I hadn't the faintest idea. It was intended to extract Feely from the predicament she was in, and to brook no argument.

But it didn't work.

Feely gave me one of her ten-ton looks.

"What do you mean by barging in here!" she shouted, her face already going the color of brick.

As if to defend her, one of the men put his arm around her shoulders and pulled her toward him.

"Well?" he demanded, in a parade-square voice.

I marched over to Feely, seized the man's hand between my thumb and forefinger as if it were a stinking fish, and lifted it from my sister's shoulders.

I could smell the alcohol on his breath.

It was a showdown of sorts:

"What's going on here?" a voice demanded: a voice that I would know anywhere. Anywhere! Even on the darkest desert night.

I dropped the offending hand and spun round.

Dieter, Feely's forsaken fiancé, was standing in the doorway, his face frozen at the scene before him.

"Dieter!" I shouted and flew into his arms. I wanted to squeeze him until nothing was left but a husk.

The room fell suddenly silent.

The three men with kerchiefs all let their hands fall to their sides, as if to be within handy reach of their holsters.

They stared at Dieter, as if afraid to be the first to unlock eyes.

Dieter stared back at them.

And then, on the other side of the room, a whine began: low at first, like a distant air-raid siren, then rising in pitch and volume from a whisper to a buzzing scream.

It was, all in all, an amazing vocal performance.

"Dieterrrrrrrr!"

Feely's shriek flew past my ears like an enraged hornet or a ricochet from a .45 caliber slug. Feely herself followed, knocking me out of the way with a wicked forearm.

In a lightning flash, she was in his arms and he in hers.

All, apparently, was forgiven.

Much as I wanted to gab with Dieter, I decided to leave the lovebirds alone. As far as I knew, they hadn't seen each other for a while, which meant that they would want to be alone to swap spit until they were caught up, or until they died of saturation.

In chemistry, the term "saturation" refers to the state of a compound at which all the units of affinity of the contained elements become engaged, and it is dependent upon both heat and pressure.

In this case, I could not have come up with a better definition if I tried. It was downright disgusting. I didn't want to watch.

I strolled casually out the door, whistling Thomas Morley's musical setting of Shakespeare's song "It Was a Lover and His Lass" from As You Like It, but I don't think either of them heard me.

Outside, the world seemed suddenly quiet in the warmth of a perfect English day. There was no one in the street, nor did there seem to be any further activity across the road in the churchyard.

I made my way round, under the quaint hanging signboard—THE OAK & PHEASANT, ARVEN PALMER PROPRIETOR—to the sunken garden at the back of the inn, to the enclosed area I had seen from my bedroom window.

"Go away!" said a voice.

I turned to find Daffy curled up with a notebook and a pencil, in a small bower behind the garden gate. I had walked straight past without seeing her.

"Go away," she repeated.

"Go away yourself," I said. "I am not your slave or your bondmaid, you know."

I stuck out my tongue at her to prove my point.

"Idiot," she retorted, and returned to her reading.

"Dieter's back," I said.

"*I* know that," she said. "He came round here to see me first. I told him where Feely was."

"I'm glad," I said. "I've missed him."

Daffy said nothing: a perfect indication that she had missed him, too.

"What are you writing?" I asked.

"None of your beeswax," Daffy said.

She had picked up some rather colorful American expressions from Carl Pendracka, one of Feely's—now supposedly unsuccessful—suitors.

"Oh, *here* you are, luv!" exclaimed Mrs. Palmer as she came bustling through the gate with a tray, upon which was a tall glass of milk and an artfully arranged stack of cucumber sandwiches.

I had already begun a grin, and had raised my hands to receive this most welcome feast, when the landlord's wife walked straight past me and put the tray down on Daffy's bower bench.

"I thought you were still in your room, and took it up there by mistake," she said, shaking her head in baffled amusement.

"Thank you, Mrs. Palmer. This is most kind of you," Daffy said in her smarmiest, stickiest voice.

I could have whacked her on the head with a warming pan.

"Would you like one, too, dearie?" Mrs. P asked, turning to me with dramatically raised eyebrows.

The lesson had not been learned.

"No, thank you," I managed to mumble, shaking my head.

"Headache warning still in effect, then?" she asked. Whatever she meant by that.

I nodded.

"I'll leave you to it, then," she said, and she was gone.

"You oughtn't to do that, you know," Daffy grumbled.

"Do what?" I replied, out of habit.

"Whenever anyone calls you 'dearie' you change instantly into a monster. It's like *Hocus Pocus!* or *Alakazam!* And—*poof!* You become *The Ineffable Flavia.*"

"I don't know what 'ineffable' means," I said, although I had my suspicions.

"It means you're a beast. A chump; a bufflehead; a clam; a foozle; a proper dickey-dido."

I knew that, with Daffy, it was best to let her exhaust her storehouse of exotic insults. She would eventually, like an overwound alarm clock, run down and stop her clatter.

While I waited, I examined my fingernails—which I was now rather proud of. I had finally been able to break my habit of gnawing the old keratin to the gristle, and had grown, quite to my surprise and admiration, as slick a set of claws as had ever graced a maiden's hand.

"You've made a friend," I said when Daffy's jaw had tired.

"Huh?" she said, taken by surprise.

"Mrs. Palmer. She's your lapdog. Unlike me."

Daffy scoffed: a prolonged and horrible damp process involving her sinuses.

"She's a *published poet*," she threw at me. "Her work has appeared in the *New Statesman* and in *Blackwood's*. She's spent weekends with the Sitwells, for heaven's sake! What do you say to that?"

"I hope she enjoyed the blue cows," I said.

Sir George Sitwell had caused his cows to be painted in the blue and white willow pattern so as to look better in the green landscape. Or so the vicar's wife had once told me.

"A grand triumph of aesthetics over brains," Cynthia had remarked. "So remarkably rare nowadays."

"Besides," Daffy said, lowering her voice to an excited

whisper and scanning the horizon for eavesdroppers, "she's the author of *The Mussel Bed*."

"Zip-a-dee-doo-dah," I said.

"You're so ignorant!" Daffy spat. "*The Mussel Bed* was a literary sensation. It was short-listed for every book prize going but they could never discover who the author was."

She closed her eyes and recited:

"On Monday morn
The maid came up
And found him there in bed,
His jaw ajar,
His face affright,
All pale,
All cold,
All dead."

Daffy shivered.

"'Brilliant but chilling,' *The Times* called it. '*Folk naïf*, but all the more effective because of it.' James Agate wrote: 'Raw, bleeding, essential,' and George Bernard Shaw suggested, mischievously, that he had taken upon himself the skin of a country barmaid and written the thing."

"And Mrs. Palmer wrote it?" I asked.

"She confided in me," Daffy said. "She made me swear never to tell, and I won't."

"You've just told me," I pointed out.

"Pfaugh!" Daffy said. "You're nobody. And if you ever tell, I shall pour poison in your ear while you're asleep."

I knew that Daffy was desperate. She was cribbing from Shakespeare: the scene in which Hamlet's wicked uncle, Claudius, pours hebenon into the ear of the sleeping king.

Hebenon, in my opinion, was simply a mangled form of henbane, misremembered by one of Shakespeare's acting pals when it came time to write down the plays. Either that, or the error was caused by a daydreaming typesetter.

My point being that the old poison-in-the-ear-of-a-sleeper was nothing new to me.

Daffy's threat was as empty as her hope chest.

"Ho-hum," I said.

But it was at that very moment that I realized something: Two pairs of ears were better than one and twice as likely to gather useful gossip.

Did that mean using my sister as a listening device?

Well, yes, frankly, it did.

We were in a strange place where we knew almost nobody. We would not likely be staying here any longer than required by the law. Time, therefore, was of the essence. I needed to collect as many ears as I could—as American soldiers were said to have done from the British during the American War of Independence.

I drew my forefinger across my mouth in the signal of the zipped lip, crossing my heart and holding my fingers up in the Girl Guide sign of honor (*Ha-ha!*), and said:

"I, Flavia Sabina de Luce, do most solemnly swear that I shall never reveal, upon pain of poison in the ear, those secrets which my dearly beloved sister Daphne de Luce is about to impart unto me."

I realized, even as I said it, that the "unto" was a bit rich, but I wanted Daffy to take me seriously.

"But why would she entrust her secret to you?" I asked. I needed to keep a bit of skepticism in the conversation, otherwise Daffy would suspect I was acting—which I was, but not in the way she thought.

"Because there are times," Daffy answered, choosing her words carefully, "when a woman needs to confide in another woman—and *only* in another woman. Doctors won't do, nor will an entire army of Freud's followers."

"True," I agreed, hoping to sound wise beyond my years.

"What would you know about it?" Daffy scoffed.

I shrugged, which was as good an answer as any. It got Daffy off my back and gave her a perfect opening to go on spilling her guts.

And it worked.

"The poor woman is petrified," Daffy told me. "It seems that her book cut a little too close to the bone. Some of the poems were far too close for comfort."

"To real life?" I asked. This could prove interesting. Especially in a town whose vicar had gone to the scaffold for vile crimes against women!

"Of course to real life!" Daffy said.

"Which poems were they—in particular?" I asked.

"She didn't tell me. I'll look them up when we get home to Buckshaw."

"You have a copy of *The Mussel Bed?*" I asked. Sometimes my sister amazed me.

"Of course," she said, "as does every discriminating woman in England. *The Times Literary Supplement* called it 'indispensable' and they weren't far off the mark."

It was at that moment that I vowed to get my hands as quickly as possible on this literary gem. Daffy's copy might be back at Buckshaw, but surely there was one within earshot of where we were sitting. In its author's bedroom, for instance.

She wouldn't have left a copy in the little library of the saloon bar of the Oak and Pheasant. No, that would have been too risky. But it was reasonable to assume that it wasn't far away.

"So no one knows that she wrote this book?" I asked. "Not even her husband?"

"No," Daffy said, glancing over her shoulder. "*Especially* not her husband."

"Then what's she got to worry about?" I asked.

Daffy bit her bottom lip as if she were making a critical decision, then beckoned me with a crooked finger.

I went to her side and put my ear close to her mouth.

"She's begun to receive blackmailing letters," she said.

"Somebody *knows*?"

I couldn't help myself.

"Shhh!" Daffy whispered. "Apparently so. Now promise you won't breathe a word."

I pantomimed the old sewing-the-lips-shut-with-an-invisible-needle-and-very-long-thread routine, which seemed to satisfy her.

"Now run along," she said, opening her notebook.

"What are you writing?" I asked. "Notes on the case?"

"No. It's a sonnet. You wouldn't be interested."

"Of course I'd be interested, Daff," I said. "I'm your sister, aren't I?"

She gave me a speculative look.

"Some say you are, yes."

"Come on, Daff. Let's hear it. I'll bet it's a killer. A masterpiece, I mean."

Vanity overcame her. She turned to a middle page.

I might not have thought of looking there.

"Well," she said, clearing her throat, "it might not be very good, but here it is—"

Why do so many poets apologize before reading their work aloud? I wondered. How many readings had we attended at St. Tancred's parish hall where the poet felt obliged to kill his own young before they ever drew breath?

"Get on with it!" you always wanted to shout—but you never did. Poets—other than the dreaded Millbank Morrison, of course, who had a hide as thick as a rhinoceros's in chain mail—were notoriously sensitive about their creations, whereas scientists never were.

Did Joseph Priestley apologize for discovering oxygen? Or Henry Cavendish for hydrogen?

Of course not! They fairly crowed about it.

"Pray go on," I said. "I'm listening."

Daffy cleared her throat again and began to read:

"What pale-flesh'd slugs or graveyard grubs do mar
Thy fair and once beguiling former face?"

"Stop!" I said, holding up a hand.

How *dare* she? How *dare* she trespass upon my personal territory? *I* was the expert on the business of the dead. *I* was the Doctor of Decay. How *dare* she?

"I'm sorry, Daff," I said. "You'll have to stop there. It's too real. You've made me queasy."

Daffy looked up, flushed with pride, then closed her book.

"Actually, that's all there is so far. I've only just begun, but I shall read you the rest of it when I'm finished."

"Don't wear out your pencil," I said as I walked out through the garden gate.

· T E N ·

"Ah, Miss de Luce," said a voice before I'd taken half a dozen paces. "A word with you, if you don't mind."

It was Constable Otter, notebook and indelible pencil poised at the ready.

How long had he been lurking outside the garden gate? How much had he overheard?

I tried to sneak a look at the page to see if it was blank, but as I stepped forward, he stepped automatically back. What a canny customer he was!

"Yes, Constable?" I said. "How may I help you?"

"By not meddling," he replied, "in things you know nothing about."

Was this a threat? Was I being warned off by a village bobby?

"I beg your pardon," I said. "I don't know what you're talking about."

"I believe you do," Constable Otter said, shutting his notebook with an elaborate single-handed flourish and, with all the art of a well-drilled sailor loading a cannon, tamping it down into his jacket pocket.

"Yes, I believe you do," he went on.

I put on Innocent Face Number 5: the full-on expression that combines injured innocence with just the slightest hint of aggression, conveyed by the rolling-out of precisely four millimeters of lower lip. I had practiced it many times in a mirror.

The next move was his—and he took it.

"I've rung up Inspector Hewitt at Hinley," he said. "I am led to believe you're rather notorious in that neck of the woods."

In that neck of the woods? Was this country bumpkin suggesting that my small successes in the solving of crimes were limited to Hinley and environs? Had Inspector Hewitt neglected to tell him that I had been thanked—in person!—by our own dear (and now, alas, late) King George VI?

What was the inspector thinking of? Had he forgotten already that I had sent him—and his wife, Antigone, whom I adored—a wicker hamper of apples and oranges upon the birth of their daughter, and first child, in January?

Antigone, of course, had sent back a card thanking me for my thoughtfulness, but since then, I had heard nothing.

It was, I must admit, quite soon after Father's death, and the Hewitts, perhaps, had wanted to respect my family's privacy.

There had been a discreet card of sympathy, edged in

black, but that was all, which came as a keen disappointment when I had been expecting to be asked to stand as
the baby's godmother: to stand with the child at the font
as she was christened Flavia Antigone Hewitt.

And now this!

"Notorious in that neck of the woods," the constable had
said.

"Yes, Constable Otter," I replied. "I have been known
to solve a crime or two."

The hairs on the back of my neck were fairly bristling.

"Perhaps you have, miss, but what makes you think
that a crime has been committed here? What makes you
think that the young man's death was anything more
than misadventure?"

Sharp as a tinker's tack, this constable! He was giving
nothing away.

Since I already knew that Orlando Whitbread was a
young man, Otter wasn't being indiscreet. But, obviously,
he wasn't yet aware I knew the dead man's name.

"I didn't *say* it was a crime," I shot back.

Two can play at this game, you saucy Peeler! I thought.
Didn't he realize he was taking on a master?

"I merely observed that I have been known to solve a
crime or two. Elsewhere. In the past."

That ought to put him in his place. I had given away
nothing.

"Perhaps you have, miss," he said. "But in any event, it
won't be called for in this case, will it?

"Besides," he added, almost as an afterthought, "the

Chief Constable doesn't fancy interference on his own turf. No, that he doesn't. Not by a long chalk."

There was no doubt about it. I *was* being warned.

Constable Otter knew a great deal more than he was telling, which was proper, I suppose, for a policeman, but still, if no crime had been committed, why had he gone to the trouble and expense of ringing up Inspector Hewitt to check on my background?

Something here was fishy, and it wasn't just Orlando Whitbread.

Or perhaps it was.

I needed to get to the bottom of this business about Blue Boy and his scarlet dancing slippers, but how was I to do so?

The answer seemed obvious.

The low-beamed kitchen of the Oak and Pheasant was hot and hellish, like some turkey-tainted inferno. Pots bubbled busily on the cooker, giving off odors of gravy, potatoes, and mushy peas.

In spite of it being midsummer, the pub seemed to be doing a roaring business in hearty meals. Who ate them? I wondered.

Could it be the local farmers, who came in starving from the fields? If so, I hadn't seen any tractors parked outside. Or the droves of tourists who, with petrol rationing ended, were everywhere in England, driving cars with names like Hawk or Snipe, suggesting that their tin wings could whisk you through the air over vast distances to anywhere your heart desired.

Perhaps the resting turkey on the sideboard was destined for the tummies of the roustabouts from Shadrach's Circus & Menagerie. Other than my brief encounter with Polka-Dot Kerchief at the fair, I hadn't had a chance to look into their presence.

I needed to ask some questions.

Brushing wet strands of hair out of her face, Mrs. Palmer looked up from stirring something that looked like a glue pot. She was not exactly delighted to find me in her kitchen.

I made an after-the-fact knock at the doorframe.

"Sorry to bother you, Mrs. Palmer," I began, letting the words gush out like water from a hose, "but I want to apologize for the way I spoke to you. It wasn't right. I don't know what got into me. It may have been the shock of finding the body of that poor drowned man on the riverbank, I don't know, but even that is no excuse. I beg your pardon and I promise it will never happen again."

I moved my hand closer to my heart to emphasize the point.

I was proud of myself! I had groveled, made good, and brought the subject round to the corpse all in one breath.

I lowered my head and stood there looking abject.

Who could resist?

Not Mrs. Palmer, at any rate.

Slowly, as if to savor the moment, she removed her oven gloves and, with an audible sigh, placed them tenderly on the table.

"Who told you to come in here?" she asked. "Your sister Daphne?"

Darling Daphne obviously had Mrs. Palmer eating out of her hand.

"No," I said. "I came of my own volition."

I don't know where the word came from. It popped out of me like the filling from a squeezed pimple.

"I don't believe you," Mrs. Palmer said, taking up her gloves again.

"You don't have to," I returned, taking the plunge. "But it's true."

It was masks off. Very seldom did I ever show the real Flavia de Luce to anyone, especially to strangers. But now? Well, she had asked for it.

"As Professor Cooke pointed out more than sixty years ago," I said, taking a deep breath, "you cannot unite the chemical elements in any proportion you please. Twenty-three ounces of sodium will unite precisely with thirty-five and a half ounces of chlorine to produce table salt. But if you have carelessly added an extra half ounce of either substance, Nature will set aside the surplus. All the wishing in the world cannot force the extra to mix."

Mrs. Palmer looked rather stunned. I think it was my use of table salt as an example that got through to her. She understood table salt.

"And your point is?" she demanded.

"I am here because I will myself to be here," I told her. "And all the king's horses and all the king's men couldn't keep me here if I didn't want to be," I said, waving my hands in the air to add a bit of drama.

"Well," Mrs. Palmer said, "if even half of what you tell me is true, I can only say that you're a Force to Be Reckoned With."

She spoke the last few words in capital letters. You could actually *hear* them!

I dropped my eyes modestly.

Spot-on! I thought. Her assessment was spot-on.

"Your sister told me you had dynamite for brains, but I had no idea—"

Dynamite for brains? Daffy told her that?

I might have to rethink my sister.

Mrs. Palmer seemed to have come to a sudden decision.

"Help yourself to the Mercy Seat," she said, pointing to the kitchen's only chair, an ancient wingback in the corner.

She saw my puzzled look.

"That's what Arven calls it—the Mercy Seat. He lugged it down from the attics. In case I ever took a break, he said. Not that I ever have, mind. Belonged to his father, the Old Gaffer. Go on, sit yourself."

I lowered my carcass reluctantly into the ancient upholstery, which reeked of departed dogs and so forth. I was expecting the chair to be uncomfortable and oppressive, but I was pleasantly surprised to find that it fit me like a glove. The Old Gaffer must have been quite slight of frame.

"I'll make you a nice cup of tea," Mrs. Palmer said, and I did not object. "Don't mind me if I keep working. To a cook, the world consists of open mouths.

"Not that I'm complaining," she went on. "Those lads from Shadrach's Circus shoveling in their pies and pints in the summer is what keeps us in coal in the winter."

Although Mrs. Palmer had not said so directly, it was obvious she had accepted my apology.

As she worked, she talked to me over her shoulder, clattering away like some wonderful automaton, bustling about the kitchen, lifting lids, sniffing sauces, pulling pies from the pantry, and dismembering the turkey. In an earlier century she might have been called *The Marvelous Mechanical Maid. Wind her up—see her sweep!*

People would have paid to see her, but now I had her all to myself.

I was trying to think of the best way to make my questions seem casual when she said suddenly, "You poor child!"

It took me a moment to realize she was referring to me.

"What a shock it must have been, finding Orlando's body like that, without any warning. Your fingers in his mouth, so to speak. Just the thought of it gives me the heebie-jeebies."

I nodded and widened my eyes a bit.

"Did you know him?" I asked.

"Orlando? Everybody knew Orlando. He was what you might call a local character."

"In what way?" I said.

"Oh, in every way: the way he behaved, the way he talked, the way he dressed. Orlando was an original—one of a kind."

"Wasn't he the son of a former vicar?"

"Dear old Canon Whitbread, poor lamb . . . dear old soul. God rest him."

Poor lamb? Dear old soul?

What kind of description was that? The man had gone to the scaffold for sending a clutch of communicants to an early grave by means of a poisoned chalice.

Poor lamb? Dear old soul? My great-aunt Fanny!

"God rest him," I repeated, making the sign of the cross on my breast. "A good man, was he?"

Mrs. Palmer put down a pot roast and dabbed at her eyes with the corner of her apron.

"He was a martyr," she said. "Put to death by the Powers of Darkness."

"The powers of darkness?" I asked.

"Clement Atlee," she said, "and the Labor Party. Curse them all!"

Mr. Atlee, the former prime minister, had, by only a slender margin, been defeated last autumn by Winston Churchill, who had returned for his second term.

Because I had been incarcerated in Canada at Miss Bodycote's Female Academy, I had heard little about Churchill's victory, although I was quite fond of the man himself, who had taken the trouble to attend my mother's funeral.

"Amen," I said, and Mrs. Palmer beamed upon me.

"Hanged by the neck until he was dead. An innocent old man led to the slaughter," she said, pulling open the oven to baste a large pan of roasting potatoes. "That's what some say—including me."

"But how is that possible? Surely someone—"

"Listen, sweetie," Mrs. Palmer interrupted. "When good old Gabriel blows his horn, 'Surely someone' will be the last words ever to be spoken on this earth. When nothing's left of the world but ashes and a smoking jaw-bone, that ruined mouth will still be croaking 'Surely someone . . .' You can count on it."

I had begun to like this Mrs. Palmer. Immensely.

It was as if, somewhere in our vast universe, a giant planet had rolled over in its sleep—some great force had shifted, quaked, and then subsided once more into silence.

It left me numb for a moment—but only for a moment. Until I realized that this innkeeper's wife, in her low, hot, greasy kitchen, had been the first person in my entire life to explain why there was a Flavia de Luce.

I was necessary. *I* was *Someone*.

I felt as if I had shed an invisible skin. A fresh layer of the onion had been exposed.

Had Mrs. Palmer noticed as the change came over me? Probably not. But if she did she gave no sign of it.

"Orlando had to live with that," she continued. "And so did all the rest of us. We knew we had to get on with our lives. That's why, when Orlando turned up to audition for the Puddle Lane Little Theatre just days after his father's funeral, he was welcomed with open arms."

"By everyone?" I asked.

"Well, almost everyone," she replied. "Poppy Mandrill grumbled a bit. But then she always does. Poppy has a remarkable theatrical career behind her, with emphasis on *behind*. She just doesn't realize it yet, as most faded actors don't. But I think she realized from the start that this rather unusual young man had what it took to be a star."

"And what about Canon Whitbread? Did he? Realize it, I mean?"

Mrs. Palmer shot me a penetrating look.

"About Orlando?"

I nodded.

"Canon Whitbread was under no illusions about anything or *anyone*. Including himself—or his son. Every canon, you must remember, has a cathedral somewhere in his past. The country canons are mostly lovely old gentlemen who have been given the title as a garment to keep them warm on their way to the grave, and no one was more aware of that than Canon Whitbread."

"And Poppy Mandrill?"

"Well . . ." Mrs. P said, letting the word out in a long breath, "our dear canon was under no illusions about her, either. *Particularly* about her. St. Mildred's is not exactly known for its High Church practices—not by a long chalk—and yet she insisted on his hearing her confessions every Saturday afternoon. 'The Saturday Afternoon Matinées,' he always called them."

"He told you that?" I gasped.

As the child of a devout Catholic family, I could hardly believe that a churchman would break his vows of silence. The sanctity of the confessional was sacred no matter what the circumstances.

"He was joking, of course. Poppy wasn't the only one of his flock who wanted to whisper in the vestry. We were very close, the canon and I," she announced, brushing up her hair with the back of a damp hand. "I served as vicar's warden when all but I had fled."

"The boy stood on the burning deck," I said.

Daffy had recited that horrific old potboiler to me when I was still in my pram, waving in great, swashbuckling circles around her head a smoking string mop whose strands she had set alight to simulate the breech-loading of Nelson's cannon at the Battle of the Nile.

I knew what Mrs. P meant, though. Suspected of murder, old Canon Whitbread must have often found himself alone in his protested innocence. Nobody wants to be on cozy terms with a killer.

"It must have been difficult," I remarked.

"Difficult is an understatement," Mrs. Palmer said. "At times, toward the end, it seemed as if it were the two of us against the world."

"What about Orlando?" I asked. "Surely he—"

"Orlando was estranged from his father, and had been for some time. Poor soul. He had a devil of a time trying to make both ends meet. He worked for a time delivering ale casks, but it got the better of him, if you know what I mean. And he filled in from time to time at the chemist's, but that—well, let's just say that didn't work out, either. I even gave him whatever work I could find for him washing dishes, but Arven didn't like having him underfoot, or so he claimed."

She sighed.

"Orlando lived in a boathouse down by the river—

Scull Cottage, they call it, although it's not quite so grand as it sounds. A leaky boathouse with a bed and paraffin camp stove is more like it."

She saw me looking at her.

"I only went down there once or twice," she told me. "Toward the end. To try to talk some sense into him."

"And did you?" I asked.

It was quite a long time before she answered. I could see her going over that visit, minute by minute in her mind.

"No," she said at last. "I didn't."

"You didn't?" the landlord said, appearing suddenly in the kitchen as if from a magic lamp. "You didn't what?"

"Oh, nothing, Arven," Mrs. Palmer said. "Dearie here was just asking me if I'd made her cucumber sandwich. It clear slipped my mind. Too many cooks."

How fascinating, I thought, *that she should both lie to her husband and, in the same breath, scold him for being in the kitchen.*

Or was she scolding *me*?

Whatever the case, I noted that she was a lightning liar. As a connoisseur of the untruth myself, I was quick to recognize the gift in others.

"Well, I'd better be going," I said, leaping up out of the Mercy Seat as if scalded (for the landlord's sake). "Thank you, anyway, Mrs. Palmer. I'll eat later. After I've picked up my snapshots."

It was far too early for Hob's photographs to have been processed: They would not be ready until tomorrow at the earliest. But it was a good excuse and I escaped with an—almost—clear conscience.

·ELEVEN·

WHEN YOU'RE PLANNING MISCHIEF, it's always a good idea to throw up a smokescreen in advance. Excuses made *after* the fact are seldom successful.

Which is why I made a point of mentioning to the Palmers that I was departing the Oak and Pheasant to pick up photographs. One would not ordinarily bother, or feel it necessary, to explain to a landlord where you were going or why. My real intent was to draw attention to the fact that I was taking myself elsewhere: which ought always to be your first concern when you plan to burgle someone's bedroom.

The second step is timing. It is only logical to plan your attack while the burglee is away from the intended target.

Say, for instance, that you were planning to rifle the bedroom of a country publican's wife in search of a certain book of poems. Logic would dictate that the best time to do so would be when the said publican's wife, being up to her ears in sauces in the kitchen, would be least likely to return to her sleeping chambers.

Which was now.

There wasn't a moment to lose.

Up the stairs I went, as if returning to my bedroom. At the first landing, I stopped to examine the shelf of books which Daffy had scoffed at.

Under Two Flags . . . The Sea Hawk . . . Piracy . . . Eric Brighteyes . . .

The titles alone made me seasick except the last one, which made me gag.

How could people waste their lives writing—or reading— such utter bilge?

There was no sign of anything slender enough to be poetry. Mrs. Palmer was not foolhardy enough to leave her explosive little book in plain sight where any commercial traveler might pick it up for a bit of bedtime reading. *Hide in plain sight* was a well-worn plot device used by legions of detective novelists, but not in this case.

Resuming my upward climb, I peered up through the old oak banisters and newel posts, but the landing above looked deserted. On tiptoe, I crept slowly up the last five steps.

The coast was clear.

The bedrooms rented out were at the front of the inn, facing the church, except mine and Dogger's, which both overlooked the sunken garden at the rear. This left only one room unaccounted for: the one I had decided belonged to the Palmers.

The door of this room was painted with buttermilk emulsion in a peculiar shade of blue, a color which reminded me not of buttermilk, but watery milk of the thin, skimmed variety: the skin of a decrepit duchess.

I pressed my ear tightly against one of the door panels. The only sound to be heard was that of my own heart.

I seized the knob and twisted. The door opened and I stepped inside.

How often fortune favors the brave!

In spite of its tall four-poster bed—which surely must be the very one that Good Queen Bess had slept in—the room was surprisingly small and crowded: clothespress, dresser, chair, table with alarm clock, faded red Turkey carpet on the floor, washstand, sink, shaving gear, skin cream. Aside from those few personal belongings, it was as spare as if the landlord and his wife were transients themselves, stopping overnight at the inn on their way to visit an expiring aunt in Exeter: hardly the room of a longtime landlord and his churchwarden wife who had lived here since the year dot.

The ancient wallpaper—surely no newer than the eighteenth century—portrayed a smoke-darkened Chinese landscape with repetitive fishing boats, mountains, cranes, bamboo, and pagodas.

I began my search for *The Mussel Bed* in the most obvious place: under the mattress. The high bedstead itself was shaky and precarious. Its elderly bed slats clattered horribly, like old bones raining down on a slate roof, and I eased the bedding back into its original position, hoping the noise would not be heard in the kitchen directly below.

I rifled the drawers of the dresser, fingering each item of clothing, and peered into the depths of the clothes-press, plunging my hand into the deep pockets of the hanging bathrobes.

All to no avail.

I looked behind the curtains and under the carpet, behind framed pictures, and (against my will) into the flowered chamber pots.

I was about to turn my attention to the contents of the washstand when there was the creak of a floorboard: the sound of a footstep in the hall.

I froze.

Someone had paused at the top of the stairs. Another guest, perhaps, stopping to get their bearings in the dim, mazelike, up-again-down-again passageways of the old inn.

But then as I watched, the doorknob began—slowly—to turn.

I stepped back into the corner at the head of the bed. There wasn't quite enough material in the drapes of the canopy with which to wind myself a shroud.

I pressed myself against the wallpaper, hoping, somehow, miraculously to blend into those dreadful water-stained pagodas.

The door opened. A shoe appeared . . . a leg . . .

"What the devil are you doing in here?"

Needless to say, it was Daffy.

"I might ask you the same question," I told her, with a flick of my head so that my flying braids would give her a symbolic whip-lashing.

For a long moment, we stood there glaring at each other, both of us unwilling to give an inch.

De Luce v. de Luce, as the law liked to put it.

And not for the first time. Far from it!

There is an old scientific paradox: What happens when an irresistible object meets an immovable object? One solution to this stumper was proposed in a tale from Greek mythology in which an irresistible fox encounters an immovable hound—or vice versa. In that particular case, the great god Zeus turned both of them to stone, thus cleverly solving the problem.

And that was precisely what was happening here. My sister and I stood glowering at each other like a couple of calcified garden ornaments, a situation which persisted until I decided to give in. Otherwise, we would have still been standing there when we were gray-haired old ladies with hearing trumpets and china choppers.

"Looking for *The Mussel Bed*," I said, catching Daffy by surprise.

"So am I," she replied. "Let's search together."

I had begun listing all the places I had already looked when Daffy strode confidently across the room, climbed up onto the high mattress, and, standing fully upright, stretched her arm and felt along the top of the canopy.

"The spell for finding books," she whispered, closing her eyes before pronouncing the incantation: "*Abraca-dabra, Alakazam, Angela Thirkell, and Omar Khayyam.*"

I had never seen my sister so excited.

Slowly Daffy retracted her extended arm, and—to my

amazement—clutched in her hand was a slender book with yellow marbled covers.

"Eureka!" she said, for once not following the word with the usual offensive pun.

"How did you know it was up there?" I asked, not believing what I had just seen.

"When you have eliminated the impossible, whatever remains, however improbable, must indicate the four-poster."

"Huh?" I said, perhaps for the first time in my entire life.

"Elementary," Daffy said. "The Mussel Bed."

Only slowly did her words seep into the thinking part of my brain.

"Oh! I see," I said. "The Mussel *Bed.*"

"Wonderful," Daffy echoed dryly, rolling her eyes up beseechingly to Heaven. "Now let's amscray."

Daffy had learned Pig Latin from Carl Pendracka and was inordinately proud of her ability to baffle Mrs. Mullet by lapsing into that tongue—or whatever you wish to call it—when she wished to convey a confidence, or deliver an insult.

"The eans-bay are urned-bay," she would say. "My ummy-tay is urning-tay to ar-tay."

Mrs. Mullet would beam upon her as if the king himself had complimented her on the glories of her cooking.

"Amscray," of course, meant "Scram."

"Ighty-ho-ray!" I said, and again Heaven was harrowed by my sister's scorching gaze.

Daffy held the slender volume up to her lips and blew. A small atomic dust cloud appeared and dissipated.

Then she tucked the book into the folds of her woolen cardigan. She had for the past six months or so begun complaining of the cold, even when the summer temperatures were tending toward the tropical, and never went anywhere without an old brown baggy knitted jumper which I realized only now, with a sudden shock, had belonged to Father.

I wanted to hug her but I didn't.

Hopping down from the bed, she gestured with her head and eyes that I was to follow.

Back in Daffy's room, we huddled over the book.

"The dust dictates that it has lain undisturbed. No fingerprints other than mine," she said.

"Which means that whoever is blackmailing her has their own copy," I suggested.

"Unless, of course, they borrowed it from a friend or from a library—or read it in a bookshop. The latter seems unlikely, though. A blackmailing letter is no casual thing. Like tough beef, it requires a certain amount of stewing on the part of the writer."

"Or cold-blooded calculating on the spur of the moment," I added.

This was a situation of which I had considerable first-hand experience.

"Precisely," Daffy said.

Precisely? Could this actually be Daphne speaking? To me?

To *me*?

Where were the razor words?—the acid accusations?

Had it come to pass that the fullness of time and a drowned dandy had finally brought my sister and me together? Was I witnessing a miracle?

And if that were true, was the miracle mine? Or was I merely caught in the crosswinds of someone else's heavenly intervention?

There was no time now to worry about such things. I would sort it out later.

But miracles, I knew, above all, required acknowledgment. Some sign must be given before the bestowing angel took it into his or her head to throw in the towel; to wander off in a sulk and give the gift to someone else instead, out of sheer spite, such as the ruddy traveling wine salesman in the room across the hall.

Accordingly, I crossed my eyes at Daffy.

If we were to be colleagues in crime—even just this once—then priorities needed to be established at the outset.

"Open the book," I commanded, perhaps a little too forcefully. "Let's get on with it."

She looked at me. I looked at her.

"I can't wait to hear your professional opinion, Daff," I improvised. "I'm a complete duffer when it comes to literary excellence."

With all the cool confidence of a Mona Lisa with all

the aces, she cradled the book in her left palm and opened it to the first page. She let out a whistle.

"Crikey!" she said. "Listen to this. It's the dedication. There's also a dedicatory poem:

"To Mine Own Leander.
The copper mare and
The brass stallion graze
In Flecker's Field.
He paws the turf,
While she the wind tastes.
And when he trots to her
She turns tail."

"I don't understand it," I said. "Does it mean anything?"

"Only to the discerning eye," Daffy said.

"Then you'd better explain," I told her. "I have no time to piddle about with poetry."

"Pity," Daffy said. "You might learn something."

"Such as?"

I was already becoming impatient.

"To begin with, Leander was a character in Greek mythology. He fell in love with a nun named Hero."

"Hold on," I said. "Hero is a man's name."

"It is now, yes. But in those days, it was a woman's. Before men reduced real history to rubble, then raked over the ruins, like a dog burying and digging up its . . . well, you know."

"Bone," I said, but Daffy ignored me.

"This Leander tried to swim the Hellespont at night, but a storm blew up and drowned him."

Drowned? At night?

This was becoming intriguing.

"What about Flecker's Field?" I asked. "I've never heard of the place. Is it around here somewhere?"

"Possibly," Daffy said, "but James Elroy Flecker was the name of a poet who died during the Great War."

"In battle?" I asked.

"In bed," Daffy said. "Not in the field, but in bed. Of tuberculosis. In Switzerland."

"I don't see the point," I said. I was glad I had taken up poisons, rather than poetry, which seems to me more baffling than belladonna.

"The point is," Daffy said, "that Flecker's Field—in one of its senses—was poetry. You know:

". . . *Have you heard*
That silence where the birds are dead yet something pipeth
  like a bird?"

Invisible feathers tickled my spine. I was going to have to look into this Flecker chap. Perhaps I was even going to have to rethink poetry.

"Aha!" I said. "I understand!" Although actually, I didn't.

"So obviously," she went on, "the reference could be to some poet other than herself."

"But wait!" I said. "If Flecker's Field refers to poetry,

then it might just as well be Mrs. Palmer's *own* field, since she's a poet herself."

Daffy gave me a skeptical look.

"Or," I said, holding up a forefinger to emphasize a brilliant idea, "it might be an *actual* field. Is there a field belonging to the Oak and Pheasant?"

"Hmmm, I doubt it." Daffy frowned. "Modern poets are seldom literal—unless they live abroad in the colonies, of course. Still, I expect your idea might be worth looking into."

"Do you think we might find a *real* copper mare and a *real* brass stallion? Maybe it's a horse breeder we're looking for—or a racetrack."

"Or a railway," Daffy added, clapping me on the shoulders. "The Iron Horse, and all that."

Although I nearly fainted with surprise, I bore up remarkably well.

"And what about the rest of it?" I asked. "All that pawing of the turf and the tasting of the wind, and so forth?"

Daffy got up from the bed and went to the window, peering down into the sunken garden where Feely and Dieter were strolling round and round in circles, arm in arm.

She turned and gave me a long, cold, calculated look as if she were weighing whether to entrust me with some deep, dark secret. After what seemed to me like hours, but couldn't have been more than a quarter of a minute, she said:

"Leave that to me."

"Righty-ho," I said.

We had agreed, Daffy and I, that each of us would follow her own lines of investigation.

Not that I intended to, of course. Not for a mayfly's minute.

What Daffy didn't realize was that we were aiming at two different targets. While her intent was to unravel the mysteries of a book of poetry, mine was to catch a killer.

I had no idea what she knew about Orlando Whitbread, and I didn't want to ask her. With her nose forever in a book, Daffy was no great authority on today's front page—or yesterday's, for that matter.

In her estimation, the world had come to an end in 1870. Nothing worthwhile had been written or published since the death of Charles Dickens on the ninth of June in that year.

Although she read more modern works, it was simply to exercise her eyes—or so she claimed.

And so it was I who scanned the morning papers for the lurid crimes. I had begun, of course, with the avalanches of ancient newspapers that tumbled out of every cupboard at Buckshaw, many of which dated back a century or more. From their brittle yellowing pages I had read with fascination about the cream of the criminal element: Haigh, Armstrong, Crippen; the list went on and on.

Once begun, it was hard to break the habit, and I was already hungering for much more current news. Mrs. Mullet was only too happy to bring me the latest papers every day, after her husband had finished with them.

"Alf gets up with the sparrows every morning," she told me, "so as to be at the newsagent's when they rolls up the blinds. Alf says 'e can't 'elp it. 'As to find out what they're up to at Westminster. That lot needs keepin' an eye on. Our Agnes says 'e's what's called an invertebrate reader."

Agnes Mullet had left home some years ago to study Pitman Shorthand, and had since come to be considered—at least by Alf and Mrs. M—the world's greatest authority on anything which involved printed matter.

Unlike the great Sherlock Holmes, I did not keep a commonplace book other than the one that was in my head. Who could ever forget, for instance, even the tiniest detail of the Acid Bath murders, in which John George Haigh dissolved as few as six and as many as a dozen bodies in vats of concentrated sulfuric acid?

At the risk of sounding ghoulish, I swear that these titbits were etched permanently into my brain.

To put it bluntly, I was more accustomed than Daffy to dealing with death, while she was more accustomed to dealing with Dickens—which is all right, I suppose, if you feel you might be seized suddenly by little red men from Mars in their flying saucers and transported back to Victorian times.

Which is why I decided to keep my intentions to myself.

By now, it was getting late in the day. If I got a move on, I might even be back at the Oak and Pheasant in time for tea.

·TWELVE·

SHADRACH'S CIRCUS & MENAGERIE, all in all, was rather a shabby affair. A half dozen ancient pantechnicons were drawn up in a rough circle round the market square, like a wagon train under attack. Although they had the appearance of military vehicles which had barely survived the First World War, these sagging vehicles were painted in gaudy colors with the name of the circus, as well as garish images and slogans: MAN-EATING TIGERS! LIONS! ELEPHANTS! SEE THE SAVAGE BEASTS!

All of these, and more, were portrayed on the panels with oversized heads, snarling mouths, and teeth the size of icicles. A crouching cheetah was preparing to bring down a white Arabian stallion, which was rearing up, red nostrils flaring and eyes rolling in terror.

What would Hob think of such a dramatic scene? I wondered. *Or was it too unreal?*

Nearby, in a wheeled cage, a rather moth-eaten lion was sleeping on its back with feet in the air. To one side of the cage, the lone elephant, still chained by its leg to a post in the ground, munched thoughtfully on a stray newspaper. There were no tigers in sight.

A steam organ, sadly out of tune and sounding like defective plumbing, was playing the opening theme song for the wireless program *The Archers*, which seemed especially pathetic: *DUM-dee-DUMP-ity-DUM-dee-DUM, DUM-dee-DUM-dee-DUM-dee* . . . and so on, almost to distraction. Every one of the piercing notes was a new assault upon my ears. It was like being under attack by a swarm of those wasps that drill through the skin of baby figs to lay their eggs.

On a raised platform, a tall, thin man with a bare chest, but wearing suspenders, was swallowing a sword for an audience of two small boys who were fighting over a bag of apples. The sword-swallower put down his blade and began juggling five metal rings, but it made no difference: The apple war raged on.

I was wondering where to begin my investigations when a voice behind me said, "Look who's here again. Missed us, did you?"

I spun round to find myself face-to-face with the man in the polka-dot kerchief. This time, he was with his two friends. I stepped back instinctively.

All three of them had their hands in their pockets and all three had something in their mouths: one a toothpick, one a wooden matchstick, and Polka-Dot a cigarette.

"Come to see the menagerie, 'ave yer?" Matchstick asked. "Come to see the man-eating tigers?"

Polka-Dot snickered and blew a showy smoke ring.

That did it.

"Actually," I said, "I'm looking into the death of Orlando Whitbread—the man who was fished out of the river this morning."

I realized as soon as I said it that this was a hugely risky business. I was not only tossing away my anonymity but also, possibly, putting my life in jeopardy.

What if one of these bruisers was the killer? What if one—or two—or perhaps even all three of them had dumped Orlando into the water? Any one of these muscle-bound hulks could have overpowered his thin body with ease.

I watched their eyes carefully for the slightest sign of alarm, but there seemed to be no reaction other than amusement.

"Friend of yours, was he?" Polka-Dot asked, looking from one to the other of his pals as if he had made a capital joke.

"A relative, actually," I lied. "A cousin. A distant cousin, to be sure, but a cousin nonetheless."

"Nonetheless!" Polka-Dot coughed out the word in a cloud of smoke. "Hark her, Nigel! Nonetheless! *Nonetheless*, she says."

"Nonetheless," Matchstick replied with a grin, and I deduced that he must be Nigel.

"One of the Torquay Whitbreads," I went on, ignoring their stupid banter. "On my grandmother's side, obviously. My aunt Gregoria always predicted that Orlando would meet a watery death. 'You can count on it,' she used to say. And she was right. Of course, Aunt Gregoria had more than a little of the psychic about her, which might have given her a bit of an unfair advantage, don't you think, Mister . . . ?"

"Terence," Polka-Dot said.

"How do you do?" I asked, sticking out my hand and trying not to gag.

Terence's paw was black with circus grease and grime and knobbly with hardened calluses. To the touch it was like hand-wrestling with an engine-room oiler.

I would need to concoct a disinfectant as soon as I got back to the Oak and Pheasant.

"And you are?" I asked, offering my tainted hand to Matchstick.

"Nigel," he said, taking my fingers in his fist, and I almost laughed. "You don't look like a Nigel," I said gaily. "More like a Pierre, or a Jean Baptiste. But perhaps it's your neckerchief."

His neckerchief was gaily striped with blue, white, and red, like the French tricolor flag. I suppose it could equally have been red, white, and blue, like the British, but I wanted to flatter him.

I held out my hand to the third ruffian—Toothpick—and raised my eyebrows. His light blue neckerchief matched his eyes.

"Cornell," he said quietly. "Pleased to meet you, Miss—"

"Dorchester," I said. "Arabella Dorchester. But you can call me Arab. Everybody else does."

"Hold on," Terence protested. "That's not the name your sister gave us."

I arranged my features into a look of surprise.

"Betty?" I asked, letting my mouth fall open in disbelief. "Oh, she's such an awful liar! She's always telling people she's Lady Lancaster, or Dame Agatha Dimbleby. Who did she tell you she was?"

"Ophelia de Luce," said Nigel, looking like a man bamboozled.

"That scallywag," I said, shaking my head. "I'm so ashamed of her. I really must apologize on Betty's behalf."

The three roustabouts were looking distinctly uneasy. I had deftly turned the tables on them and got the upper hand. There was no time to lose.

"Now then," I asked, taking command as if it were I who had arranged our meeting, "how long have you gentlemen been in town?"

"Three days," Cornell answered obediently. "Counting today, that is."

I shot him a beaming smile as a reward, and from that moment on the poor lad was eating out of my hand.

"And you," I said, turning to Terence. I had already sized him up as the ringleader. "Are you in charge of these great beastly machines?" I asked, waving a hand toward the parked pantechnicons. "Gosh, they must be jolly difficult to drive."

I almost reached out to feel one of his bulging biceps, but I restrained myself.

Terence drew in a deep breath.

I had him.

"Well, then," I said, rubbing my hands together. "About Cousin Orlando. I'm sure Aunt Gregoria would be willing to offer a generous reward for information. Just to put her mind to rest, you understand. Orlando was more or less her pet, you know. Actually, she spoiled him outrageously."

"We seen 'im round about—'ere and there," Terence said, shifting his shoulders and looking away, trying to disguise the telltale glitter in his eyes.

"I'm surprised to hear that," I said. "I should have thought you'd have seen a great deal more of him. Cousin Orlando was simply mad about circuses. More than mad: He had a bee in his bonnet about them. He didn't beg to run away with you, did he? To be trained as a clown? Offered to work for nothing?"

"'E never said anything like that to us," Nigel volunteered.

Which told me what I wanted to know: They *had* talked to Orlando. He had still been alive when they arrived in town the day before yesterday. More to the point, they had been here when he died.

"What did he say, then?" I asked, turning to Cornell.

"We had a few drinks with him is all," Cornell said, "at the Wooden Bird."

"The Wooden Bird?" I asked.

"The Oak and Pheasant. It's a kind of joke. We've always called it that."

"Why?" I asked.

Cornell shrugged.

"Who knows? Same reason the landlord is always

called Gov', no matter his real name. It's a tradition. You might as well ask why they always drop bread in the churchyard, or dance round the Maypole with wooden hobbyhorses!"

"Always?" I asked. "You've been here before?"

"Shadrach's has been stopping here since Napoleon was in nappies," Terence said.

"And which of you is Mr. Shadrach?" I said.

All three of them laughed at once, as if their mouths were tied together with a string.

"Mr. Shadrach went to his reward when Queen Victoria was on the throne, if you'll pardon the expression," Terence said.

Again came the clockwork laughs—but only two, this time.

"Then who's the proprietor nowadays?" I asked. "Cousin Orlando may have approached him."

"Approached *her,* you mean," Terence told me. "Mrs. Dandyman. 'Dreadnought Dandyman,' we call her."

The three of them broke into sniggers, and I noticed that Cornell looked cautiously over his shoulder.

"Because she's an old battleship," he explained. "A dreadnought is a battle cruiser from the time of World War One."

"HMS *Colossus* and HMS *Collingwood,* for instance," I said.

I'd show them I knew my peas from my pickles. I had often enough pored over the ancient picture magazines which simply bulged to bursting with photographs of British Naval Power.

Not one of the three seemed to be able to come up with a reply.

"And where might I find Mrs. Dandyman?" I asked, following the line of Cornell's glance, which was toward the largest of the pantechnicons—the one with the stallion and the cheetah.

"Over there—in Bucking Horse Palace," Nigel said. "Just don't tell her we told you."

"Bit of a tartar, is she?" I asked.

Terence gave off a noise that sounded as if his sinuses had collapsed.

"Judge for yourself," he said as he turned and walked away with Nigel and Cornell hard on his heels. Behind the backs of his two pals, Cornell twiddled his fingers goodbye.

A slight chill touched my bare arms as I stepped into the shadow of the pantechnicon. The sheer tonnage of the thing loomed over me like a vast red whale.

My first task was to find the entrance, which was not easy. The metal skin of the thing appeared to be seamless, and the enormous murals of the beasts made it even more difficult to find a door. After a complete walk-around without success, I finally spotted a small set of folding stairs, cunningly concealed among the roots of a painted jungle tree. Only then did I spot the door, its hinges hidden by the artist's idea of bark.

Someone, I thought, *is particular about her privacy.* And I couldn't help but wonder *why?*

I gave the steps a gentle pull—more as a test than anything—and was astonished when they folded out and down without a sound.

"Hello?" I called. "Mrs. Dandyman, are you there?"

Again in silence, the steps folded themselves up as they retracted and locked into place with a metallic *click*. It was as if they had never existed.

Hydraulic, I thought. *How clever*. They could be opened and closed from the inside as well as from the outside, which made sense.

All I needed to do was find the push button.

Which wasn't all that difficult once you knew what you were looking for.

And yes! Here it was: not a button, but a switch, cunningly disguised as one of the tiger's claws.

I looked round to see if anyone was watching me, but Terence and his chums had wandered away from the pantechnicon, leaving me alone in the shadow of the thing.

No one would see me climb aboard (if I was able to). If I vanished from the face of the earth, no one would ever know where I had gone. Orlando's fish-nibbled features sprang suddenly into my mind.

"Mrs. Dandyman?" I called again. "I'd like to speak with you."

When there was no answer, I reached out and flipped the switch.

The silent steps came down and, with the slightest hiss of air such as you might expect from an alien spaceship, like the one Michael Rennie stepped out of in *The Day the Earth Stood Still*, the metal door slowly began to open.

"Hello?" I called out into the darkness, placing a foot on the lowest tread.

When no one told me to keep out, or to go away, I took it as an invitation and climbed aboard.

To my right was a heavy hanging curtain. I pulled it aside—foolhardy, perhaps, but I did it anyway—and walked through.

I couldn't suppress a gasp.

The cavernous space—I hesitate to call it a room— was filled with paintings: a dozen or so, each on its own altar and each illuminated by a row of flickering candles.

A *private chapel*, I thought.

In one of the paintings, a man flayed to his bare muscles stood holding his own skin draped over his arm like a toga. In another, a nearly naked man was being grilled over a makeshift stove by men with lances. And in yet another, a woman armed only with a crucifix was using it as a blade to cut her way out of a dragon's belly.

"Chamber of horrors, isn't it?" said a voice. "Better run away before something nasty happens to you."

I hadn't seen her there, half hidden, as she was, by a hanging curtain.

She took a step toward me, a pointed object in her hand.

I was already preparing to take to my heels when I realized that her weapon was an artist's paintbrush.

As she stepped out of the shadows, I could see that the woman had been working on a canvas of a group of men, bound together by weighted chains, being tossed over the side of a ship and into the sea while, nearby on the shore, another man hung from a cross surrounded by a swarm of bees.

"They're beautiful!" I exclaimed. "Every one of them. That's Saint Astius on the cross, isn't it? He was covered in honey and left in the hot sun to be stung to death by bees."

The woman took another step toward me, her candlelit face blazing like a comet in the half-darkness, her gray hair streaming out behind her like the comet's tail.

Closer and closer she came until her nose was nearly touching mine. The odor of garlic on her breath was so overwhelming that when she spoke, I could smell every word.

"Blimey!" she said. "You do know your saints, don't you?"

I was afraid that her next question would be to ask my name, but I needn't have worried.

"Who's this, then?" she asked, pointing to the group of men who were being forced to walk the plank.

Was it my imagination, or did one of them look uncannily like Orlando Whitbread? I had only seen him dead, of course, so it was difficult to tell.

"The seven martyrs of Dyrrachium," I said, ticking them off on my fingers. "Germanus, Hesychius, Lucian, Papius, Peregrinus, Pompeius, and Saturninus—alphabetically, that is."

I did not tell her that I had once won a prize by being able to regurgitate those names on demand. Poor Father Duffy, back in Hinley, was probably still shaking his head at the defeat of his house Goliath, Mary Rose Trethewey, who had a photographic memory but whom Fate had dealt a losing hand when I was given her question by mistake.

Feely (who knew him from one of the music festivals) had tipped me off that Father Duffy was obsessed with the Albanian Martyrs, and that they were more likely than not to be hauled out of the hat like white rabbits, in order to defeat the Bishop's Lacey home team.

I had got their names off by heart by making a mnemonic of the first letters of the martyrs' names: Give Him Large Portions of Potted Plums and Strychnine.

G, H, L, P, P, P, S.

Germanus, Hesychius, Lucian, Papius, Peregrinus, Pompeius, and Saturninus.

Just like that, and I had come away with the trophy: a rather cheesy china teacup with my name (misspelled) painted on the back by Mary Margaret Tackaberry, the captain of the Crafts League.

I didn't notice until I got home that the Virgin Mary on the front of the cup was sticking out her tongue.

"Very impressive," Mrs. Dandyman said, turning to the skinned man.

"Saint Bartholomew," I said. "The patron saint of tanners."

"And this?"

"The bloke on the barbecue?" I asked, becoming more sure of myself by the minute. "That's easy: Saint Lawrence. I believe they still have the grill on display in a church in Rome."

Before she could question me further, it was time to gain the upper hand. I pointed to the woman escaping from the dragon's gut.

"Margaret of Antioch. The dragon is the devil in disguise. Serves him right. You'd think that he, of all people, would know that crucifixes are not just used against vampires."

Mrs. Dandyman lifted one of Saint Bartholomew's candles out of its socket and held it up in front of my face. For a long time she examined my features, moving her light from right to left.

"I've seen you before, somewhere," she said. "But I can't for the life of me remember where."

I shrugged.

"I'm just a girl," I said, hating myself even as I said it. "Ever so many girls have mousy hair. I'm just one of the mice."

Sometimes, you must manufacture camouflage with whatever is within easy reach, which, in this case, was my mouth. And my brain, of course.

I needed to divert her attempt to put a name to my face. She might have seen my photograph in the newspaper not long ago.

"I feel that I can trust you, Mrs. Dandyman, but you must give me your word that you won't share with a soul what I'm about to confide in you."

Who, in the entire history of the world since Adam and Eve, has ever been able to resist so downright juicy an offer?

"I give you my word," she said, already licking her lips in anticipation.

I touched the back of her hand with my fingers to change her promise into an unbreakable bond.

"I'm the one who found Orlando Whitbread's body," I said, and I watched her eyes. "I need to talk to you."

·THIRTEEN·

"ORLANDO?" SHE GASPED. "HE'S dead?"

Even by the warm light of the flickering flames I could see the color draining from her face, an effect which is virtually impossible to fake—and goodness knows, I've tried.

If this woman wasn't honestly shocked, she was the greatest actress I had ever seen.

"When?" she asked. "Where? What happened?"

"This morning," I told her. "In the river."

"Was it suicide?"

I said nothing, a trick I had learned from Inspector Hewitt, which had proved to be one of the most useful weapons in my arsenal.

"But no, that's not possible," she said, answering her own question. "That's simply not possible."

"Perhaps it was an accident," I suggested, sparing her

what I believed to be the truth—at least for the time being.

"Not likely," she insisted. "Orlando grew up on the riverbank."

I continued my silence.

"He was always as much at home in the water as Mole and Ratty. Boats, swimming, fishing. I'm surprised he hadn't grown gills."

I recognized at once that she was referring to the animal characters from *The Wind in the Willows*.

"Always?" I asked, choosing my question with care.

"It seems like always. Shadrach's Circus has been coming here year in and year out since the old man himself—blast him—was alive."

"Your father?" I asked, meaning Shadrach, whomever he might be.

This produced an ironic and tight little laugh.

"My great step-uncle," she said. "He was a monster. Even the tigers lived in fear of him. In the days when we *had* tigers, I mean. Nowadays, we have only one: Saladin. Near-blind and toothless. He only growls because his bones ache."

"So you've known Orlando for a long time," I said helpfully.

"Since he was a boy, poor lad. He used to beg us to take him away with us. Not that he had any illusions of becoming a showman, but simply to escape from his father."

"Canon Whitbread," I said, matter-of-factly. "The one who—"

Mrs. Dandyman held up a restraining hand.

"Yes, *that* one. Say no more about it. I find it distressing."

"But I thought everyone loved Canon Whitbread."

"And so they did—until he did away with three harmless old ladies who dared disagree with him. Love can forgive only so many murders."

She was being ironic, I was quite sure of it.

Daffy had once explained to me that irony consisted of words from another world: that they did not seem to mean what you thought they meant, which was a contradiction in itself.

"They're words from the other side of the looking-glass," Daffy told me, "and ought always to be answered as such."

Could I trust Daffy? In cases like this, I had no other choice.

I took a deep breath, counted to three, looked Mrs. Dandyman in the eye, and asked: "How many murders have *you* forgiven?"

"None," she answered. "Nor will I—ever."

I was flabbergasted by her words. Here was a woman after my own heart! How I rejoiced in meeting her!

And yet I mustn't let her know.

In my own short life I had come to believe that murder is unforgiveable. Perhaps, in time, when I was older, I would come to see things differently, though for now, I was happy enough to be lumped with Saint Augustine, who prayed for purity—but, as he said, not yet.

"Who were they?" I asked. "The women he did away with, I mean."

"The Three Graces, we used to call them, if somewhat

inaccurately. Two Graces and an Annie, in fact, but there's no sense in nicknames, is there? Grace Willoughby, Grace Harcourt, and Annie Cray. Faith, Hope, and Treachery. The Weird Sisters, others called them."

"Were they actually sisters?"

"Good lord, no! It was just that they all stirred the cauldron of gossip more than was good for them—or for anyone else. There's nothing so deadly as an acid tongue driven by a pious mind. That's what Canon Whitbread said in one of his last sermons."

"Just before he poisoned them?" I asked.

"Some say that, yes."

"And you?"

"I keep to myself," Mrs. Dandyman replied.

She turned back to her easel and I suspected I was being dismissed.

I was, after all, trespassing.

"Why martyrs?" I blurted. "Why do you paint only martyrs?"

"This world we live in," she said, keeping her back to me, "is made up of saints and sinners. And of the two, there's a shortage of saints. It's as simple as that."

But was it? Did her words—which seemed to me to come too easily, as if she'd been asked this question before—mean that she saw it as her duty to supply the world with saints, even painted ones?

Or to rid the world of sinners?

Flavia, I thought, *you are developing a suspicious mind.*

"One more question, if I may," I persisted. "And then I'll leave you to your work."

She didn't answer, so I asked it anyway.

"Who hated Orlando enough to kill him?"

Mrs. Dandyman spun round and dropped her brush, splattering the hem of her dress and the legs of the easel with an ax-murderer scarlet.

"Nobody!" she exclaimed. "And don't you dare suggest otherwise. Don't you dare even think about it."

"What about Poppy Mandrill?" I asked brazenly. If I were to be tossed out on my ear I desperately needed one last morsel of information.

"Out!" Mrs. Dandyman shouted. "Out with you before I call the police."

I wondered idly how she could carry out this threat with no telephone in the pantechnicon, but it was no time to anger the woman further.

"I'm sorry," I said, and walked out the door, down the folding steps, and into the sunshine, my head in the air, not sorry in the least.

On the far side of the market square, Constable Otter was engaged in conversation with the three roustabouts, Terence, Nigel, and Cornell.

I put on a carefree expression and, with a careless whistle, became absorbed in kicking an empty ginger-beer bottle ahead of me as I walked. The greatest thing about being twelve is that you can turn it on and off as the situation requires.

The instant Constable Otter spotted me, he touched the front of his helmet with a long forefinger and made a beeline toward me. I angled away slightly—not too obviously, I hoped—and began to tack back toward the Oak and Pheasant.

It was no use. The blasted man had me on his radar and changed course even as I did. He reminded me of Inspector Bucket in *Bleak House,* that relentless hound who seemed to be everywhere at the same time.

"Miss de Luce," he called out.

Picking up speed slightly and changing direction again, I pretended I hadn't heard him.

"Miss de Luce!" he called again, more persistent this time.

I couldn't possibly evade him without breaking into a full gallop.

By now he was at my heels, and with my peripheral vision, I could see that he was reaching for my arm. I did the only thing I could think of: I stopped dead in my tracks.

Constable Otter crashed into me at speed, and down I went, ark over teakettle into the dust.

Intentionally, of course.

I lay there looking dazed—allowing the man to scramble to his feet, pick up his helmet, dust himself off, and regain his dignity. Meanwhile, I began, slowly and painfully, contorting my limbs into the most bizarre angles I could conjure up on a moment's notice from my monkey ancestors.

Laboriously, I hauled myself to my knees.

I set my drooping head to vibrating at high speed, like the clanger on an alarm clock, as if I were on the verge of a seizure, all the while groping for my elbows, knees, shoulders, and giving off a few pitiful moans.

"Are you all right?" he asked. "I'm sorry, but—"

"Shappened?" I said, slurring the word and letting my tongue thicken and loll out the corner of my mouth. "Hoss hit me?"

It wasn't a bad plan to raise the specter of concussion right at the outset.

"I'm sorry," the constable said again, reaching for my elbow to help me up, but I shook him off.

A small crowd had begun to gather. I gaped at them blearily, letting my eyes roll a little, as if I had never seen human beings before.

I grasped Otter's hand and hauled myself agonizingly to my feet.

"What's she done, then, Constable?" a man in rubber boots called out. "Broke into the Bank of England?"

In spite of my grave injuries, most of the onlookers laughed at this sudden flash of wit.

"He attacked her!" called out a small birdlike woman with white hair and spectacles the thickness of railway signal lamps. "I saw it with my own two eyes!"

Another laugh went up.

"Pick on someone your own size, Jimmy!" the rubber-booted man called out.

I could see that, round his official police collar, Constable Otter was turning red as rubies. I decided that he had had enough.

"Sorright," I said. "My fault. I tripped. I shurrna stopped so . . . so . . ."

I rolled my eyes again, fishing for an elusive word.

"Fasht," I concluded triumphantly.

There! I had done it!

Constable Otter was suddenly beaming upon me like some pagan Sun God of beaten gold.

"Are you all right?" I asked, reaching out a solicitous (but trembling) hand toward him for extra points.

I shook my head to clear it and then I took his arm.

"I'm still a little shaky," I said. "Perhaps you could walk me back to the Oak and Pheasant, and you can question me over a nice cup of tea."

That's how it's done.

At least in *my* books.

And so it came to pass that PC Otter and I were alone at last in the saloon bar of the Oak and Pheasant, safely away from any danger of being overheard.

"Please have a seat, Constable," I said. The place was my residence, after all, even if only temporarily. Besides, it cost nothing to be polite.

"Thank you, miss," he said, pulling his inevitable notebook from his pocket. "But I'm on duty."

"I hope you won't mind if I sit," I said. "I'm sorry to be so much trouble. I expect your wife will be wondering what's become of you."

"No, she won't," he replied, "as I don't have a wife. Now then, about the . . . uh . . . deceased, which you discovered in the river this morning."

"Orlando Whitbread?" I asked, as if I had an endless

string of corpses up my sleeve, which I suppose in a way I did.

"How did you know his name?" he pounced, his pencil poised.

"Poppy Mandrill was screaming it. You could hear her a mile away. Besides, everyone in the county knows it by now."

Constable Otter made a brief scribble in his notebook as he arranged his features into a look of Official Gravity.

"You're not withholding anything from me, are you, miss?"

"Withholding?"

I wanted to add *"What could I possibly be withholding?"* but with the slip of paper from Orlando's trousers still soggy in my pocket, I didn't want to say too much.

I was beginning to learn that in criminal investigation, as in chair design and poetry, less is more.

At that moment, the landlord appeared with the tray of tea I had ordered on the way in.

"I've brought a few shortbread biscuits," Mr. Palmer said. "Some people like a few shortbread biscuits with their tea."

Since neither I nor the constable said anything, he gave the table a quick wipe and left us to our discussion.

I took a biscuit and dipped it into my tea. Etiquette be hanged.

"I expect Scotland Yard will be arriving at any moment," I remarked pleasantly. "And I shall be grilled again. It's such a bore, isn't it?"

"Scotland Yard?" Constable Otter said, not touching his tea. "Why would we bring in the Yard? They're not called out for every little accident, you know."

He shook his head and gave me a rueful smile.

"What would they think if we bothered them with every bruise—every skinned knee?" he said, glancing pointedly at my own knee which was scraped raw from my tumble. I hadn't even noticed.

So he still believed Orlando's death to be an accident, did he? Not worth reporting.

Investigation wrapped up in ribbons by the local constable. A discreet inquest which would find that the victim met his death through misadventure. A trip in the dark. Nobody's fault. Case closed.

Which left the field to me.

If I played my hand properly, I would get to the bottom of this affair, and present it myself—solved—to the appropriate inspector at the Yard. Providing I could discover who he was.

And perhaps—yes, perhaps—I could ring up Inspector Hewitt and lay the whole thing at his feet much as a dog brings a bone.

The important thing was to lie low; to say nothing to anyone.

From here on in, I would be as silent as the tomb.

I took a last sip from my teacup, and set it back on the saucer, taking great care to let my hand shake enough to produce a noticeable clatter of chinaware.

"I'm afraid I'm not as well as I thought I was," I said to

Constable Otter, summoning up a sickly, insipid smile. "I still feel quite shaken. If you'll excuse me, I think I'll go to my room and lie down."

I could see the relief on his face.

No more competition, he was thinking. *No more interference from that de Luce brat.*

In his eyes, I was already a dead duck.

Well, *"Quack! Quack! Quack!"*

I had just reached the top of the stairs when Mrs. Palmer came suddenly out of her room. She seemed surprised to see me.

"Oh, there you are," she said. "Did the undertaker find you?"

"Undertaker?" I asked, genuinely puzzled.

"Mr. Nightingale. He was looking for you. Arven told him you were in the saloon bar with Constable Otter. Didn't he look in?"

"No," I said. "Perhaps he didn't want to disturb us. Did he say what it was about?"

"He was looking for his son. Thought you might have been the last to see him."

My heart gave a leap.

"Is he missing?" I asked.

"Only in a general sort of way," Mrs. Palmer replied. "Hob is not your usual boy. Without a mother, and his father busy with the graves and so forth, he comes and goes when he pleases. He wouldn't if he were my son. I'd put a string on him."

I was reminded instantly of Hob and his kite. And his camera. Perhaps I could kill two birds with one stone by locating the little boy—probably gone back to Shadrach's Circus, I thought—and by retrieving his processed film from the chemist's shop.

But here was a pretty kettle of fish: Why would Mr. Nightingale keep clear of me when he knew I was with Constable Otter? Wasn't the constable, after all, the official eyes and ears of Volesthorpe, who probably knew to within a square yard the location of every single inhabitant at any given moment—as well as what they were up to?

It simply didn't make sense.

I vowed then and there to ask Mr. Nightingale that very question as soon as I was able to locate him. I was confident that he would give me a frank answer.

Undertakers were, I had discovered, decent men. Once you had got past the black crepe, the polished ebony, and the closely shaven chins, they were a tribe of hail-fellows-well-met, who enjoyed a joke as much as the next fellow, and sometimes more.

But aside from that, and perhaps more importantly, they knew—not to put too fine a point upon it—where all the bodies were buried.

I needed to buff up my acquaintanceship with Hob's Da, I realized, and I needed to do so immediately.

And this was the perfect opportunity.

"Thanks, Mrs. Palmer," I said. "Hob can't be far away. I saw him just a while ago. He's probably gone back for another squint at the elephant."

*

Outside, in the garden bower, Feely and Dieter were still clutching both of each other's hands, each gazing into the eyes of the other as if they were about to burst into song, like Jeanette MacDonald and Nelson Eddy in *Maytime* or one of those boring but unsettling films featuring advanced wrestling holds.

They didn't even see me.

Which was just as well, because I didn't wish to be seen.

An older sister in love is an unexploded bomb (UXB) at the best of times, but when she's just been reunited with her intended mate after a nerve-shredding separation of more than half a year, she's as touchy and unstable as a rusty bucket of old nitroglycerine ($C_3H_5O_9N_3$), and consequently best steered clear of.

I made my way back to the high street and to the premises of Wanless & Sons Dispensing Chemists, taking great care by stopping to gape like a tourist at the half-timbered shops and the tiny leaded windows of the adjoining houses.

I dawdled on the pavement for a couple of minutes, shaking my head at the quaintness of it all.

And then I stepped casually into the dimness of the shop.

"We're closed," said the man in white behind the counter. He looked as if he hadn't budged since I was here hours ago.

"I'm sorry," I replied. "But I wondered if there's the slightest chance my prints are ready? I don't mean to bother you, but there's been a family emergency and we've been summoned home immediately."

"Summoned" was a perfect choice of words, I thought. It added such great gravity to the situation.

He gave me that stare that chemists have.

"I don't know," he said, "but I doubt it. I had to step out for a while, you understand. We're very busy.

"Howland!" he bellowed, but this time there was no reply from the underworld.

He stamped on the floorboards. "Howland!"

"Would you mind checking?" I asked. "I'm afraid that it's . . . it's . . ."

I stifled a sob. Pressure works best when applied at precisely the right moment.

The chemist clicked his tongue with that sound which is usually written "Tch," and which suggests martyrdom: "Give me the strength to suffer this fool gladly."

Bending down, he pulled at an iron ring that was inset into the trapdoor and lifted it, revealing the top of a steep and narrow set of stairs—more of a ladder than anything.

I leaned round the wicket for a better view, but the chemist, with that crablike secrecy natural to his profession, scuttled down the hole, pulling the hatch closed behind him, and I, tiptoeing as silently as I could, stepped onto it.

I'd have to be quick.

A lightning scan of the counter did not reveal what I was hoping to find. An apothecary's pill roller of wood and marble and a brass balance were on one side and a paper-dispensing roll on the other.

No, it wasn't here. It would be put away somewhere out of sight, as official objects often are.

I pulled out one of the two deep drawers in which were a surprising number of loose coins, bills, and a few slips of scribbled paper which I guessed to be IOUs.

Don't touch, Flavia, I thought. *Fingerprints and so forth.*

I closed the first drawer and pulled out the second.

"Fortune favors girls with guts," some ancient Roman had once written, or ought to have written, because it was true.

I was instantly rewarded: There before my very eyes was a tall, black slender volume. *Sale of Poisons Register Book* was stamped on the cover in gold letters.

I hauled it out and opened it, fingerprints be hanged. It couldn't possibly be a crime to examine an official document. Could it?

I turned the pages with trembling fingers, beginning at the back, where the latest entries were written in a black and official-looking ink.

Each page had space for four entries, each detailing the date, the name and address of the purchaser, the name and quantity of the poison sold to them, the purpose for which it was required, and their signature, along with the name of the person who had introduced the purchaser to the chemist, which, in most cases, had been signed or initialed by the chemist himself: E. B. Wanless, presumably the name of that white-jacketed gentleman who was presently rummaging around somewhere in the depths beneath my feet.

My eyes widened as the secrets of Volesthorpe were laid bare. Here, in page after page, among the purchases of lead and opium to treat spasms, were the names and addresses of everyone who had bought sixpennyworth of rat poison and mouse poison; arsenic for psoriasis, or—four pounds of it at a time!—to tan or cure skins; potassium cyanide to destroy wasp's nests, or for photographic purposes.

As I leafed back toward the entries of two years ago, a notation fairly leapt at me off the page: HCN.

Prussic acid!

An ounce of the stuff had been sold to the Volesthorpe Constabulary. My pulse leapt as I read the reason given for the purchase: "Poison injured dog," it said.

And it had been signed for by J. R. Otter, Constable 997.

A wooden clatter beneath my feet indicated that the chemist was coming back up the ladder.

There was no time to waste: I shifted my brain into its speed-reading setting, tuning my eye for any occurrence of HCN, prussic acid, or cyanide.

And there were, I'm sorry to say, many—most requiring an ounce to poison a dog or a cat. And Hob's photographer brother, Pippin Nightingale, had, in an entry dated 1st November, 1949, signed for two ounces of "Cyanide of Potash," his given reason being "Silver Bath."

And in August of the same year, Canon Whitbread, of

"The Vicarage, St. Mildred's" had bought two ounces of potassium cyanide for the purpose of "destroying wasps' nests."

I touched the dead man's signature with my forefinger. I pictured him standing here at this very wicket as the cyanide was handed over. What was in his mind? What was in his heart?

I remembered, too, that according to Mrs. Palmer, Orlando had worked part-time at the chemist's shop, but as far as I could see, he had never signed this register, either as a buyer or a dispenser of poison. Which made sense, I suppose, since he was not licensed as a pharmaceutical dispenser.

The floor was now beginning to quake beneath my feet as the chemist applied his shoulder to the trapdoor. A string of muffled, but still clearly naughty, curses filtered up through the heavy floorboards.

"Hello?" I called out, injecting a note of surprise into my voice as I slipped the poison register back into the drawer and shoved it shut with my hip. "Is something wrong?"

At the same moment, with both feet still firmly on the trap, I bent down, seized the iron ring, and gave it a jolly good rattling.

"Blast!" I said in a frustrated voice, kicking at the ring. "I think it's stuck."

More chemical profanity floated up from under the floorboards.

"Hold on," I shouted. "I need to get something to lift it."

A few more heavy but useless heaves from below con-
vinced my captive that I was telling him the truth.

I smeared a bit of dust from the floor onto my cheek-
bones, tousled my hair, then bent and threaded one of my
pigtails through the ring. Then, in one single and con-
tinuous motion, in a fluid movement that would have
delighted both Sexton Blake and Philip Odell, the BBC
wireless detective, I stepped off the trap and pulled open
the hatch, using my hair as a rope.

I stared down for a moment into the lobster-red face of
the chemist.

I held the pose just long enough that the astonished
Wanless could see what I had done. Then, freeing my
hair from the ring with a flick of my head, I stuck out a
helping hand and began to haul him up out of the hole.

"Oh, you poor soul," I cooed, hoping it would sound
genuine. "The beastly ring was jammed. I had a very dickens of a time getting it open. How brave of you not to
have panicked! If it were me"—I shuddered—"I should
have shed a kidney."

I know . . . I know. But sometimes it's necessary.

I steadied his shaking arm as he came scrambling up
out of the open hatch like a sailor escaping a sinking sub-
marine.

It was easy enough to see that the man had worked
himself up into a tizzy. *Claustrophobia,* I thought. *No point
in staring and embarrassing him.*

"I'll just take my prints, then, and be on my way," I
said, in that cheery voice that makes people want to
strangle you.

I was simply dying to whistle "Someday My Prints Will Come," but I thought better of it.

"There are no prints," Wanless muttered, running his finger round the inside of his collar.

"They didn't turn out?" I asked. My heart began to sink.

"I expect they did," he said. "Howland had to charge extra for the expedited service."

"That's all right," I said blithely. "I don't mind paying. How much will it be?"

"You don't understand," the chemist said. "Howland must have dealt with it while I was out. They've already been picked up. Picked up and paid for. Less than an hour ago. It's marked in his receipt book."

He pointed toward the cellar.

My jaw fell open.

"Picked up by whom, may I ask?" I demanded, stiffening my spine like Aunt Felicity. I'd show this impertinent tradesman a thing or two! "They were my photographs."

But wait—best not to get too shirty. Perhaps Hob had picked up the snapshots and was lurking somewhere, chortling at the thought of surprising me with the finished prints.

"Ah," I said, relieved at the idea. "My friend—the little lad . . ."

Wanless gave me a quizzical look.

"They were signed for by Constable Otter," he said.

How did Otter know about the prints? I thought. *Had Hob told him? Or had he spotted the camera at the riverbank after all and decided to let it lead where it may—as I should have done, in his boots.*

I tried not to gulp. I mustn't panic. If Hob's aerial photographs showed anything at all—which I wasn't sure of—I didn't want them falling into the hands of Constable Otter.

I'll admit my reasons were selfish ones, but Otter had the full force of the law at his command, while I had only my wits. Would he have been so bold as to open the envelope and have a peep at someone's private prints? If he was any kind of investigator, he almost certainly would. I had already noted his keenness.

One thing was certain: I needed to find Constable Otter immediately, and to recover the photographs without arousing suspicion.

I have always believed that it's better to seize the bull by the horns than to be bitten in the backside. At the risk of dragging in too many animals, I would beard the lion in his den.

And, like Daniel in the book of the same name, I would trust in the Almighty to zip the lion's lips.

·FOURTEEN·

THE VOLESTHORPE CONSTABULARY—A DANK and moss-covered stone guardhouse—was located in the market square. It must once have been used as the village lockup.

One could easily imagine a set of wooden stocks at the door, facing the village green, where the village rowdies and hotheads were left to cool their heels—and their heads—until the alcohol wore off.

Attached to the rear, as an afterthought, were what I took to be the bachelor living quarters of Constable Otter: a wooden lean-to built along the lines of a Quonset hut cut in half and rammed up against the original medieval jail.

The constable's bicycle, with his rainproof cape lashed to the carrier, was parked out in front under the blue lamp.

The lion was at home.

I threw back my shoulders and straightened my back. "Don't slouch," Daffy was always telling me, "otherwise you'll look like me."

My sister affected a scholarly slouch of which she was particularly proud. "Bent under the burden of knowledge," she was fond of saying. "A cripple for culture."

I took a deep breath, stuck out my chin, stuffed make-believe shoulder pads into my blouse, arranged my features into what I thought Joan Crawford might look like in such a situation, and marched in the door.

Constable Otter looked up from the battered-looking counter at which he was writing.

"Well?" he asked.

"I believe you have my photographs," I said coldly, holding out my hand, palm up, to receive them.

"Have I, now?" he asked in a teasing tone.

So! It was going to be one of *those* conversations. A catalog of condescension.

Well, two could play at that game. I was glad I had been alerted so early on.

"Yes," I said. "You have. The chemist gave them to you—to give to me."

I moved closer and stuck out my hand again—too close to his face to be ignored.

"Is that what he said?"

Actually, he hadn't. I was bluffing and he knew it.

We were eye to eye. Which of us would blink first?

"Well?" he asked again.

Maddening.

He pulled them from under the counter, running a finger teasingly along the flap of the envelope, as if he was about to open it and remove the prints. The man was toying with me. I had to do something—and quickly.

"Constable," I said, "I wish to remind you that those photographs are my personal property. As such, they are protected by several Acts of Parliament. Unless you are seizing them in evidence, you have no right of possession. You are breaching my privacy."

Otter ought to have known better. I saw a slight haziness come into his eyes, like a scattering of cloud beginning to cross the moon.

I had made him think.

I was still bluffing, of course, but that's just part of the game and, in my opinion, one of the most enjoyable. She who bluffs last bluffs best.

Taking care not to lay it on too thick, I moved my hand even closer, making it easier for him to give up the envelope.

He began to gnaw, almost invisibly, at his lower lip.

"And did you take these pictures yourself, miss?" he asked, thrusting his face forward in a determined manner.

Of course I had taken them. Hadn't I removed the film cartridge from Hob's camera with my own hands?

Does God forgive you when you intentionally pretend to misunderstand? This was probably one of those questions that tormented the ancient saints in their lonely cells in the tiny hours of the night.

Would the Creator actually cast you, forever, into Hell's deepest coal cellars, merely for using the wits that He gave you?

It seemed most unlikely.

And yet, I didn't want to perjure myself—at least not officially—by lying aloud.

I would compromise.

"Surely, in your profession, Constable," I said, "you will recall the case of *Nottage v. Jackson* (1883), in which Justice Bowen ruled that the prints taken from a negative are to be appropriated to the use of the customer only."

It wasn't for nothing that I kept a complete set of the *Encyclopaedia Britannica,* Eleventh Edition, in the eastern upstairs loo at Buckshaw.

Were the constable's eyes clotting, or was it just my imagination?

"You're a regular clever clogs, aren't you?" he said at last.

"No, Constable Otter, I am not," I replied, holding out my hand again. "But I *am* a girl who knows her rights. My pictures, if you please."

And by the jingling Jeremiah, he handed them over, holding the packet between his thumb and middle finger as if it had suddenly begun to reek.

I offered up a rapid prayer of thanks to Bernardine of Siena, the patron saint of bluffers and gamblers.

"Thank you," I said, removing the envelope slowly from his hand, and trying to keep my voice from sounding too shirty.

No need to rush. Keep a cool head, Flavia.

Taking my time, I looked slowly round the barren room, then back to the glaring policeman.

"Quite a nice place you have here, Constable Otter. But I think a few flowers would vastly improve it."

I left him to work out what I meant.

And then, shooting him a horrible smile that was a half inch short of a grimace, I sailed out the door of the constabulary as grandly as if I were the *Queen Elizabeth*.

I had made an enemy. I just knew it.

I was strolling up the high street, looking for a place to study the snapshots undisturbed. Because of the circus, I supposed, there were little knots of people everywhere, with privacy nowhere in sight.

I was walking past a shop whose window was full of yarn: skeins and balls of yarn of every color imaginable— and a few shades that weren't. I had just paused for a closer look at an antique colander full of wicked-looking knitting needles, when a voice said:

"Pssst! Flavia."

I spun round. There was no one there. No one within fifteen or twenty feet of me.

"Pssst! Flavia!"

More urgent this time.

Failing any other choice, I looked up: up into the branches of a plane tree that overhung the pavement. And there, perched like a cocky sparrow, grinning down at me, legs dangling from a limb, was Hob.

"Come on up!" he hissed, making the universal beckoning signs with his hands and fingers.

I made a hasty reconnaissance of the street to make sure no one was watching, then, with a sudden leap, hauled myself up amongst the branches and settled on the limb beside him.

It was like a cool, green cathedral here in the tree. A slight breeze stirred the leaves, providing a welcome refreshment from the hot, tired air of a summer afternoon.

"Oh, good! You got the snapshots," Hob said, reaching for the envelope. "Let's have a look and see how they turned out."

Something in me resisted handing them over, but I realized at once that in spite of Constable Otter, in spite of *Nottage v. Jackson*, and in spite of Justice Bowen, when it came to Hob's ownership of these snaps, I hadn't a chance.

My inner dog-in-the-manger crawled back into its bed of straw.

"Of course!" I said, overcompensating with cheerfulness. "You go first."

I passed him the envelope and watched impatiently as he slowly lifted the flap, peered into the envelope as if he were applying his eye to a telescope, looked up to grin at me, stuck two fingers into the packet, and pulled the photos halfway out.

I could have strangled him.

And yet, in my heart, I remembered having done things every bit as maddening myself on many occasions. Manufactured mysticism was such a wonderful way of stretching a happy instant to the breaking point; a way of causing a brief moment of sharing to form even a fraction of some new infinity. And I realized now, for the first time, that these brief and fleeting joys were little more than sadness with a mask on.

"Let's have a dekko," I said, pretending to grab for the photos, but Hob jerked them away, giggling.

"Bags it me," he said, settling the matter beyond dispute. It is a fact of life that, among civilized people anywhere in the world, a basic "bags it" trumps everything, including, I suspect, even Judgment Day.

Pretending to be bored, I gazed off into the distance, waiting impatiently for Hob to thumb his way through the prints.

He made a rude noise with his mouth.

"Spoiled," he said. "All of them."

"Oh?" I said airily. "Why?"

"The camera moved. They're blurry."

"What do you expect when the camera's bobbing around on the end of a kite? Let's have a look."

Hob handed over the photos with no further interest.

"You have to wait until the string tied to the shutter is already tight. You mustn't jerk it too hard. I tried to wait until the wind was pulling steadily."

"Well, there wasn't much of a wind, as I recall," I said, thumbing through the photos.

Hob was right. Most of them were no more than hopeless smudges of light and shadow.

All except one.

"Hold on," I said. "This one's almost perfect."

Hob leaned over for a second look.

"It's looking in the wrong direction," he said. "I was trying to take a view of the river and the circus."

"And so you did," I said, pointing to the foreground. "Look: Here's our punt on the river. That's me dabbling my hand over the side."

I did not draw attention to the dark submerged mass in whose dead mouth my fingers were firmly hooked.

"Pfah!" Hob said. "You can have it. That's not what I wanted."

How well I knew the feeling! As a scientist, I'd learned to incorporate unexpected results into my data. There was, for instance, the time I had charged Feely's hot water bottle with a mixture of naphtha and turpentine, both of which are capable, after a certain delay, of dissolving India rubber. Although Feely had been too embarrassed to report the outcome, I knew by her looks next morning at the breakfast table that I was the prime suspect.

When I retrieved the wreckage later that day from the refuse bin, I found that I had accidentally discovered what I believed to be a previously unknown solvent, a single whiff of which was powerful enough to strip paint from battleships at a distance of six miles.

Spirit of Flavia, I intended to call the stuff, but not until I had got around to writing it up for the chemical journals. So far, I simply hadn't had the time.

I slipped Hob's print into my pocket. I would study it later at my leisure under a magnifying glass.

"Did your father find you?" I asked, trying to change

the subject and—yes, I admit it—draw attention away from the photographs.

I had almost forgotten that I'd been looking for Hob when I happened upon him.

"No," Hob said.

"Then you'd better run home," I told him. "He was asking for you at the Oak and Pheasant."

Hob sniffed.

"I'm not a boozer, you know."

"Perhaps he'd looked everywhere else," I suggested. "Perhaps he thought someone had seen you."

"He's checking up on me," Hob said, examining his fingernails. "He's afraid I'm hanging round the circus."

"Like Orlando Whitbread?" I asked. The words slipped out before I could stop them.

Hob's mouth fell open.

"How could you know that?" he asked. "Are you a witch?"

"Yes, I am," I told him, enjoying the moment. "I practice a specialized kind of witchcraft called thinking. It's a very mysterious power. Quite unknown to the average person."

I wiggled my fingers at him like a nest of little worms, as if casting a spell. "Now then, tell me about Orlando Whitbread before I turn you into a turnip."

Hob shrugged, unimpressed.

"Orlando played the Widow Twankey in the panto. He pulled a string of sausages out of the horse's—well, you know. I'm not allowed to say the word."

"Bottom?" I suggested.

He nodded furiously.

"He made me laugh until I sicked," he said. "Da had to take me home. I ruined the new jumper I got for Christmas."

I wrinkled my face in appreciation.

"'Cause we had spaghetti for dinner," he added, trying to outdo himself.

Although, like Mr. Gradgrind in Dickens, I have always had a fondness for facts, this was a little too much sauce even for my liking.

"What a good memory you have," I said, trying to be encouraging, but not *too* encouraging.

It was odd. Although I had never experienced such a thing before, I was suddenly feeling the need to display a certain maturity. I must tread carefully.

"What did Orlando do when he wasn't pulling sausages out of horses?" I asked. "Did he have a job?"

"He walked by the river," Hob said. "Talking to himself—or someone invisible. Waving his arms around."

"Is that all?"

"I guess so."

It seemed obvious that Orlando must have been either a madman or an actor rehearsing his lines.

"Well, I'd better be on my way, then," I said.

The day was getting on, and the heat was having its effect. I suddenly wanted nothing more than to put my head on a cool pillow and allow my thoughts to collect themselves.

What a disaster it would be—and how embarrassing—to fall out of a tree from fatigue.

I needed to eat and I needed to sleep.

Murder would simply have to wait.

"Wait," Hob said, as I began to pick my way down the tree.

"What?" I asked snappishly.

"Nothing," he said, seemingly hurt. "I just didn't want you to go."

I felt like a heel.

I was beginning to feel a headache coming on, and this time it was genuine. I could already feel the invisible octopus wrapping its tentacles round my temples.

I'd barely eaten for hours, I realized. Even in a young person such as myself, the finely tuned chemical factory that is the human body cannot run forever on cheese and pickled onions.

Little has been written about the exhausting effects of a late summer afternoon's heat, but I intend to do so. Like the weather, everyone knows about it, but no one does anything about it.

I would use myself as a guinea pig. Yes, that was it! With proper microscopic examination of blood samples taken at regular intervals and chemically analyzed at every step, I would show that lack of food in a hot environment and in the presence of mental stress could result in a kind of blood poisoning.

It was a brilliant insight and I couldn't wait to get back to Buckshaw.

"Hold on," I said, brightening suddenly. The word "poisoning" had triggered something in my mind. "You said Orlando walked by the river. *Where* by the river, in particular?"

Hob shrugged.

"In the churchyard. By the dock."

"Waving his arms and talking to himself."

"Mostly," Hob said.

"What do you mean, *mostly?*"

"Just hanging around. Like he lost something. Staring at the water."

Cold fingers caressed the back of my neck. There is an old saying or belief that a criminal always returns to the scene of his crime. Whether this is true or not I have no way of knowing, but the tired old idea was suddenly speaking to my blood. Could it be that Orlando was drawn back to the spot where his father was supposed to have ditched the silver chalice? The same spot where Fate would later, eerily, arrange for me to find his corpse? Had Orlando's death been staged to make it seem like suicide?

I nearly lost my grip on the branch.

"Hob," I wanted to say, *"you are a treasure. A bucketful of gems. Your price is far above rubies."*

I also wanted to hug him.

But I didn't, of course.

"Hmm," I said in what I hoped was a disinterested voice. "Anything else?"

Hob shrugged.

"Sometimes he helps Da in the shop. He used to, I mean. Da said it didn't work out."

·FIFTEEN·

THERE WENT ANY IDEA I'd had of sleep. Farewell food, and farewell cool pillow, also. There wasn't a minute to be wasted.

The way ahead was marked in my mind as clearly as a map drawn in flame.

Having thanked Hob, I made my not-so-graceful exit by parachuting down out of the tree and into the street. Thankfully, there was no one about to witness this display.

I would return at once to the Oak and Pheasant. I would quiz Dogger about his day's investigations, then turn my attention, full force, to the late Orlando.

But back at the inn, disappointment awaited me. Dogger was nowhere in sight. And the Rolls was gone, which meant, I hoped, that he had uncovered something interesting.

I went to my room to wait for him.

I sat for a time on the edge of my bed, drumming impatiently on my knees. My stomach was giving off noises like a jungle at sunset and could no longer be ignored. There was nothing in the room to eat but fingernails.

Had Dogger been there, I'd have asked him to fetch me up a whole hog on a plate, which I'd tuck into with fangs and flying fat, like Henry VIII. I would let out a belch of gratitude, and then we'd be off, renewed: a pair of old hounds hot on the trail of a cold-blooded murderer.

When I opened my eyes, I was lying on my back and the room was suffused with a gray and watery light.

I thought at first that I had been deprived of color vision as punishment for some forgotten sin.

I struggled into a sitting position.

Beside me on the table was a packet wrapped in wax paper which, when I opened it, turned out to be a cold ham sandwich, with salt, pepper, and mustard, just the way I preferred it.

"Bless you, Dogger," I said aloud, and fell upon the food.

Henry VIII, by the Grace of God King of England, France, and Ireland, Defender of the Faith, and of the Church of England and also of Ireland on Earth Supreme Head, would have been proud of me.

I washed down the feast with the cup of cocoa—still slightly warm—which Dogger had left. He had been here not so long ago.

I gave my arms and legs a good waggle to shake off sleep.

In spite of the weather, it would be chilly outside in the early morning. I dug a wool jumper out of my suitcase, a garment insisted upon by Aunt Felicity:

"*Only a fool would go without wool,*" she had said.

It was almost a poem, and having once remembered it, I could not get the blasted thing out of my head.

"*Only a fool would go without wool,*" I said to myself as I shrugged into the jumper.

"*Only a fool would go without wool.*"

I wondered idly if Mrs. Palmer had ever written so instructive a poem, or whether she confined herself to obscure musings about wild animals, such as copper mares and brass stallions.

Hold on, I thought. Hadn't there been a rearing Arab stallion painted on the side of Mrs. Dandyman's pantechnicon?

My heart accelerated at the thought—although it might have been the sudden influx of ham.

I switched off the bedside lamp. No need to signal to anyone outside that I was up and about. One of the prime rules of sneakiness is to attract no undue attention.

I opened and closed my door soundlessly. The stairs were in darkness so that I had to make my way down, step by step, holding on tightly to the banister.

Clinking noises from the direction of the kitchen told me that Mrs. Palmer was already up and preparing for another busy day.

I slunk with ferret footsteps across the entranceway and eased myself out the door.

Well done, Flavia, I thought. Even a ghost could not have made a more soundless exit.

It was only when I was outside, breathing the chill morning air, that I came to my senses and realized I didn't know where I was going.

Scull Cottage, I knew, was somewhere on the river-bank, but on which side and in which direction?

Mrs. Palmer had said that it was little more than a boathouse, and that it was leaky. How many structures of that description could there be? I could hardly barge into the kitchen now and ask for directions.

No one must know what I was up to.

I would simply have to flip a mental coin and proceed by elimination.

I glanced up quickly at the casement windows, hoping my face wouldn't show up white in the half-light of the early morning. Feely would not be awake yet anyway, I decided. Courting is strenuous work, and if I knew my sister, she would now be snoring away like half a hundred pigs, her mouth gaping open and her hair a buzzard's nest.

Having decided I would begin in the churchyard and work my way downstream, I was partway across the gravel sweep when I heard the sudden and unmistakable sound of car tires.

Someone was coming and there was nowhere to hide. In the open road I would be a sitting duck.

I did the only thing that I could think of: I froze.

It is a well-known law of nature that a moving object attracts more attention than one which is motionless.

Every rabbit and every squirrel—in fact, every living creature subject to being eaten by predators—is born with the ability to freeze instantly when danger is detected.

I was standing there awkwardly in mid-stride, trying not to blink—not even to breathe. If my strategy worked, whoever it was would drive by without noticing me.

The crunching sound came closer and closer. It was eerie. Even in the silence of the morning I could hear no motor.

Crrrunch!

And then it stopped.

There was a soft thump, as of a sturdy door coming open, followed by the sound of boots on gravel.

I turned my head slowly, like an owl, hoping the whites of my eyes would not give me away.

Dogger was standing beside the Rolls, holding the door open for me. The car's sidelights glowed with a soft, warm welcome.

"Good morning, Miss Flavia," he said. "I trust you slept well?"

"Very well, thank you, Dogger," I answered. "I knew you'd be waiting for me."

It was a bluff. Dogger knew it and I knew it, but in spite of that, it somehow served as a bond between us.

To those of us who truly love one another, the occasional flaming fib serves only to strengthen the ties.

"Scull Cottage, please," I said, climbing into the front seat of the car's deliciously toasty interior.

"Indeed," Dogger said as he let in the clutch and we floated away in near-silence from the inn.

"You will have already had a good look round," I remarked, as we drove along the deserted high street—in the opposite direction, actually, of the way I had intended to go.

"I'm afraid not," Dogger said. "I did make something of a reconnaissance, but I'm afraid I was spotted by a neighbor."

"Spotted?" I asked. That could mean anything from a quick glance to the ringing up of Constable Otter.

"Recognized," Dogger elaborated, looking straight ahead. "A person from the past."

Aha! I thought. Dogger had already admitted to having been here before. "In another life," as he had put it.

"A woman?" I asked, staking everything on a wild surmise.

"I'm sorry, Dogger," I threw in at once. "I have no right to ask that. It just slipped out. Forget I said it."

Dogger turned and smiled.

"As it happens, you're right. A dear friend, merely, but one, I'm afraid, I have—"

"Never mind," I interrupted, still embarrassed for my breach of manners. "Let's talk about something else. Orlando Whitbread, for instance. Shall I tell you what I've found out about him?"

Dogger shook his head.

"Not until later, Miss Flavia, if you don't mind. After we've had a look round. I've found it useful to come at things with an untainted mind."

Even though I agreed with his principle—indeed, Inspector Hewitt had once told me much the same thing—it did not occur to me until later that Dogger had already visited Scull Cottage. This would be his second look.

Dogger turned off the road and onto a narrow track—no more than a cow path, really, that ran along the edge of a field, at the far side of which it began to slope downward toward the river.

Ahead was a grove of willows, which, in the first light of day, clustered together in the slight fog with a vaguely literary look. Beyond these, a hawthorn hedge blocked the view of the water.

Dogger brought the Rolls to a stop and engaged the parking brake.

"This is as far as we can drive," he said.

As we climbed out of the car, I had a good look at our surroundings: at the bottom of the sloping field, glimpses of the river through the trees and bushes; above us, the greater expanse of the field. No houses were visible. In fact, no structures of any kind. In the pale light of the early morning, the entire landscape seemed composed of water, earth, and sky.

What a remote place, I thought, *for skulduggery.*

How odd it seemed to find such a wilderness on the very doorstep of a busy market town.

"This way," Dogger said, leading me along a barely visible path which appeared to lead directly into the heart of the hawthorns.

What seemed at first to be an impenetrable tangle opened quickly up into a pleasant track among the trees that ran down to the water's edge, and to a quaint but sadly neglected structure.

"Scull Cottage," Dogger said, almost to himself.

The place had the look of an abandoned pagoda. Its sagging roof, curving down in a swayback shape, was decorated, at the end of each joist, with a carved dragon's head. Once painted Chinese red, these formerly fearsome creatures were now sadly weathered and peeling, their wooden faces looking half hopeful, as if they were awaiting rescue.

We walked slowly round the structure, taking it all in: the mossy shingles, the drooping window frames, and the general air of brackishness.

The cottage itself might have been some relic of a drained Atlantis: a greenish, almost shapeless mound, a loaf of forgotten bread caught in the act of moldering back into the earth.

As in the presence of all fungi, there was a feeling of slight but detectable uneasiness about the place.

At the water's edge, beneath the trees, a dock of decomposing planks was crumbling quietly into the river. Beyond it, a stile marked the end of an overgrown lane: a former towpath, I guessed.

Old boards groaned as I stepped onto the porch.

"Careful," Dogger warned.

I nodded to indicate that I was heeding his words. The hush of the place was uncanny.

It was like that weird poem of the German hero-adventurers so admired by Daffy in which "all seemed quiet in the iland"; in which "no bird sang in the bushes"; in which "no tree rustled in the breeze"; and in which "no beast brushed athwart the thicket."

Even the thought of the words made me shiver.

I cupped my hands against one of the grimy windows.

It was useless. With the dishwater light of the early morning behind me and darkness within the cottage, I could see nothing of its interior.

"Were you here yesterday, Dogger?" I asked. It was just a sudden feeling I had, and I wondered why I was whispering.

Dogger nodded his head. He did not elaborate and I did not ask. It seemed somehow wrong, in this strange place, to make a sound.

I pressed my nose to the glass again, hoping for miraculous vision to be suddenly bestowed upon me.

Something touched my elbow and I nearly leapt—like Saint Bartholomew—out of my skin.

I whipped round, wide-eyed, to find Dogger offering the torch. I had not noticed him bringing it from the Rolls.

With a curt, professional nod, as if leaping out of my skin were part of my plan and no more than an everyday occurrence, I took it from his hand, switched it on, and held the light against the windowpane.

A woman's face was staring back at me from the darkness.

"Bugger!" I said—regretting it at once.

Get a grip, Flavia, I thought. Dogger was here. What possible harm could come from a moldering old house on the riverbank?

The house of a dead man, some part of my mind insisted. *The house of a murdered man.*

"Look here, Dogger," I said, pretending to sound no more than mildly interested, even though it took every ounce of my willpower to keep from taking to my heels.

Dogger stepped carefully up beside me on the porch and applied his eye to the window.

"Interesting," he said. "I should imagine 1910, or thereabouts."

I placed my eye next to his, our faces next to one another against the glass.

In the yellow light of the torch, I could see that we were looking at a large theatrical poster pasted to a wall. On it, in garish colors, a woman in a Victorian girdle, and not much else except for a few ostrich feathers, swung upon a trapeze, her painted lips open in simpering laughter.

"A bird in a gilded cage," Dogger said softly at my ear. "Back then, women were often portrayed as captives, their cages being life upon the stage."

"Did they ever escape?" I asked, instantly aware that we had slipped into a topic in which I was out of my depth.

But I would persist. Perhaps I would learn something.

"Some did," Dogger said. "This one—if I'm not mistaken—"

He took the torch from my hand and directed its beam to the bottom of the poster.

Lady Babylon, it said, in garish yellow lettering of a theatrical nature, *A Musical Play Written and Composed by Leonard Bostwich. Sung and Performed by Miss Poppy Mandrill.*

"Gosh!" I said.

"Quite," Dogger agreed.

"Is that actually her?" I asked. "She was a stunner when she was young."

Dogger did not reply.

I could now see in the gloom of the interior that there were many more posters and photographs of a similar nature covering the walls. In fact, the place looked more like a picture gallery than a home.

Had Orlando actually collected these relics himself and constructed a shrine of sorts to his mentor?

I was pressing my face flat against the window to permit a better view of the far corners when a voice said:

"Arthur?"

I spun round, startled by the sound.

In the dawn, a woman was standing at the stile, a hoe in her hand.

I'll admit I must have gaped.

She was dressed in rubber boots and a pair of muddy trousers tied at the waist with binder twine. A khaki shirt, open at the neck, was obviously a military castoff, as was the broad-brimmed, sweat-stained hat, which would have been more appropriate in the jungles of the Far East than in this remote British backwater.

"Arthur?" she said again, and it was only then I realized she was talking to Dogger.

Dogger lowered the torch and began to turn round, but I noted the slight hesitation, as if he needed to gather his wits before answering to his Christian name. His jaw muscles were ever so slightly tightening.

"Claire?" he asked, turning fully to meet her gaze at last.

Dogger was always a man of few words, and never more than now.

The woman had put down her hoe and was climbing over the stile. A moment later she stood facing us, a definite blush creeping up her tanned neck from the depths of the khaki shirt toward her glorious red hair.

"I thought it was you," she said, gulping to keep her voice calm.

As a female myself, I knew instinctively that she was fighting back an almost irresistible urge to hug him. The joy in her eyes stood out like diamonds.

"I saw you here yesterday," she said. "I couldn't believe my eyes. I thought I must have been mistaken. I called out to you from my garden, but you mustn't have heard me."

She spoke with an accent which I couldn't immediately identify: the vowels tightly wound, like Cockney, but even more so.

"No, I heard you, Claire," Dogger said. "You must forgive me. I was unprepared—"

"Nonsense!" Claire exclaimed. "You mustn't explain. I understand perfectly."

And I could tell from the calmness creeping back into Dogger's face that he believed her.

"It has been a long time," he said. "A very long time, indeed. How have you been?"

I couldn't help noticing his deliberate choice of words: "How have you *been*," rather than "How *are* you?"

How she was *now* was evident to everyone for a quarter of a mile: Even in the early light, her smile was a hundred suns.

"Getting by," she said. "Same as always. And you?"

"I manage," Dogger said, and I knew in my heart that he was telling this woman the brutal truth.

I couldn't help myself. I slipped my arm in his.

Could it be jealousy, this creeping in my throat? This almost imperceptible swelling of my brain?

Is this what the green-eyed monster looked like from the inside?

"Dogger has been of very great service to my family," I heard myself saying. "He has been a rock."

I wanted to say more but I didn't. I wanted to quote one of Daffy's favorite lines from *Cyrano de Bergerac:* ". . . A rock, a crag, a cape! . . . Say rather . . . a *peninsula!*"

But Dogger would have been embarrassed and so would I.

I was learning to keep my mouth shut.

"Miss Tetlock," Dogger said, "may I introduce you to Miss de Luce."

"Flavia," I said, sticking out my hand and seizing hers, not caring about the agricultural debris with which it was covered. How very different, I thought, from the black and unpleasant handshake Terence had given me at Shadrach's Circus.

This handshake was, by comparison, wholesome, and I beamed my approval toothily at this woman, in spite of the fact that we had only just been introduced.

"Claire," Miss Tetlock said, tightening her grip to show she meant it. "Call me Claire."

For a moment, we all of us stood there, as if in a tableau or a trance, waiting for the next word to come, and yet each of us reluctant to be the one to speak it.

"Well, then," Claire said at last, "I expect you'll be wanting to have a look through Orlando's belongings. Such a tragedy."

She saw my jaw drop open in disbelief.

"It's all right," she continued. "Orlando entrusted me with a key. I kept an eye on the place when he was away and he, in return, drove off invaders, human or otherwise, from my allotment garden."

She waved in the direction of the stile.

"Constable Otter may not approve," Dogger said. "But if you insist—"

"Hang Constable Otter," Claire cut in, to my surprise. "I don't mean that literally, of course, but there are times when, in order to be maintained, the law must be broken.

"Or at least *bent*," she added.

I beamed upon her as she stepped up onto the creaking porch and pulled a key from her shirt pocket. This was a woman from the same mold as myself.

"All I expect is justice," she said, as she turned it in the lock. "Orlando is going to need all the help he can get."

What a curious thing to say about a dead man, I thought.

A moment later we were inside.

·SIXTEEN·

HANGING ALMOST OVER THE water as it did, Scull Cottage had a brackish smell, like an aquarium that belonged to an absentminded fish enthusiast.

I shivered as I recalled my fingers caught in the dead Orlando's mouth: good experience, to be sure, but not one that I would care to have often repeated.

"I'm sorry there's no electricity laid on," Claire told us. "The place is really little more than a converted boathouse. If the truth be told, no one is supposed to be living in it. Orlando had his ups and downs with the authorities, but Orlando being Orlando . . ."

She let her voice trail off to end in a wry smile.

"What was he like?" I asked suddenly, taking advantage of the opportunity.

"He was a clergyman's son, the son of a canon," Claire replied, "which ought to explain everything, but doesn't.

That he enjoyed telling people he was a son of a gun is perhaps more revealing."

I grinned because I knew she wanted me to.

"A joker," I said.

"Not entirely. An attention seeker, perhaps, which is often the force driving those who seek the stage. His mother died when Orlando was a baby."

"A very good actor, I understand."

I did not bother mentioning where I had heard this, but Daffy had once told me that all actors and all murderers are attention seekers.

"The only difference," she had said, "is that the one fulfills his fantasies in a darkened alley or a shabby room, while the other does it on a raised platform in full public view."

"Astonishing," Claire said, interrupting my thoughts. "Anyone who saw him as Eliza Doolittle in *Pygmalion,* or as Hamlet, realized that Orlando was larger than the stage itself. He was not just *touched* with genius, but totally saturated with it."

"Eliza Doolittle?" I asked. "He played the role of Eliza Doolittle?"

"And on less than an hour's notice," Claire told me. "Millie Plumb, who works part-time at the chemist's, fell suddenly ill after rehearsing the part for months. Orlando stepped in and . . . well, the rest is—or ought to be— theatrical history. Those of us who saw the performance knew that something far more than greatness had been revealed to us. I still have to pinch myself to realize I didn't dream the whole thing."

"Genius is often accompanied by an inexplicable chill," Dogger observed. "Professor Merlino of Mantua published some most suggestive notes upon the topic, but they have gained little attention outside of Italy."

"Didn't Orlando also help out occasionally at the chemist's?" I asked. I didn't want to interrupt Claire's story, but the coincidence popped into my mind.

"Did he poison Millie to get the part, you mean?" Claire smiled. "Because Orlando's name was involved in both cases, that very point was raised at the inquest into the deaths of three old ladies who died quite soon after his singular performance. The coroner, quite rightly, refused to hear it."

"Canon Whitbread," I said, wanting to let her know I hadn't just fallen off a lettuce lorry.

"Canon Whitbread, indeed," she said.

Dogger had all the while been standing quietly by, listening with great interest but saying little.

"As a trial run," he said. "Both to secure the role for himself and to practice up his poisons."

"Something of the sort," Claire said. "It was later proven—by a chemical analyst employed by Scotland Yard—that Millie's gastric catastrophe had been caused by a surfeit of green apples: the result of courting in an orchard with the wrong sort of person and the wrong sort of fruit."

"The old, old story," Dogger said.

"Yes, the old, old story," Claire echoed, and for a moment there was silence.

"Listen," she said abruptly, fidgeting with her collar.

"How would you like to come over to my cottage for a cup of tea? Quite frankly, this place gives me the jim-jams."

She jabbed a thumb in the direction of Poppy Mandrill, who from her painted poster was grinning horribly over Claire's shoulder.

"Very kind of you," Dogger said. "But since we're here, we'd like to have a look around, don't you think, Miss Flavia?"

I nodded agreement, torn between the two of them, but drawn most powerfully to the prospect of having a good old rummage through Orlando's goods.

"I'm sorry," Claire said. "I was being selfish."

"Not at all," Dogger said. "It gives me the jimjams, as you say, also. But your assistance would be of immense help. Perhaps with the three of us, things will proceed more quickly."

"What are we looking for?" Claire asked. "Is it something I may already know about?"

"Letters," Dogger answered. "Address books, telephone numbers, bottles, books, and refuse. Anything that will give us insight into the life—if I may say so—of the deceased."

Could this be yet another of what I took to be Dogger's jokes?

He's enjoying himself! I realized. In spite of the gravity of the situation, and of our many troubles, dear old Dogger was having the time of his life.

It did my heart good.

But at the same time it made me break out into a cold

sweat, since in my pocket was the slip of paper I had removed from Orlando's corpse.

Should I confess to withholding evidence and hand it
over?

It was no wonder that so many of the ancient philoso-
phers had spent so much time and ink chewing over—
digesting and redigesting—moral issues.

Philosophy had always seemed to me like the four
stomachs of a cow, but now I might have to rethink my
position.

Was I guilty or was I not? And if so, of what?

I suddenly knew how poor old Plato must have felt,
and in that moment, I made my decision.

"Look at this," I said, pointing to a black-and-white
photograph of the young Poppy Mandrill on a bicycle,
her skirts raised to show a risky bit of ankle.

"It's signed: *'To my Pegasus, from Poppy.'* Inscribed
with a Biro. Much more modern than the photo."

"Good lord," Claire breathed, shooting a look at Dogger.

Pegasus, I recalled from hearing Daffy read aloud some
of the steamier passages from *Bulfinch's Mythology*, was
the winged horse in Greek mythology who sprang from
the soil stained by the blood of the decapitated Medusa.

We British are far behind other countries when it
comes to inventing stories.

Still, was it any accident that Poppy Mandrill handed
out autographs to a horse, while Mrs. Palmer wrote poems
to one?

Well, stranger things have happened. You never knew

what you were going to run into in the English country-side.

As Dogger shone the light from wall to wall, the shadows dissolved, revealing poster after ancient poster, photo after curling photo, all of them of Poppy Mandrill.

"She must have been very famous," I remarked.

"Incredibly famous," Claire said. "She was the toast of the London stage. It was said that gentlemen drank champagne from her silk slippers and snippets of her hair were auctioned off to millionaires."

"But what happened to her?" I asked, thinking of the old woman hunched in her bath chair, directing amateur plays in a backwater town.

"Poppy committed the deadly sin of growing old," Claire said. "The gentlemen slunk away to sip from other slippers. Millionaires have no interest in gray hair."

"Rather like Medusa," I said. "Orlando was to be her winged horse, wasn't he? The one who flew to new heights from her wreckage?"

"Flavia," Claire said, "you fascinate me. You really do. You also frighten me."

I tried not to look too smug.

"I have very clever sisters," I said modestly, including both of them at the last minute for good measure. A handful of flattery, spread like seed, costs nothing.

As no one said anything, I continued snooping round the little cottage. Aside from a cubicle containing a WC, it was all one room, with a bed and books in one corner, and a small kitchen area with a primitive paraffin cooker, kettle, cup, and saucer.

The little larder, housed in a tin tea chest, consisted of bread, milk, cheese, and half an apple.

Had Orlando gone to his death hungry? I wondered.

This riverside shanty must have been a comedown from living in the vicarage.

"How did he get on with his father?" I asked. "Orlando, I mean."

"Remarkably well," Claire replied. "Canon Whitbread had sufficient knowledge of human nature to leave well enough alone. He knew that genius cannot be put in a box."

"But sometimes in a bottle," Dogger said, holding up a bottle with a glass stopper. He held it out toward my nose.

"Paraldehyde," I said. I would recognize the sharp unpleasant smell of acetic or ethanoic acid from across a cricket pitch. It was vinegar with a chip on its shoulder.

"Where did you find it?" I asked Dogger.

"Behind the Bible on the bookshelf," he said. "The hiding place most often chosen as the spot least likely to be searched."

I rewarded him with one of Winston Churchill's famous two-fingered "V for Victory" signs.

Now that the stuff had come to light, there was no further point in trying to hide my light under a bushel.

"I smelled it on the body," I explained to Claire. "At the riverbank."

"As did I," Dogger said.

You could have knocked me over with a shadow! Whatever detailed observations Dogger had made as we were fishing Orlando out of the river, he had kept the specific details to himself.

But hadn't we agreed to do so?

Although I was agog at his powers of observation, I decided not to draw attention to them.

"And what did you conclude?" I asked.

"That the poor young man had most probably been treated clinically for alcoholism, most likely in a private hospital. That a course of paraldehyde injections had been prescribed—perhaps something on the order of five to ten cc's—but that, as is often the case, he had become addicted to the very stuff that was meant to cure him."

"You deduced that based simply on the smell?"

"It is another old, but sad, story," Dogger said. "One hypothesizes certain fixed outcomes.

"As if that weren't enough," he added, "there was also the evidence of the skin: the allergic rash and the yellow-ish discoloration, the latter appearing also, although to a lesser degree, in the eyes."

"Drat!" I said. "I missed that entirely. I knew that certain people became addicted to it, but I didn't know why."

"It is much like a drawing room puzzle," Dogger said. "The more pieces you put into position, the larger the picture becomes."

"I think I can add a piece, too," Claire said. "Now that Orlando's dead—and because Arthur and I are old friends—I suppose there's no harm in telling you . . . as long as you keep it confidential."

She said this looking at me.

I crossed my heart and gave the Girl Guide sign of honor. Not that it counted: I was an outcast.

"Orlando did receive treatment at Dollylands for his drinking . . . difficulties. It's a very discreet private hospital in Highgate, founded by Sir Ernest Dolly to treat wealthy Victorian . . ."

She paused.

"Unfortunates," Dogger supplied.

"Thank you, Arthur." Claire nodded. "Yes, unfortunates. A precise description of Orlando."

"They'll have wanted to keep that quiet," I remarked, "what with his father being a canon, and so forth.

"But," I added, my curiosity suddenly tickled, "how did *you* find out about it, then?"

"Because my profession required it," Claire answered. "I was formerly a nurse."

Eureka! I thought. As Dogger had said, the more pieces that fall into place, the bigger—and clearer—the picture becomes.

I slapped my stupid brow. How could I not have realized?

"Of course," I said. "You're Australian! You were in the Australian Army Nursing prisoner-of-war camp!"

Daffy had once scared me silly—beneath the blankets and well after lights-out—by telling me how Japanese soldiers had machine-gunned the brave Australian nurses at Bangka Island, off the coast of Sumatra.

It was a topic never again to be spoken of aloud: not then, not ever.

I glanced at Dogger to see how he was taking it.

I shrank inside.

Dogger's eyes were in the past. They had taken flight at my words, and gone to another place.

Please, God, I prayed. *Don't let him have another of his episodes.*

I reached out and took his hand—squeezed his fingers fiercely.

"Dogger," I said, "I'm sorry. I didn't mean to—I didn't mean to—"

"Sit down, Arthur," Claire said, pulling out a chair from under the rickety table. She took Dogger's elbow and guided him into the seat.

She did not look at me.

Slowly, and with great gentleness, she began stroking the back of his hand.

"The trees are lovely this time of year," she said, "don't you think?"

Dogger looked up at her, seemingly dazed.

He opened his mouth and then, after what seemed like simply ice ages, said: "Yes . . . yes . . . So they are."

"I'm sorry," I said, forming the words silently.

It had all happened so quickly. One moment we had been efficiently searching Scull Cottage and the next my impulsive mouth had flung Dogger into some deep hell of the past.

For someone like myself who is used to having her own way, there is nothing worse than the feeling of helplessness, of not knowing what to do.

All I could think of was to touch the back of Dogger's neck. Perhaps the warmth of my fingers would calm his brain.

I noticed, as I made contact, how neatly barbered he was. When had he got a haircut, and where, I wondered? I supposed he had been clean-shaven back and front for as long as I could remember, and yet I couldn't recall his ever visiting a barber.

There was so much I didn't know about the man!

At the touch of my hand, Dogger turned his head slowly round, looked up at me, and smiled. Well, perhaps it wasn't quite a smile, but the corners of his eyes wrinkled slightly.

"Thank you," he said. "I shall be all right in a few moments."

"Shall we take a little stroll?" Claire suggested. "Over to my place? It's not far—just beyond the stile. I'll make a nice cup of tea.

"This place is not conducive," she added with a shiver.

Even though I didn't know the meaning of the word, I knew what she meant.

"Besides," she continued, "we don't want to be caught tampering with the evidence, do we?"

I questioned the wisdom of having to move Dogger so soon after his "turn," but wasn't Claire, after all, a nurse? Mustn't she have been accustomed to Dogger's episodes, and how best to deal with them?

She was already helping Dogger out of the chair.

"A stroll in the fresh air will do us all some good," Claire said, with a glance at me, and I felt a flush of shame arising.

"It's such a lovely day," she added, opening the door.

Outside, the sun had suddenly sprung up as it does in midsummer, as if night had never existed.

We stepped out onto the porch and she turned the key in the lock. "What is it Housman said about such beautiful summer weather?

"'June suns, you cannot store them / To warm the winter's cold . . . ' I forget the rest."

"'The lad that hopes for heaven,'" Dogger said, "'Shall fill his mouth with mould.'"

"Of course!" Claire said. "Your memory always amazes me, Arthur."

By now we were approaching the stile. I lifted down one of the crosspieces and we stepped over easily without having to scramble across like a herd of schoolboys.

We stopped for a few moments under the willows to admire a mute swan with its two cygnets, both of which were dabbling about in circles.

"The mute swans belong to the king," Claire told us. "They're his personal property. At least, they did. Now they shall belong to the queen. How very odd it will seem to have a Queen Elizabeth on the throne again after three hundred and fifty years! It's going to take some getting used to, I expect."

A metallic clatter behind us made me turn round. Through the hanging branches I could see Scull Cottage, and someone dismounting from a bicycle.

"Shhh!" I said. "It's Constable Otter."

"Just in the nick of time," said Claire.

·SEVENTEEN·

CLAIRE'S COTTAGE WAS EVERYTHING Orlando's wasn't: neat, compact, and filled with the morning light. A pair of wingback chairs, upholstered in cheery chintz, faced the fireplace. Dogger, with deliberate movements, lowered himself into one of them and I took the other.

Claire made herself busy with the teapot and the kettle, setting out three cups and saucers on the blue-painted kitchen table.

"Pleasant," Dogger remarked.

I was happy to see that he seemed to be recovering himself. Having been exposed to his terrors in the past, I knew that they might be mild or severe, and of either short or horrifically long duration.

At least this time he hadn't been haunted by visions.

As Claire was pouring the tea, I had a sudden vision of

my own: of the Rolls sitting parked in the field beyond Orlando's cottage.

Before I could say anything there came the clatter of boots on the porch and an abrupt, official-sounding knock on the door.

Claire seemed in no hurry to answer it.

"Yes, Constable?" she asked. "Is there a problem?"

Constable Otter made no secret that he was craning his neck to look past Claire to Dogger and me, who were still seated at the fireplace.

"I wondered, miss," he said, "if you had noticed anyone about in the past twenty minutes or so?"

I knew perfectly well that he had spotted the Rolls in the field, and had done as any good policeman would do: checked the temperature of the radiator. He had estimated the time based upon the cooling rate and the time of day, taking into consideration the outside temperature.

Not bad, I thought. As I had noted before, young Otter was going places.

"No one other than my two guests, Constable. We're just sitting down to a cup of tea. Would you care to join us?"

"Not while I'm on duty, thank you, Miss Tetlock," he said.

Constable Otter was *definitely* going places.

"Anyone at Scull Cottage, I mean."

"We walked through the property," I volunteered, "on the way here."

Careful, Flavia! I thought. *Don't slice it too fine.*

"We parked in the field beyond," I explained, hoping to shift attention from the cottage.

With great ceremony and a few fancy flourishes, Constable Otter produced his little black book and made a note.

"Miss de Luce and Mr. Dogger," he said, pronouncing our names as he wrote them down.

Which seemed to satisfy him.

He closed his notebook and looked narrowly from one of us to the other. I recognized the technique.

Was the constable trying to intimidate us—or simply to assert his authority?

He turned as if to go, then paused and looked me in the eye.

"You seem to get about a good deal, Miss de Luce."

"We're on holiday," I replied. "Trying to see as many of the sights as we can, yet remaining ready to hand, should you require us."

That "ready to hand" and "require us" were both masterstrokes. They suggested availability and a willingness to please without actually fawning.

Still, I mustn't risk being too clever with this man.

But then he turned and was gone.

Dogger, I realized, had said nothing during the constable's visit.

I stared at him, wondering how he was feeling.

"Better, thank you," he said.

It was remarkable! Dogger and I were as attuned to each other as two wireless sets operating on a private frequency.

At the same time, I could tell that he needed time to recuperate. It would be up to me to make good use of the meantime.

"I must admit I'm curious," I said to Claire, who had come to stand behind Dogger. Although she appeared not to be, she, too, was keeping a close eye on him.

"About the Three Graces, I mean."

"Ah, the Three Graces," she said. "Miss Willoughby, Miss Harcourt, and Miss Cray. Where did you hear about *them?*"

"Mrs. Dandyman at the circus told me about them. I didn't want to pry too much."

"Probably a wise choice," Claire remarked, and left it at that.

"We should be happy to hear their story," Dogger said, settling back into his chair.

This was an excellent sign, and I could see that Claire thought so, too.

"Well," she began, "it all had to do with the church. St. Mildred's had just begun to drag itself out of the Middle Ages. For the first time since the Creation, women were beginning to take on certain roles—not ordination, to be sure, but important roles nevertheless."

"Such as vicar's warden," I said.

"Precisely. And as you can well imagine, because of the very novelty of these appointments, the competition to fill them was fierce. Until this time, Miss Willoughby, Miss Harcourt, and Miss Cray had been the greatest of friends—cronies, you might have called them. They played bridge and euchre together, they took holidays together, they made up half of the Volesthorpe 'Bitter Knitters,' as they called their little circle—jokingly, of course, but as you know, a joke, in order to be effective, must be at least half true.

"And then there was the gossip. It was said that those three had refined rumors into razor blades. There was nothing they didn't know and weren't willing to talk about: from the color of Annie Trout's knickers, which were said to be Venetian red, to the precise amount to the penny in little Albert Morrow's piggy bank . . . two shillings, fourpence, ha'penny.

"But when the vicar's warden, dear old Dr. Glandley, died suddenly after catching a chill during a midnight house call, everything changed.

"It wasn't exactly open warfare, but it wasn't far from it. Oh, they were still polite enough to one another when they met, but it was as if each of them had mysteriously grown bristles. There were odd visits in odd hours to the vicarage: forgotten gloves, borrowed books, promised recipes . . . any pretext to get Canon Whitbread alone and press their case."

"Who was it that called them the Three Graces?" I asked.

"Funnily enough, it was Canon Whitbread himself. Initially, I think, he tried to make light of the situation, but he finally realized that it was no joking matter. In the end, he said, he had to fall back on the wisdom of Solomon and let them take turns: a year for each, in strict rotation."

"And what about Mrs. Palmer?" I pressed. "She told me she was vicar's warden, too."

"And so she was," Claire said. "Although that happened a bit later—after Miss Cray came down with a severe colic."

"Colic?" I asked. "I thought that was something babies got."

"In adults," Dogger said, "it may, among other things, be caused by kidney stones or gallstones."

I couldn't help shooting him a beaming smile.

"At any rate," Claire went on, "Canon Whitbread ruled that, rather than disrupt the business of the parish with 'temps,' as they call them nowadays, a fourth volunteer be appointed to step in when any of the 'Three Graces,' as he called them, was indisposed."

"That doesn't make sense," I objected. "A fourth person serving part-time would be no less disruptive than one of the other three filling in."

"That very point was raised at a meeting," Claire said, "but the canon pointed out that a temporary substitution, based upon the random bouts of illness in another, might result in an unjust division of duties. Or so he claimed. Frankly, I think he was not above inventing convenient excuses.

"The Three Graces had to pretend to be satisfied with that solution, and so Greta was allowed to join their company."

"Greta?" I asked.

"Greta Palmer. Your present landlady."

"Did anyone object to that?" I couldn't resist the question.

"Oh, there was some grumbling, mostly among the Graces. There was the usual chin-wagging that Greta wasn't as good as she ought to be—that there was some past scandal that hadn't been properly aired—"

"And was there?" I interrupted.

Claire paused and looked up toward the ceiling as if to find an answer.

"And of which of us is there not?" she asked, finally.

I had to admit she had a point. Even I, Flavia de Luce, have done certain things in the past of which I am not particularly proud, although I don't need to bother listing them here.

"I suppose," I agreed, a little too weakly for my own liking.

"Now then," Claire said, "I expect you're wanting me to get on with it—to get to the poisonings."

This woman knew me like the inside of her eyelids.

I shrugged.

"If you wish," I said, the best I could do on the spur of the moment.

She laughed: not a laugh as of silvery bells, as you might expect, but a wholehearted guffaw that grew from the gut and exploded into the room.

Dogger smiled.

Life had never been sweeter.

"The poisonings," Claire said, as if she were reading aloud the title of a scientific paper at the beginning of a speech. "It was given in evidence at the trial of Canon

Whitbread that on the morning of the murders, he got out of bed and, having overslept, put on his vestments at the vicarage, rather than in the vestry of the church, as he usually did."

"Was it a Sunday?" I asked.

"Yes, it must have been. St. Mildred's has not conducted early Communion services on a weekday for as long as I can remember—except on certain occasions."

"Such as when Christmas falls on a weekday or a Saturday," I said.

Claire nodded and went on.

"He left the vicarage directly—without breakfast, as is usual for one about to partake in Holy Communion—and hurried across to the church. He was several minutes late, a fact which was later confirmed by members of the congregation."

"Was Orlando living with his father at the time?" I asked.

"As a matter of fact, he was," Claire said. "Although it was claimed by the Crown Prosecutor at Canon Whitbread's trial that he had taken the 7:02 up to London the previous evening."

"Hmmm," I said. I would need to look into this later, I thought. Alibis involving railway timetables do not happen nearly as often in real life as they do in detective novels. Not that it much mattered now anyway, since Orlando was dead.

Or did it?

"Sorry," I said to Claire. "I was woolgathering. Go ahead."

"Well, Canon Whitbread began the service. The congregation was sparse, as it so often is on early summer mornings. No more than a handful of people."

"Including the Three Graces, obviously," I said.

"Obviously. None of them would ever dream of missing a service. Couldn't allow the other two to get one up on them. It might have been funny if it weren't so pitiful.

"Everything was quite normal right up to Communion. Miss Willoughby, Miss Harcourt, and Miss Cray came up to the rail together, Canon Whitbread administered the Sacraments, and they returned to their pew."

"The same pew?" I asked.

"Oh yes—they always sat together."

"Who else?" I asked. "In the other pews, I mean."

"Only three others. Lettice Farnsworth and her husband, Hugo, and . . . oh yes, the undertaker's lad."

"Hob Nightingale?"

"Yes, that's right. The little lad. Sat in the front row out of habit. Anyway, it wasn't long—no more than a couple of minutes—before the Three Graces began dropping like flies. I'm sorry to put it so crudely, but that's how Lettice described it at the inquest."

Lettice Farnsworth was to be congratulated. She had given a remarkably vivid—and accurate—description of cyanide poisoning.

In its most lethal form, hydrocyanic acid (HCN), in sufficient dosage, can kill within a minute. It does so by paralyzing the central nervous system and, perhaps more important, by paralyzing the heart directly.

It is always pleasant to reflect, also, that the same cyanogen is found in the kernels of peaches and cherries, and that the glucoside amygdalin, which is contained in the essential oil of bitter almonds, as well as in the kernels of plums and apricots, is converted into hydrogen cyanide in the presence of certain enzymes and a bit of moisture, and is often used to provide the characteristic taste and odor in the manufacture of certain sweets.

Do I enthuse too much? Very well, then, I enthuse too much.

The point is that, by dropping like flies, the Three Graces reacted exactly as I should have expected.

"Mrs. Farnsworth didn't go up for Communion herself?" I asked Claire.

"No," Claire said. "She was made to sign the pledge with the Band of Hope when she was a child that liquor would never pass her lips."

"Not even when it's the blood of our Lord Jesus Christ?" I asked.

"Not even," Claire said, shaking her head.

"What about her husband? What was his name . . . Hugo?"

"Poor Hugo has had his struggles with alcohol, but he's been abstinent for years. He and Lettice go to church for reasons of their own, but when it comes to Holy Communion, they both sit on their hands."

"It seems un-Anglican," I said.

Claire laughed that laugh again.

"Someone once said that all Roman Catholics are Roman Catholics for the same reason, but every Anglican is Anglican for reasons of their own."

Dogger smiled. In spite of his silence, he was following our conversation intently.

"Now then," Claire said. "Let me get on with my story, and you can save your questions for later."

Had I just been put in my place?

If so, she had done it so gently that I could hardly take offense.

I gave her a grin, to show that there were no hard feelings.

"Dropping like flies," I prompted.

"Oh, yes—dropping like flies. Well . . . Canon Whitbread had returned what remained of the consecrated elements to the altar. Before they could finish the recital of the Lord's Prayer, the Three Graces were dead."

How fascinating, I thought, *that "Feed on him in thy heart" and "preserve thy body and soul unto everlasting life" would be the last words that the Three Graces would ever hear in this life before the cyanide froze their hearts, and they were plummeted into Eternity.*

But what could they have done to deserve so dire a death?

"Hold on," I said. "One more question: Why would Canon Whitbread poison three harmless old ladies? What was his motive?"

"Well," Claire said, "it came out at his trial that there had been some jiggering of the church funds. Not a great deal, mind, but enough that the various vicar's wardens could no longer ignore it. They had decided to join together as a body"—*how apt,* I thought—"in order to confront him."

"Was Mrs. Palmer one of those?" Dogger had been sitting so quietly I'd almost forgotten he was in the room.

"Yes," Claire answered. "They arranged to meet in the vestry. Canon Whitbread reportedly didn't take it very well."

"All of this came out at the trial, I presume?" Dogger asked.

"Yes, and most—but not all—of it was reported in the newspapers. The Church still has long arms where certain interests are involved."

Dogger nodded, satisfied, and subsided into his thoughts.

"Now comes the interesting part," Claire went on, resuming her story. "After the Three Graces had collapsed into their pew—like circus contortionists, Lettice told me later—Canon Whitbread went on to the Gloria and the Blessing. He didn't come down from the altar until he had completed the service."

"To give the cyanide time to work!" I exclaimed. "He wanted to be certain they were dead."

"So the Crown Prosecutor suggested at his trial. But the defense suggested—quite brilliantly, at least in this instance—that the older clergy had been taught to carry on 'come hell or high water,' as he put it (begging M'lud's pardon) and citing the instance of the Vicar of Chittleford who, despite a direct hit on the nave of his church during the Blitz, had gone on to the completion of Holy Communion though not a single member of the congregation remained alive. The defense then, changing course slightly, began to put forward an argument for shock, but the judge was having none of it. In the case of the Three Graces, no one from the congregation had come to their assistance until it was too late."

"The Farnsworths and Hob Nightingale, you mean," I said. "It wouldn't have mattered much if they had—unless they'd just happened to have three doses of the antidote to cyanide up their sleeves, and got to the victims within seconds."

"I suppose," Claire said. "But Lettice claimed that they hadn't really noticed anything untoward until Hope Harcourt slipped out of her pew and crumpled to the floor. It is not uncommon for elderly ladies to doze off at early morning services on warm summer mornings—not uncommon at all.

"Although they don't anymore," she added. "Since the Three Graces died, it's believed bad luck to sit in that pew. Some say it's haunted, some say you can still smell the poison."

"Hold on," I said. "What about Hob—did he see them fall?"

"Hob didn't give direct evidence. He's underage. But he gave a statement to the police saying that, since he was seated in front of the three victims, he would hardly have noticed anyway. Smart as a whip. A very clever thinker, our Hob is, for so young a lad."

I realized that no matter how fascinating Claire's story might be, there were several things I needed to do at once. I could always catch up on the details later.

"I'm sorry," I said, glancing at Dogger, "but I think it would be best if we got back to the Oak and Pheasant."

Dogger, bless his finely tuned soul forever, nodded assent and began to get up out of his chair.

"I wonder if I might trouble you to drive?" I asked Claire.

She scrambled to her feet and took Dogger's elbow, as if in friendship.

"Of course," she said.

And a few minutes later we were riding in comfort back toward the inn, with Claire at the wheel and Dogger beside her.

"I shouldn't feel right riding in the passenger compartment," Dogger had insisted.

"First time I've ever driven a Rolls-Royce," Claire told us. "Actually, it's the first time I've ever *ridden* in one. I shall be spoiled forever."

I glanced over at Dogger, who was gazing out with seeming disinterest at the passing riverbank.

"I shall see you in, then take the shortcut home."

"No need," Dogger said. "I am quite all right. It was pleasant seeing you again, Claire."

He offered his hand and she took it.

I'd swear that a look passed between them, but I couldn't be sure. My heart gave a little lollop.

Had I been witness, this morning, to a carefully produced drama? Had Dogger staged an episode in order to be in the company of Claire Tetlock? Would Dogger even be capable of such a thing?

There are times when eyes and ears are not enough, times when you need to go inside yourself, to listen to the Whisperers in the Pit who, although they may sometimes shock you, are very seldom wrong.

After seeing Dogger to the door and waving goodbye to Claire, I made a beeline across the road to St. Mildred's.

I needed to be alone.

·EIGHTEEN·

THE CHURCH, AS I had hoped it would be, was empty.

Inside, I made a slow circuit of the nave and the chancel, reading the ancient memorial marble tablets that seemed to cover every inch of the walls, and a grim old lot they were, most of them recalling in stifling detail the lives of military men back to the time of "William Conker," as Mrs. Mullet referred to the tour operator who had brought the de Luces to England in 1066.

Everything was coated heavily with dust, some of it, I knew, the remains of those happy warriors and their loved ones, who must be jammed, judging by the number of plaques, heel-to-jowl inside the walls and underneath the floor's stone slabs. You couldn't walk down the aisle without having Sir Morton Stackpole and "Maud his dearly biluved wife" rise up in a cloud to greet you, as if they had been too long without company, and settle in a chummy way on your hands, your face, your neck, and in your hair.

On the Epistle side of the church, just outside the chancel, let into the floor at the foot of the lectern, was a bit of stone: a gray-flecked square of marble, no more than three and a half or four inches on each side. In the crumbling antiquity of the church, its relative lack of age had caught my eye. In short, to someone with my powers of observation, the marble stuck out like a sore thumb: too new, too polished, too freshly chiseled.

I got down on my hands and knees to examine the surface, On it, carved in half-inch letters, was the word G.L.O.W.

Glow?

What on earth could that mean? Could it possibly be a family name? I had never met or heard of anyone with the surname Glow, but in England such a thing is not beyond belief. Or was it, perhaps, a discreet marker placed by some organization, such as the General Laborers and Office Workers, to commemorate a certain occasion, or a gift of money to one of the church funds?

There was no point wasting time in speculation. I would simply ask the present vicar for an explanation: Clemm, I believe Mr. Palmer had said his name was—the plump gentleman who had come to the riverbank with Constable Otter.

I made a second circuit, pausing this time to run my fingers along the back of the pew—the second row from the front—where I deduced from all accounts that the Three Graces must have met their end, or ends. There wasn't a trace left of their passing—which in a few cases can be remarkably messy, cyanide working as it occasionally does. If such was the case, someone had done a wizard job of mopping up.

I slid gently sideways into the pew, closed my eyes, clasped my hands, and tried to project myself into the past: into the minds of those three old ladies at the very moment the poison had taken hold.

There would have been, at first, the realization that the sacramental wine was stronger than usual. Perhaps a cracked or otherwise defective cork, overlooked by Canon Whitbread, had allowed it to go sour—although I recalled from my chemical readings that, in 1922, the Holy Office had given permission to the Archbishop of Tarragona, in Spain, for the sacramental wine to be treated with either sulfurous anhydride or potassium bisulfite to keep it from going off.

That, of course, was the Roman Catholic Church, which is far more advanced in such matters than the Church of England.

After that first taste, there would have been a couple of blissful moments which would, alas, be their last; and then the sudden onrush of sensations: the taste of bitterness, the burning in the throat and bowels, the tightening of the jaw, the foaming at the lips, the perspiration, the inability to move any of the muscles—not even time, probably, for a final "Uh-oh."

How pleasant it is, as you sit in an ancient church, to ponder poisons, surrounded as you are by the towering toxicity of the stained-glass windows. The yellow cloak of that staring saint, for instance, was most likely achieved by adding cadmium, which, with its several compounds, is quite poisonous; whereas the startling emerald green of all that glassy grass at Galilee is most likely due to arsenic.

To say nothing of the lead.

Such happy thoughts are proof that I have become an adult. I am now ruled by not only what I see, what I hear, what I taste, and what I smell, but also, and perhaps most important, by what I think.

That very thought in itself ought to be certain proof that my brain has developed satisfactorily.

Pleased with myself, I turned the attention of my expanding brain to my surroundings.

Old churches, like old humans, give off occasional creaks and groans as bits of dried wood and old stones shift in their sockets. Also like old humans, they tend to hum a bit, although it's nothing to be alarmed about.

The slightly sickening smell of long-departed lilies and longer-departed perspiration hangs like an invisible mist in the air. There is an almost imperceptible whiff of roast beef, as if the ghosts of John Bull and his fellow squires were banqueting in the crypt. Added to this, almost as an afterthought, is the dry, pious odor of Bibles and hymnals.

Why do the printers of these books use so sober-smelling an ink? Why don't they stir your nostrils and your imagination with the sharp, tantalizing stink of, say, the *News of the World*, or the *Daily Mirror*?

To verify this observation, I reached out and lifted a Bible from the book rack of the pew in front of me, and gave it a sniff. Slightly moldy, but still recognizable as a

Bible. I'd put money on being able to identify one in the dark.

As is almost always the case, the book was bound in black, the title stamped in gold on the cover and spine. This particular edition contained not only the Bible, but also the complete *Book of Common Prayer*, along with maps of the Holy Land, charts of weights and coins of Scripture, and botany of the Bible (from which I was delighted to learn that the Vine of Sodom in Deuteronomy is in fact a kind of giant milkweed with poisonous juice which, in spite of its tasty appearance, dissolves, upon being bitten, into smoke and ashes): all of this in one handy—although slightly bulky—volume. It was a churchgoer's dream, a Boy Scout knife for Bible class.

But something had caught my eye. The word "poison" had leapt at me off the page.

Yes, here it was: Deuteronomy 32, verses 32 and 33:

*For their vine is of the vine of Sodom, and of the fields of
    Gomorrah: Their grapes are grapes of gall, their
    clusters are bitter:*
*Their wine is the poison of dragons, and the cruel venom
    of asps.*

If I had stuck my finger at random into the Bible as fortune-tellers do, I couldn't have hit upon a more apt entry. Wasn't this a direct warning against poisoned wine?

Could "the poison of dragons" and "the cruel venom of asps" refer to gossip?

Both passages were underlined in pencil.

Scarcely daring to breathe, I turned slowly back to the flyleaf, almost afraid of what I might find.

Written in black gall ink, the words made my eyes swim:

Anne Elizabeth Cray,
Hassock Cottage, Volesthorpe

Annie Cray! Of the Three Graces: "Faith, Hope, and Treachery," Mrs. Dandyman had called them.

And of the three, Annie Cray was Treachery.

Was it possible that she had brought this Bible to church the day of her murder, and that it had lain here unnoticed ever since? Two years had passed since Annie and her fellow gossips had been trundled off to meet their Maker. Could it be that the police—the whip-smart Constable Otter included—had overlooked the harmless Bible nestled in its book rack, not two feet from where the dead women would have lain?

Obviously, it was. Hadn't Claire Tetlock told me that the pew was believed to be haunted? That no one would sit in the spot where I was sitting now?

Besides, a Bible or a hymnbook is as invisible in a church as the walls and windows. No one would think to take a second look at the contents of the book rack.

It had lain there all this time, untouched, waiting for someone with the eyes to see.

Waiting for me. Flavia de Luce.

As I flipped the pages idly, the names of the books in the Old and New Testaments, the page numbers, as well as the numbers of the chapters and verses, fluttered by

like those animated cartoons which you make by drawing, in the corner of each page with a pencil, a slightly
different sketch of a galloping horse or a stick man having
his hat blown off by the wind.

I was riffling through Revelation when I had one.

A revelation, I mean.

It must have been the flying numbers, racing by before
my eyes at dizzying speed: Perhaps not, but something
in my freshly attentive brain went *Click!* as clearly
audible—inside my head, at least—as the slow breathing
of the ancient oaken beams above my head.

For an instant, I felt as if I myself had swallowed cyanide:
My mouth went dry and my breath snagged in my throat.

Slowly, so as not to break the spell, I reached into my
pocket and pulled out the crumpled bit of paper I had
found in Orlando's pocket.

The numbers danced before my eyes: *54, 6, 7, 8, 9.*

I had supposed them at first to be the numbers of
hymns, but I was wrong.

What if they were books, chapters, and verses?

With trembling hands I turned to the general index.
Beginning with Genesis, I counted off the entries. The
fifty-fourth book of the Bible was the First Epistle of Paul
the Apostle to Timothy.

I followed my finger to chapter 6, and then to verses 7,
8, and 9:

*For we brought nothing into this world, and it is certain
we can carry nothing out.
And having food and raiment let us be therefore content.*

But they that will be rich, fall into temptation, and a
snare, and into many foolish and hurtful lusts, which
drown men in destruction and perdition.

A passage about drowning found in the pocket of a drowned man?

It was beyond coincidence.

But what did it mean? Could it have been a warning? A threat? And if it was, who gave it or sent it to Orlando, and how did it come to be in his pocket?

I read the remaining lines of Timothy, which, although they were few, contained the famous saying that the love of money is the root of all evil, and that those who covet it have pierced themselves through with arrows.

Poor Orlando was fortunate, in a way, that whoever had it in for him hadn't used a crossbow.

But what had it all to do with money? As far as I knew, Orlando had been as poor as a church mouse, brought up by a rural clergyman who had to embezzle funds from the collection plate in order to heat the vicarage.

There were so many unanswered questions. Why, for instance, had someone chosen Saint Paul's First Epistle to Timothy as a warning? Surely, there were many much more threatening passages in the Old Testament, such as those in which God is shaking His fist at Moses and his tribes.

Could it be that the Timothy letter was the only reference in the entire Bible to drowning? If that was the case, it would prove beyond a doubt that Orlando's killing was meditated. It takes a certain amount of calculation to select a biblical text and then plan and execute a murder to match.

It would have been too much to ask—too much of a coincidence—for the fat black volume in my hands to contain a Bible Concordance and, of course, it did not. I would need to get my hands on one of these at the earliest possible moment to check out the drowning angle.

Again I opened the pages of Annie Cray's Bible in search of inspiration. Anything would do: I needed help.

Like the attached Bible, *The Book of Common Prayer* contained a great deal of reference material: a calendar of the church year, including the various saints' days; a table of the Moveable Feasts according to the several days that Easter can possibly fall upon; a complicated set of tables of rules for finding the Golden Number and, once having found it, determining the date of Easter in any given year.

It was like a holy treasure hunt.

Fortunately, I had learned something about the topic from our own vicar, Denwyn Richardson, in Bishop's Lacey, who, having caught me fishing—illegally—in the river behind St. Tancred's, had sat down beside me in the warm summer grass and begun rattling on about one of his greatest enthusiasms: *The Book of Common Prayer and How to Use It.*

He had delivered several sermons upon the topic, not only from the pulpit, but also at various meetings and functions in the parish hall. If there was a single topic which the Anglican parishioners of Bishop's Lacey were prepared to be quizzed upon at the Golden Gate, it was *The Book of Common Prayer.*

Not only were there charts and tables of the saints' days and holy days, but also complex decrees about which chapters and verses of the Old and New Testaments were to be read aloud as lessons, depending upon the calendar and the time of day.

"It may seem rather left-handed," Denwyn had said, "but it's all perfectly logical. It all comes down to the moon, Flavia, when you stop to think about it."

Which, I suppose, is as good a thing to base a religion upon as any.

But just when I thought I had wrapped my mind around the codes and calendars of Christian prayer, Denwyn had mentioned, almost apologetically, that there was also an alternative table of lessons, and it was this which we used at St. Tancred's, rather than the original.

"But why?" I asked.

"Because the bishop wishes it," he had said, slipping me a furtive wink after a hasty glance round to make sure that no one was watching.

So there it is, then, I remember thinking. *Down here on earth, a bishop is mightier than the moon.*

Although this was an obvious case of misguided thinking, I did not say so to Denwyn. The poor man had a living to earn.

I dragged my mind back to the present—to the Alternative Tables.

If St.-Mildred's-in-the-Marsh used the same timetables we used in Bishop's Lacey, I ought to have an answer in two flicks of a dead lamb's tail.

Timothy 1 ought to be easy enough to spot.

I let my eyes float slowly down the long columns, like a deflating balloon, beginning with the first Sunday in

Advent, which, of course, would be in December—then onward through Christmas, Epiphany, Lent, and Easter.

Surprisingly, Timothy did not make his appearance until several Sundays after Trinity, at which time he was taken out for a rather good trot.

Ah! Here he was: First Timothy, chapter 6, verses 7 to 9—the very verses I had found listed in the dead Orlando's pocket!

My blood was already beginning to jingle.

With the knowledge absorbed during Denwyn's riverside lecture, as well as various exposures at Girl Guide meetings, I was able to work out—with remarkable speed and efficiency—the precise date of that reading in the present Year of Our Lord, One Thousand Nine Hundred and Fifty-Two.

But they that will be rich, fall into temptation, and a
snare, and into many foolish and hurtful lusts, which
drown men in destruction and perdition.

Those now-chilling words would be read aloud from the lectern as the Second Lesson of Evensong on the third Sunday after Trinity. Here, at this very spot, they would echo among these very stones and hammer beams.

June the twenty-ninth. Tomorrow evening!

The first Sunday—and just two days—after I fished Orlando Whitbread's drowned body out of the river.

Had it been planned?

Was this a message—or a warning to others—from Orlando's killer?

·NINETEEN·

THE TIME HAD COME to "shrug off the mantle of the present," as Daffy puts it when she's reading her beloved Dickens, and project myself two years into the past to the morning of the three earlier murders.

The successful solving of any crime depends, more than anything, upon accurate reconstruction, which is the closest thing we have in the modern world to time travel. Most detectives wouldn't admit that it's a form of self-hypnosis, but they have their reputations to think of.

Think how the court would laugh—even the magistrate on the bench in his wig and robes—if the detective, asked how he came to a certain conclusion, replied: "I put myself in a trance, M'lud."

There wouldn't be a dry eye in the house!

I squirmed and settled myself into the pew, closed my

eyes, and folded my hands daintily in my lap. In my mind, I let the pages of the calendar tear loose and fly away, one by one, month by month. June of 1952 became May, then April, and so forth.

Christmas flew by and I was back in 1951: November, October, September, the months of summer, spring, then Christmas again.

It was 1950. I allowed the pages to slow a little: I didn't want to overshoot.

August . . . July . . . June . . . and here we were.

I took a deep breath and slowly opened my eyes.

The church was the same as it always had been, but then it would be, wouldn't it?

There was a stir of air behind me as the door opened and the Three Graces entered: Grace Willoughby, Grace Harcourt, and Annie Cray, looking much as I remembered them from the grainy photographs on the front pages of the tabloid newspapers, except that now their faces were in color.

Grace Willoughby, as tall and slender as her name, was wearing a smart black tailored suit with a cameo brooch at her throat, and had perched on her head a curved winglike thing which looked as if it had been forcibly detached from a duck. Grace Harcourt, somewhat shorter and broad-shouldered, with grayish-blond hair, wore a summer dress of dusky rose and a smart straw hat, while Annie Cray, dark, short, and squat, and rather toadlike, I thought (uncharitably, seeing as she was dead), had draped herself in a kind of loose rug or blanket in which holes had been cut out for her head and arms. A floppy-brimmed black hat gave her the appearance of a villain in a cowboy film.

I slid over to make room for them as they entered the pew. Even though the poor creatures couldn't see me, I didn't want to be caught staring.

More footsteps at the rear and the clatter of kneeling benches announced the arrival of Mr. and Mrs. Farnsworth—Lettice and Hugo—and moments later, the much lighter footfall of Hob Nightingale.

Because of the summer season, and the sparseness of the congregation, there would be no processional this morning: no choir, no organ—just the bare bones, so to speak.

As far as I knew, the entire cast of characters—with the exception of Canon Whitbread—had now taken up their positions to act out the tragedy.

And now—yes!—here comes Canon Whitbread, hurrying in from the vestry: late for the service, just as Claire had told me he had been, and empty-handed.

Which meant that the wine and wafers were already in the tabernacle on the altar.

In my mind, I lit a flame in the altar lamp to indicate that fact.

I would need to check these details later with the witnesses, of course, but lighting a flame with the mind is a powerful aid to understanding.

The canon genuflected before the altar, and without further ado, launched into the Holy Communion service.

With my acute hearing, I could actually hear his dusty words.

After the Lord's Prayer, he began the Collect:

"Almighty God, unto whom all hearts be open, all desires known, and from whom no secrets are hid . . ."

What had Almighty God seen that morning, I wondered, as He looked into the secret hearts and desires of those three women who were about to die, and into the heart of the clergyman who was about to murder them?

Now Canon Whitbread had begun the recital of the Ten Commandments.

Well, there was no need to re-create the entire service. The part I was most interested in wouldn't come until near the end.

In my mind, I sped up the action, so that Canon Whitbread was racing through the order of service like the Keystone Kops.

It might have been funny if it hadn't been murder.

I waited until he and the little congregation dropped to their knees for the general Confession, then reduced the speed to normal.

Turning to face the people, Canon Whitbread now begged God to pardon and deliver them from all their sins, confirm and strengthen them in all goodness, and bring them to everlasting life.

As he did so, I was able for the first time to study his face.

My immediate impression was that the man was *tired*; that he had been awake for much of the night. One of his eyelids twitched incessantly; the other seemed to droop a little. The hollows of his rather gaunt face showed up as shadows, his chin and cheeks darkened with new whiskers. There had been an unsuccessful attempt to hide the morning's bristles with a rose-tinted talcum powder. He had not taken the time to shave.

My second impression was that this was not the countenance of a killer. I had several times come face-to-face with killers. Not one of them had had the gentle features of this rather worried-looking man.

I was recalling his face, of course, from the dozens of black-and-white photographs I had seen in the newspapers, but never until now did it ever occur to me that an innocent man might have been sent to the gallows.

The very thought of it caused my blood to bubble.

I focused my attention on the hands of the man at the altar.

Having transformed the host and the wine into the body and blood of Christ, Canon Whitbread genuflected deeply and administered Communion to himself, consuming the broken host and draining the chalice. I knew already that there was no danger of his poisoning himself—that he would go on living until the day he died at the hands of the hangman.

But now he was turning again to the altar—turning his back upon those of us seated in the pews. I watched, transfixed, as he brought reverently out from the tabernacle the silver vessel—the ciborium—which contained the wafers.

I could hardly believe it! They had been there all night!

I froze the action to let my mind catch up.

Normally, with a decent attendance, Canon Whitbread would have consecrated only as many of the hosts as were needed. Any remaining would be kept in the tabernacle for use during the week, including visitation of the sick and so forth.

But this morning, with only a handful in attendance, he would make use of the hosts that were already consecrated. Of course, he had newly consecrated one of the larger wafers for his own consumption, but the rest of the congregation would be given the leftovers, so to speak.

The point was this: The hosts and the wine which were about to be administered to the unsuspecting congregation had been left in an unlocked church overnight—and perhaps even longer.

Anyone in England—and perhaps even beyond—could have sneaked in the old cyanide.

This case was becoming far more difficult than I could ever have imagined.

I needed to find out—and as quickly as possible—whether the poison had been contained in the wine or the wafers—or both.

With mounting horror—and, I must admit, with mounting excitement—I watched as he turned to face us. Annie, who had been last into the pew, was already hoisting herself to her feet and shuffling sideways into the aisle.

In her mind, there was probably some imagined heavenly prize for being first at the rail.

Well, she'd soon find out, I thought.

The two remaining Graces, Harcourt and Willoughby, were breathing down her neck.

I slowed the image down a little. I didn't want to miss a single detail.

It flashed briefly into my mind that I could stop their motion and reverse it like a comic film, but I quickly dismissed the idea. I could only make them walk backward out of the church and home again, bottoms first. I could not really change what had already happened. I was unable to save these three women from a certain death.

"These are but shadows of the things that have been," as the Ghost of Christmas Past told Ebenezer Scrooge.

I could not change their destiny. I might as well sit back and learn from it.

Now they had reached the rail and were kneeling. Grace Willoughby, in spite of being the last at the Communion rail, was the first to receive the host from the hands of Canon Whitbread. She crossed herself rather showily. Now it was the turn of Grace Harcourt, and finally Annie Cray.

Even though Annie's back was still toward me, I could tell by the sudden slump of her shoulders that she was miffed, as First Place in Heaven was snatched unfairly out of her grasp.

And now for the wine. Or should I say, the Blood of Christ?

It all depended whether you accepted the hotly disputed doctrine of transubstantiation: the actual transformation of fermented grape juice into the Holy Blood of the Son of God.

It was a subject upon which I had already come to my own conclusions.

Six months ago, at a greatly trying time in my life and racked by loss of faith, I had whisked away—by a method which I'm still ashamed to reveal—a sample of the consecrated wine from Holy Communion at St. Tancred's, and taken it home to my laboratory, where I had subjected the supposedly holy liquid to the most rigorous analysis known to organic chemistry. I had compared the fluid and its constituents at various stages of my experiment with control samples of the ordinary, or unconsecrated, wine, nicked from the same church, I must confess, at a somewhat earlier date.

I had recorded the results—which were indisputable—in the back pages of one of Uncle Tarquin's bulging notebooks, to be discovered at some future date when the world is better prepared to receive my earth-shattering findings.

I forced my mind back from these researches to St. Mildred's, and the imminent demise of the Three Graces.

Because there were no deacons in attendance to assist with the Holy Communion on this sunny summer morning, it was left to Canon Whitbread himself to deliver both bread and wine, and I had to admire the quiet efficiency with which he administered the hosts to each of the three communicants before returning briefly to the altar to replace the ciborium in the tabernacle and to take up the chalice.

And now here it was: the moment I'd been waiting for. I took a mental snapshot of the scene.

Canon Whitbread stood poised, chalice in hand, facing the three communicants, whose heads were bowed in preparation.

I felt a shiver run down the back of my neck, down my arms, and into my elbows.

I was about to witness murder.

But whether Canon Whitbread was the killer or not, I could not yet tell. And yet he was certainly the instrument by which cruel Fate had chosen to deliver their deaths to these three unsuspecting chatterboxes.

Reluctantly, wanting to treasure the moment, and yet impatient to see the results, I allowed the action to resume.

Again, Grace Willoughby was first. She tilted her head back slightly. I could not see her mouth but I knew by the angle of her jaw that it had opened. She lengthened her life by a fraction of a second by crossing herself again. But Canon Whitbread's hand moved swiftly, and the deed was done.

He was already moving sideways to confront Grace Harcourt.

Grace, too, went like a lamb to the slaughter.

Kaboola!

Just like that. With death in her mouth, she was already halfway to her feet.

Now it was the turn of Annie Cray.

Why did I feel so suddenly sorry for this pathetic little figure in her Mexican donkey blanket and silly hat? Why did I want to rush up to the rail shouting "No! Stop!

Don't swallow that! *Spit it out!*" Why did I want to grab her by the arm and haul her out of the church to safety?

These, I would realize later, were probably the kinds of afterthoughts that came to old misers as they lay dying alone in the night, clutching at straws of salvation.

If only I had thought to . . . if only I had . . . if only . . .

But I was neither old nor a miser—nor was I dying.

Fate undoubtedly has her reasons, and I was merely a girl who had been sent by her to solve a mystery.

And, by Saint George and his dragon, and his white horse, Uffington, that's exactly what I intended to do!

I studied their faces carefully as the Three Graces arose from the Communion rail and turned toward me. Was there anything in their expressions to indicate that they smelled a rat, so to speak? That they had detected even the slightest taste of bitterness?

It was difficult to tell. There is something about receiving Holy Communion which causes even the most jolly person to look as if their face has just been suddenly and unexpectedly starched and hung out on the line to dry. The face of the average communicant is not a happy one, and the faces of the Three Graces were no exception. Pious, is the word I'm looking for.

Although it may be blasphemy to say so, the features of these three women as they made their seemingly sightless way back to their seats reminded me of nothing so much as that famous painting *The Blind Leading the Blind* by Pieter Bruegel.

I watched intently as they shimmied hip to hip into

the pew. With a muffled *thump* the kneeling bench went down and they were on their knees.

Less than a minute to zero hour, I remember thinking, as I began counting.

The first sign came precisely thirty-three seconds later as Grace Harcourt let out a slight hiccup. She covered her mouth quickly with a white-gloved hand and kept it there. Her other hand was at her heart.

Potassium cyanide—when changed to hydrogen cyanide by the body's stomach acids—is one of the swiftest of the deadly poisons. Only carbon monoxide and some of the other gases kill so quickly. Unconsciousness can occur within seconds. Even so, I was surprised at the speed with which it took her.

Grace slumped farther forward, her right shoulder coming to rest against the back of the front pew. I watched as she drew a couple of noisy breaths and collapsed slowly sideways, her summer hat falling to the floor, her chin coming to rest grotesquely against the polished oak seat of the pew, her eyes staring blindly up at the hammer beams above.

While I was still marveling at the sight—and still fighting the instinct to leap to her assistance, as I had done once before with a victim of cyanide—Grace Willoughby jerked suddenly halfway to her feet, looked round in wild-eyed panic, and flopped, backward at first, and then sideways, into the pew.

She seemed unaware of her already dead friend beside her.

One of her legs twitched, then kicked convulsively—and was still.

It was not a graceful death.

Now only Annie Cray remained, still on her knees, her eyes fixed fiercely on the altar, upon which Canon Whitbread was replacing what remained of the consecrated Elements.

Then Annie, too, crumpled: slowly, beautifully, lightly, like a falling leaf that has detached itself from the parent bough and launched itself upon the air, rocking slightly from side to side, lower and ever lower, until settling on the welcoming earth.

It was just that easy.

I was happy that none of them had died that ghastly, frothing, foaming death that sometimes signals cyanide.

And now, Canon Whitbread turned toward us and began to pray:

"Our Father which art in Heaven . . ."

If there was, actually, such as place as Heaven, the Three Graces were already safely in it. I couldn't help smiling at the thought as the canon went on:

"Hallowed be Thy name. Thy kingdom come, Thy will be done in earth, as it is in Heaven. Give us this day our daily bread. And forgive us our trespasses, as we forgive them that trespass against us."

Had God already forgiven the trespasses of these three gossips, even as they lay entangled among the furniture of a country church? Was forgiveness as fast as cyanide?

For their sakes, I hoped so.

"*And lead us not into temptation, but deliver us from evil . . .*"

Yes, that was the thing, wasn't it? To deliver us from evil, which was surely still among us. Somewhere, not far from this very spot, was the person—or persons—who had callously murdered Grace Willoughby, Grace Harcourt, Annie Cray, and—yes, I was now quite sure of it—Canon Whitbread himself, albeit in a very complicated way.

To say nothing of his son, Orlando.

Father, Son . . . and Holy Ghosts.

In a weird way, it had all begun to make sense.

Not seeming to have seen what had happened before his very eyes, Canon Whitbread recited quickly, and quite quietly, the prayer of thanksgiving. He then began the closing prayer:

"Almighty and everliving God, we most heartily thank Thee, for that Thou dost vouchsafe to feed us," and so forth.

As he spoke, I turned to glance at Lettice and Hugo Farnsworth, who were clutching one another, wide-eyed, like a pair of frightened monkeys in a tree. In front of me, Hob Nightingale was fiddling idly with the buttons of his jacket, apparently lost in some kind of boyhood daydream.

I turned my attention again to Canon Whitbread as he gave us the final Blessing:

"The peace of God, which passeth all understanding, keep your hearts and minds in the knowledge and love of God, and of His son Jesus Christ, our Lord: and the blessing . . ." (here, he made the sign of the cross) ". . . of the Almighty, the Father, the Son, and the Holy Ghost, be amongst you and remain with you always. Amen."

Only then did he let out a howl of such unearthly agony that surely it must have been heard in the farthest reaches of Hell.

When I summoned up the courage and turned to look at the Three Graces, I saw to my amazement that they had begun to become transparent; to shimmer and to dim. I could clearly see the floorboards and part of the kneeling bench through Annie Cray's feet and legs.

Loss of opacity, I remember thinking. *A slight change in the index of refraction. A trick of the light.*

But in spite of my clutching at scientific straws, the Three Graces were becoming ever less and less substantial, fading away before my very eyes.

Even as I watched, they had become vague and indistinct, like receding nebulae in the haze of the starry heavens, until at last they gave a faint and final shiver . . . and were gone without a trace.

And to tell you the truth, I was devastated by their loss.

On the verge of tears, I sat there motionless for many long minutes in a perfect vacuum which, although previously unknown to science, is now known to me.

It was as if the world around me had darkened. My vision narrowed until only the altar remained visible at its center, lighted now by the low rays of the suddenly cold, weak sun lancing in through the stained-glass windows.

Somebody seized my shoulder.

·TWENTY·

WITH A DEAFENING WOODEN-SOUNDING *Bang!* I shot up out of the pew like an overcharged skyrocket, my feet tangling with the kneeling bench.

"Are you all right?" inquired an unfamiliar voice.

"What the blue blazes do you think you're doing?" I shouted, church or no church. "You might have given me a heart attack!"

I added a couple of other choice words which I will not quote here, as I am not proud of them.

I spun round to face the intruder, who withdrew his hand from my shoulder instantly. His pale face stared back at me, mouth hanging open in disbelief. Except for the white dog collar which completely encircled his neck, he was the spitting image of Humpty Dumpty.

It was the vicar: the same roly-poly gentleman I had seen talking to Constable Otter as I waited with Orlando's body on the riverbank. A Mr. Clemm, if I remembered rightly.

He had cut himself shaving, I noticed. A small scrap of bloodied tissue peeped out distastefully from his wilted white clerical collar. What could it mean?

Was he careless? Distracted? Shortsighted? Lazy? Forgetful?

These and other possibilities flashed through my mind. It's amazing what even the slightest glimpse of animal blood can do to the human brain.

On the one hand, I felt sorry for the vicar in a complicated way. I wished I hadn't seen his careless toilet habits. At the same time, I wished he hadn't let me see them.

Which of us was guilty of this small—but important— breach of good manners?

I couldn't possibly know. I wasn't old enough and hadn't enough experience.

So the fault must be his.

We stood there, the two of us, staring at each other with bug eyes, like rival dogs, each of us unwilling to be the first to speak. I could feel my hackles rising at the back of my neck, feel my nostrils flaring.

I wanted to bite him.

Mr. Clemm was as astonished by my ferocity as I was.

"I . . . I'm sorry, young lady," he began. "I thought you might have been in some distress."

You clever old hound, I thought. *Some distress* indeed!

This was a game, and both of us knew it. The next move was mine.

Hadn't Mr. Clemm been the assistant to Canon Whitbread at the time of the murders? Where had he been that fateful morning? Surely he must have been among the suspects. Until this very moment, that thought had never crossed my mind.

I pressed my wrist—first the back of it, then the front of it—to my forehead, then lowered myself gingerly into the pew.

Mr. Clemm sank slowly down beside me. He placed his hand on my shoulder.

"Here," he said, offering me a white linen handkerchief. "Wipe your nose and tell me all about it."

I was about to give him a piece of my mind when I realized my nose was running.

"Thank you," I whispered, and put the cloth to work with a surprisingly loud *honk*. When I was finished, I handed it back to him with a weak but appreciative smile.

"You may keep it," he said, with a glance at the thing. "You might need it later."

Was this a threat? Was I sitting here cheek to cheek in a pew with a mass murderer?

A mass murderer? That's a good one, Flavia. Even in the heat of the moment I made a mental note of my little joke. I would tell it to Dogger, and he would smile— perhaps even give a little whistle—at my brave wit even in the face of peril.

"It's just, you see," I whispered confidentially, "that I need to be able to lay the ghost of my great-auntie to rest. I thought that if I could see the spot where she . . ."

"I understand," Mr. Clemm murmured, patting my hand. I resisted the urge to pull away.

He had probably been made to take classes at divinity school in the art of Sucking Up to Survivors.

I gave a frail smile and went on, just to encourage him a little.

"I couldn't believe it when I found that we had landed our punt almost at the very spot where ... where—I thought it wouldn't hurt to come inside and say a little prayer for Great-Aunt Grace."

I raised my eyes to the stained-glass windows, as if to Heaven.

Don't whimper, *Flavia,* I thought. *She was supposed to be, after all, only a* great-aunt, *a distant twig on the family tree . . .*

I did what any intelligent girl would do: I batted my eyelashes becomingly and lowered my gaze modestly toward the floor.

When God has given you a great brain and long lashes, they may sometimes be the only weapons you have at your disposal, and it is best to know how to use them effectively.

"God hears all prayers," Mr. Clemm said. "Prayers both great *and* small."

"Thank you," I whispered, dabbing furtively at my eyes with his handkerchief, which was still clutched in my hand.

"You must have been shaken by your discovery," Mr. Clemm said, referring, I assumed, to Orlando's corpse laid out like a salmon in the grass.

"You can't imagine," I said, nodding frantically with rolling eyes, covering my mouth with the handkerchief and stifling what I hoped he would mistake for a sob.

Like most men of the cloth, Mr. Clemm had no idea how to deal with a damp and distressed female.

Round one to Flavia.

"Actually—" I said.

All great lies begin with the word "*actually,*" and this one was no exception.

"Actually," I said, "one of the three ladies who died so dreadfully here was a relative of mine: my great-aunt Grace."

"Grace Willoughby?" he asked.

I shook my head. "Grace Harcourt," I told him.

I'd better tread carefully, I thought. I must remember that this man, after all, had known each of the deceased personally. The fact that he had mentioned Grace Willoughby's name first probably meant that he had known her better than Grace Harcourt.

Which is why I plumped for Grace Harcourt.

Rather than volunteering any information, as I hoped he would, Mr. Clemm gave up only a sad, knowing nod.

I needed to prime the pump.

"Anything you can tell me about her last moments will help ease the pain," I said, touching his sleeve to reinforce my pleading eyes.

"I'm afraid I can't be of much help. You see, I was rather . . . ah . . . indisposed myself that morning."

Indisposed? What did he mean by that? Had he been tippling the sacramental wine the night before? Not very likely, I thought, *otherwise he'd be out in the churchyard pushing up petunias rather than sitting here evading my questions.*

Unless, of course, the cyanide had been introduced

just minutes before the Communion, which would have pointed to Canon Whitbread as the killer—or to one of the Three Graces, all of whom might have assisted in the vestry before the service.

Hard to believe, though, that any one of them would have poisoned herself. Unless, of course, it was murder/suicide.

My head was spinning.

"Indisposed?" I echoed solicitously, letting the word hang in the air.

One has to be careful about inquiring too closely into another's indisposition. You never know what torrents of ucky and disturbing detail might be spilled.

Mr. Clemm looked away—looked back—then looked away again.

"Loss of faith," he admitted, biting his lip. "I had been at that time suffering a very great loss of faith, you see. It wasn't right that I should administer Holy Communion in such a state. George was very good about it. Canon Whitbread, I mean. He told me I must confront it head-on: chin up, stiff upper lip, talk to God, 'man to Man to Man to Man,' as he put it."

"Oh?" I asked with raised eyebrows, a response which is nearly impossible to ignore.

"Yes . . . well, you see . . ."

His words trailed off in a mumble as he looked away.

"Love, was it?" I blurted, taking a shot in the dark. Still, I reckoned I had a less than fifty-percent chance of being wrong. Clergymen do not come undone over football, for instance, or even money. Jealousy, greed, re-

venge, and love were the usual motives, judging by the
newspapers, but the greatest of these is love, as Saint Paul
so wisely foresaw.

And when you boiled them down, jealousy, greed, and
revenge went usually hand in hand with love.

Quod erat demonstrandum, as Archimedes said, except
that he said it in Greek.

Mr. Clemm gasped.

"How could you possibly know that?"

"Feminine intuition," I replied. Which was an outright
lie. Feminine intuition is no more than an acceptable excuse for female brains.

I turned the famous de Luce blue eyes upon him with
full force.

Suddenly he laughed.

"All right, it *was* love. You have a very persuasive way
about you, Miss . . . ?"

"De Luce," I said. "Flavia."

He had thrown in the towel with surprisingly little effort on my part. I needed to be wary. I continued my stare.

"George was an understanding man. He told me I
needed not to condemn myself, but only to amend my
ways."

"Surely this must have come out at his trial?" I blurted.
I couldn't help myself.

"It did—in a way," Mr. Clemm answered. "However,
the coroner was one of our sidesmen here at St. Mildred's.
And so, of course, he didn't want to add unnecessarily to
the scandal."

"But why are you telling me this?" I asked, suddenly suspicious.

"Ah," Mr. Clemm breathed. "We are taught to confess, to bewail our manifold sins and wickedness, and what better way than to confess them to an innocent child such as yourself?"

I restrained a snort and favored him instead with a smile.

"Go on," I encouraged.

"Sorry," he said. "No names, no pack drill. Forgiveness," he said with a little wink, "does not demand the dirty details."

I was shocked. How could he possibly keep back the interesting bits? It wasn't fair!

"I understand," I lied, returning to the game.

All in due time, I thought.

"Come," he said. "Allow me to show you round the church. We can talk as we walk. Quite frankly, I find the atmosphere of this particular pew oppressive."

I was actually relieved to have him move. I hadn't realized how uncomfortable it had become having my escape route to the aisle blocked by a rather large clergyman.

And yet, if I wanted information, I was going to have to talk to him. Time was running out, and I was still baffled about so many points.

"This stone," I said, pointing. "It seems rather new. Stands out in such an old church. I wondered who it was?"

"A former rector," Mr. Clemm said, and began to move away.

"G.L.O.W.," I read aloud from the stone. "George L. O. Whitbread."

There was a silence of several centuries before Mr. Clemm said, "George Lancelot Orlando Whitbread. I am being very honest with you, Miss de Luce. I hope you'll not let me down."

Was he still holding me under the Seal of Confession?

"Wark! Wark!" I remembered Daffy barking, as she flapped her flippers together.

"But he was hanged!" I said. "How can he possibly be buried here?"

Mr. Clemm gave me such a long, sorrowful look that I almost forgave him his razor cuts and his shabby collar.

"Vanity," he said. "Mistakes are made. But as Jeremiah the prophet tells us, 'They are vanity, and the work of errors: in the time of their visitation they shall perish.'"

As if that explained everything.

Whom was he referring to? Who would perish? Those who made the mistakes? Or those who were their victims?

"Then it *wasn't* Canon Whitbread who killed the Three Graces?"

It was as blunt a question as I'd ever dared ask in my life.

Mr. Clemm stared at me as if he was torn between two answers. And then:

"Come," he said. "There's something I want you to see."

And without another word, he turned and walked

briskly away from me down the aisle. And I, without giving it another thought, followed him.

At the front of the church he turned sharply to the right and vanished up a steep stone staircase.

"Mind your head," his voice came echoing back between the walls of the narrow passage.

In spite of the summer heat outdoors, the staircase had a dank, musty, tonsil-clogging smell, as if it were a chimney for the churchyard.

I set my foot on the bottom step and began to climb: up and up and round and round. Because these early churches had also served as fortresses, the towers were designed to be defended. The circular staircase, with its tall risers, made fighting far more difficult for an attacker coming up the stairs, and easier for the defender fighting downward and backward, since it gave him the advantage of height and a free sword hand.

It reminded me of the mistaken belief that water went down the drain counterclockwise in the northern hemisphere and clockwise in the southern, as well as the doctor's symbol of a serpent twisting round a pole: the Staff of Asclepius, Dogger had told me it was called, and I wondered idly, as I climbed, if snakes slithered up trees counterclockwise in the northern hemisphere and clockwise in the southern.

"Are you coming?" Mr. Clemm's voice echoed from somewhere far above. He sounded impatient.

"Yes," I called up to him, wondering what he wanted to show me.

When I reached the top of the staircase and stepped out onto the flat roof, Mr. Clemm was nowhere in sight.

A dilapidated wooden structure, rather like a misplaced garden shed, stood in the very center of the roof, blocking my view of half the horizon.

I peered over the crumbling parapet at the scene below.

To my right, the river, slow and silent, glided like a lazy brown snake through the landscape, its lush willow-lined banks giving it the appearance of wearing an exotic green feather boa which had been flung aside perhaps, by some aging music hall star.

Poppy Mandrill came to mind.

From this altitude, the view was similar to the one taken by Hob Nightingale with his homemade kite camera.

A shock of remembrance rushed through my brain: *the photograph!*

I had shoved the snapshot into my pocket when Hob handed it to me in the tree, and with all the excitement, I had, quite frankly, forgotten about it.

Was it still there?

I shoved my hand carefully into my pocket and felt with my fingers.

Yes! I could feel the crisp edges and shiny surface of the photographic paper, still safely nestled where I had placed it.

Careful, Flavia, I thought. *You don't want to drop it over the edge and into the churchyard.*

Not that it would harm the photo, but I wanted to keep its existence to myself.

"Are you coming?" Mr. Clemm called again. "I'm round the other side. Round the back."

The back of the tower, I remembered, faced another stretch of the river with a view of the fields and a distant wood. More immediately, although I could not at the moment see them, it loomed directly over the lead roofing slates of the body of the church: the nave, the transept, and the chancel.

"As soon as . . . I catch . . . my breath," I called out, panting for effect like a dog in the desert.

What I needed to do needed to be done now, and I had to be quick about it. With Mr. Clemm breathing down my neck, I couldn't possibly compare Hob's snapshot with the view from the tower.

As I put my elbows on the parapet, a bit of Norman brick sheared off and went plummeting end over end into space.

"Watch out below!" I wanted to shout, but I didn't. If Fate had decided to clobber some deserving character in the churchyard below, who was I to interfere?

Besides, until I had examined the photograph, I needed to maintain silence.

As we had been taught to do in map-reading in Girl Guides, I rotated the photograph until it aligned with the landscape below.

Yes—here it was: Beyond was the dock where we had landed, and the grassy edge of the graveyard where Orlando's body had lain. The path along which Constable Otter and Mr. Clemm had come was clearly visible, a gash of gravel in the grass.

And here it was in Hob's photo. And here was our punt. Feely's sun hat was clearly visible in the bow. The pages of Daffy's open book caught the light amidships, and there was Dogger, poling us toward the riverbank.

The huddled lump in the stern was me, one arm outstretched. The ripples which trailed from my hands were due to the corpse of Orlando Whitbread. If I squinted, I could just make out his dark outline beneath the surface of the water.

I glanced rapidly back and forth from landscape to photograph. To my left—but hidden by one of the transept walls—would be the market square and Shadrach's Circus and, further along, Scull Cottage.

If I leaned over and out a bit, I could see—another stone dislodged and fell.

No time to look.

In my mind, there had been something else—

Aha! Just out of sight from where I now stood, hidden by one of the stone walls of the transept, the path began a long and gentle curve, through the churchyard, among the tombstones, toward the door.

In the photograph, a dark shape showed clearly against the light gray of the gravel.

A wicker bath chair!

And not just a bath chair, but an *empty* bath chair!

And just there, in the snapshot, look: lurking among the tombstones, the unmistakable form of the crouching Poppy Mandrill. Even from the kite's altitude, her Norfolk jacket was easy enough to see, and the bun of her white hair might as well have been a signal flag.

From behind a tall tombstone, she was watching us land the body of Orlando Whitbread.

Was her presence a coincidence, or had she herself been searching for Orlando?

On the path beside the church stood Hob, looking expectantly upward, the string of the kite and its release cord clutched tightly in his hand.

"What have you got there?" demanded a voice at my ear, and I spun round to find Mr. Clemm sticking his neck over my shoulder, trying to get a gander at Hob's photograph.

"It's just a snapshot," I said, shoving the thing quickly back into my pocket. "What did you wish to show me?" I asked, taking the offensive.

"You'll have to come round the other side of the tower," he said. "You can't see it from here."

"You go first," I said as I picked an excuse out of the air. "I'm terrified of heights."

My real reason was that I didn't want anyone between me and the top of the staircase.

"Always guard your exits," Daffy had once told me during one of our frank talks. She had been reading an English translation of an ancient Chinese text on military strategy, and was adapting its teachings to everyday life. "You never know," she warned, "what each new wind will bring."

And she was right. A light breeze had now begun to stir the flag above our heads, bringing with it the sound of faint music from Shadrach's Circus and, if I was not mistaken, the sharp odor of wild animals.

"Come," said Mr. Clemm, beckoning with a forefinger.

I followed him cautiously round the shedlike structure. The view, I must admit, was spectacular.

Far, far below us, at the bottom of a dizzying drop, were the lead roofs of the church, jutting every which way at sharklike Gothic angles.

"Behold," Mr. Clemm said, pointing, as he swept his arm round half the horizon. "All the wicked world."

Was he being facetious? Perhaps not. The man was, after all, an ordained minister of the Church of England and, as such, licensed to hear confessions. If anyone in Volesthorpe had the worldly goods on everyone, it was probably Mr. Clemm.

Perhaps even more so than Constable Otter.

"Over there," he said, pointing to the dock at the edge of the churchyard, "was where the poisoned chalice was found."

I nodded knowingly. I'd almost forgotten the poisoned chalice. Who had put it there, I wondered, after the tragedy of the Three Graces?

"*And also,*" he drew the words out with great emphasis, "the spot where you recovered the body of Orlando Whitbread."

He leered at me.

"Could it be, do you think, a coincidence?"

Was the man trying to tell me something? Was he trying to tip me off about something he had been told in confidence, without actually betraying the Seal of the Confessional, which, Daffy had told me, although it was a popular plot device and dear to the hearts of grubbing novelists and foreign film directors who were completely devoid of imagination, did not actually exist in law—not, at least, in England?

"Huh?" I said.

Mr. Clemm had on his face a look which I took to be exasperation.

"Is it not odd," he asked, moving a little closer, "that Orlando Whitbread should be found dead at precisely the same spot at which the murder weapon, so to speak, used by his own father was found?"

"Now that you mention it," I said, "I suppose it is."

"Look—Miss de Luce—" the vicar said. "I know who you are. There's no point in pretending with me. Your reputation has preceded you. I know where you've been and what you've done."

He was referring, I supposed, to my successfully solving a number of crimes which had perplexed the police. I couldn't help preening a little.

"Constable Otter has enlightened me—" he went on.

I held up a modest hand to stop him.

"What is it you wished to show me, Mr. Clemm?" I asked.

One of the greatest accomplishments of the detective's art is in learning to seem obtuse.

Another is in learning to provoke at precisely the right moment.

"Or did you simply want to get me up here alone?"

It was a bold move and, as I suspected it would, it took him by surprise.

He took another step toward me.

I stepped backward and away from him—toward the parapet.

"Hello the tower!" called a voice from somewhere below. "Miss Flavia!"

I risked a rapid glance over the edge.

Harriet's Rolls-Royce was parked on the gravel path, and beside its open door stood Dogger, calling up to me through the megaphone of his cupped hands.

·TWENTY-ONE·

IT IS UTTERLY IMPOSSIBLE for anyone ever to know what Dogger is actually thinking.

Except for me, of course.

Because of the great hardships to which he was subjected during the war, Dogger wears nothing on his sleeve but cloth. He can seem as blank as a newly whited wall, and yet—

I have learned to observe, by the minute movements of his eyelashes, the degree to which he parts his lips when he speaks, the caliber of his nostrils, and the tension of the skin at his temples (a sure indicator, which cannot be suppressed or modified by even the greatest actors of stage and cinema), his innermost thoughts.

In spite of that, the two of us always observe the ritual courtesies with each other.

"I hope you'll forgive my raising my voice, Miss Flavia," he said, as he met me at the door. "St. Mildred's has an uncommonly high tower for a fourteenth-century church. A hundred and thirty-five feet, I should say."

"A hundred and thirty-six," I told him. I had seen this fact inscribed on the tablet in the porch. "But perhaps, over the years, it has sunk a foot into the churchyard."

"Perhaps," Dogger said.

I had left Mr. Clemm on the roof to his own devices. I paused for a moment to listen for his footsteps on the winding stone staircase, but the old church was in silence.

"Dogger," I asked as we walked slowly to where the Rolls was parked, "has it ever occurred to you that Canon Whitbread may have been innocent?"

"It has indeed, Miss Flavia," he said. "It was, in fact, one of the reasons I suggested visiting Volesthorpe on our little holiday."

"You didn't!" I said, knowing perfectly well that he had. Dogger had put forward several excellent-seeming reasons for selecting this part of the river rather than Oxford or Cambridge, and in the end, even Aunt Felicity had been swayed.

"You astonish me!" I said.

"Yes." Dogger smiled.

"But," I said, remembering my visualization of the crimes from the pews of St. Mildred's, "if Canon Whitbread didn't kill those three old ladies, then who on earth did?"

"Someone," Dogger said, "who had something to hide. Someone who feared being found out."

"The poor man!" I said, thinking of Canon Whitbread.

"If that should be the case," Dogger went on, "then a very grave miscarriage of justice has occurred. Very grave indeed. Judicial murder."

"But whatever made you think so?" I asked.

"It was perhaps the speed with which he was arrested, tried, and executed," Dogger answered, holding open the front door of the car for me. "There is, of course, the so-called three Sundays rule which suggests—although not officially, of course—that three Sabbaths must be allowed to pass between the putting on of the judge's black cap and the drop from the scaffold, but still . . ."

"So much death," I said.

"Yes," Dogger agreed. "Too much death."

Without another word, he eased into first gear, and we rolled silently out of the churchyard.

"Have you had an interesting day?" I inquired.

"Most interesting," Dogger replied. "A day at the circus can be remarkably instructive."

"And not because of the elephant," I said, teasing a little.

"Not *because* of the elephant." Dogger smiled. "But perhaps in spite of it."

"Meaning?" I asked.

Before answering, Dogger turned the Rolls around and pointed its bonnet to the narrow dirt road that led along the riverbank. I knew enough to keep silent.

"In all walks of life and in all professions," he said at last, "there are those whom we might call the Invisible

Ones. No one remarks upon the presence of a clergyman at a funeral, or a policeman at the scene of a crime. No one thinks it strange to find a surgeon in the operating theater."

Although I could quite agree with him, I didn't see exactly what—or who—Dogger was driving at in this particular case.

"I suppose we usually look for the person who is out of place. '*Cherchez le stranger,*' Daffy would probably say."

"Precisely." Dogger nodded. "And often quite wrongly. Although we have no way of knowing who might or might not have been present at the death of a man in blue silk and red ballet slippers, we may be permitted to make certain deductions."

I loved it when Dogger talked like this. It made me feel that we were partners.

That we were equals.

It made me feel grown up and appreciated. It made me feel wanted.

A momentary pang struck at my heart. How could I possibly withhold from this kind and generous man the fact that I had picked the corpse's pocket as I waited on the riverbank?

Should I own up to Dogger and be done with it?

How could I admit that there was part of me that—quite desperately!—needed to have the upper hand, to intentionally withhold information: information which would all but guarantee that I should be the one to solve the murder of Orlando Whitbread?

In the Roman Catholic Church, I remembered, a sin is

covered by the grace of sacrament until you get around to confessing it, but in criminal investigation, it's an entirely different matter.

The answer was clear: I would confess later.

"Do you suppose there's any connection between Orlando's death and the deaths of the Three Graces?" I asked Dogger.

"I could hardly be persuaded otherwise," he said. "Multiple deaths in a tight-knit community prove often to be links in a single chain, however obscure that chain may seem to be. Miss A, for instance, might stab Miss B in the heart with an ice pick for love of Mr. C, while Miss D or Mrs. E might pine away in silence for the same unwitting gentleman."

"Mr. C would have a great deal to answer for," I said, "even if he was unaware of the facts."

"In a chemical reaction, I believe, the catalyst need not be aware of the reactants. It is little consumed itself, and often only a minute quantity is required to cause an infinitely larger effect. Of course, you'd know much more about this than I would, Miss Flavia, but you take my point."

Of course I did! Dogger was brilliant!

What smoldering embers had lain beneath the surface of this sleepy town, waiting only for the tiniest flash of flame to ignite the tinder?

I thought at once of Mrs. Palmer and the brass stallion in her poem. Who had he been, and who had resented him?

And the Three Graces: What tales had their tongues tattled to result in their triple murder?

288 · ALAN BRADLEY

"Why isn't Constable Otter investigating Orlando's death as suspicious?" I asked. "Why is he so anxious to treat it as a simple drowning?"

"The police move in mysterious ways," Dogger said. "Their wonders to perform."

Which opened whole realms of possibilities. Was Dogger hinting that Constable Otter himself might be involved? Could the constable be the brass stallion of the poem?

Or could it have been Orlando?

This was the most complicated case I had ever come across. Four people dead—five if you counted Canon Whitbread, who may have been wrongfully executed—and hardly a sensible clue to be had.

Everyone in town, it seemed, within the past two years, had bought cyanide for one reason or another: none attracting the slightest bit of attention, apparently, except for the good Canon Whitbread, whose campaigns against the humble wasp had resulted in a noose around his neck.

Even Mrs. Dandyman, of Shadrach's Circus, who came to Volesthorpe only once a year, seemed obsessed with ridding the world of sinners and replacing them with painted saints.

Perhaps it was too much for me, I thought. Perhaps I ought to ring up Inspector Hewitt, dump my basket of undigested trifle at his feet, and let him apply his superior brain to the evidence.

Should I? In a pig's parlor!

I would never live it down.

Flavia de Luce Fails! the headlines would scream. *Copper Solves Shocking Case Single-Handed.*

"I shouldn't worry about it," Dogger said, breaking into my thoughts. "Inspector Hewitt would be as baffled as we are."

"How did you know I was thinking of Inspector Hewitt?" I asked, taken aback.

"You straightened your hair and then you bit your thumbnail."

"Marvelous, Holmes!" I said, even though I felt like an idiot for being so transparent.

"No more so than your working out the state of my . . . health," Dogger said, with a sideways smile.

I had to laugh.

"You're observing me observing you observing me. Is that the way the world works?"

"Largely," Dogger said. "Yes."

We fell into one of those warm silences that I live for, and I stared out at the passing willows as the road narrowed to little more than a footpath.

"Where are we going?" I asked. "Back to Scull Cottage?"

"No," Dogger said. "Miss Tetlock has kindly arranged for us to visit the formidable Poppy Mandrill. We're to pick her up. They are, apparently, old friends."

I gasped.

"I told her I was keen on the history of the London stage. I'm sorry for speaking such an untruth, but I couldn't see any other way around it."

"But *are* you?" I asked. "Keen, I mean?"

"I have seen a few shows in my day. I shall manage."

"But," I said, my mind reeling, "Poppy Mandrill might well be our prime suspect."

And although I had vowed to keep back my confession until later, the whole sad story of how I had deceived him came suddenly pouring out: not just my rifling of the corpse's pockets and my finding of the crumpled paper, but also Hob Nightingale and his camera, the chemist, the aerial photos, the empty wheelchair—all of it in one breathless blurt.

I was ashamed of myself.

"Well done!" Dogger said, shaking his head.

Claire Tetlock was waiting for us at the edge of the field. Dogger got out of the Rolls and opened the back door for her.

"I feel like visiting royalty," she said, settling back into the soft leather upholstery. "Hello, Flavia."

I twisted round from my usual seat beside Dogger and gave her my warmest smile.

"Hello, Claire," I said, remembering she had given me permission to use her Christian name.

The first time I had seen her, Claire had been hot from hoeing, damp under a tropical hat. But now—dressed to kill, I thought—in a bluish-green belted summer frock with a bit of lace at the throat, she looked like nothing so much as a visiting duchess. Maureen O'Hara astray in the English countryside.

I couldn't take my eyes off her.

"I'm quite looking forward to this," she said. "I haven't

visited with Poppy for ages. She's quite a character, you know."

"I hadn't realized you were such good friends," I said, recalling how uneasy Claire had seemed at Scull Cottage in the presence of Poppy's ancient theatrical posters.

"Not quite friends," Claire corrected. "I had occasion to call upon her as a nurse. It was more of a professional association."

My ears perked up. Was Claire aware that Poppy Mandrill was able to get out of her wheelchair when the occasion demanded?

"Poor soul," I said. "She's not quite well, is she?"

Which Claire could take in any way she wanted.

She laughed.

"Poppy is an actress," she said. "And a very great one, at that. The London stage did not misjudge her. In her day she was a Titan . . . a Titaness. Or a Poppaea. That's her name, you know. Poppy. Poppaea."

Poppaea Sabina, I recalled, from Daffy's sometimes daring chatter at the breakfast table, was the woman who schemed her way into a marriage with the Roman emperor Nero, who later (Daffy had whispered over the kippers) kicked both her and her unborn child to death.

Perhaps in part because we shared the middle name Sabina, I had always felt an invisible kinship with this determined and yet somehow tragic woman. Being married to Nero must not exactly have been a piece of cake.

After turning it round, Dogger negotiated the Rolls along a narrow lane that rose, gradually, away from the river, ending in a shady grove where the yaffling call of a green woodpecker rang out among the trees like a series of rapid ricochets in an elderly Western film. Only the puffs of smoke were missing.

"Alhambra House," Claire told us. "Named after the theater."

There was nothing quite so grand about this place. A dank-looking pile whose weathered white plaster front was so cracked with an overgrowth of ivy that one longed to slash at it with a sword-stick, as Queen Mary, the Queen Mother, was said to be so fond of doing.

A couple of once-impressive pillars marked the entrance, their peeling paint betraying that they were composed of no more than worm-eaten wood, from which ants came and went in busy funeral processions.

"Poppy has fallen upon hard times," Claire said. "This place was once the Mecca of the theatrical world. Noel and Larry simply begged to be allowed to sit at the feet of the *grande dame*."

Which reminded me of something.

"What happened to her leg?" I asked.

"It was a national calamity," Claire replied. "An accident with a piece of stage machinery. Poppy's greatest, most famous scene at the end of the play. She was swinging high above the stage on an iron crescent moon when the rigging somehow failed. Although it was later determined to have been an accident, some said that the gear had been tampered with. At any rate, the heavy contraption, in falling, acted like the blade of a scimitar and . . . well . . ."

I didn't need Claire to describe the scene. I could picture it all too well: the crashing down of the mechanical moon; the single horrible, bloodcurdling scream; the audience, electrified, leaping to their feet; the hundred gasps; the hands raised to cover mouths; the sudden dimming of the stage lights; the curtain gliding slowly down to hide the blood.

"How ghastly!" I gasped.

"Quite," Claire said. "And yet in spite of it, just six weeks after the amputation, Poppy returned to the stage as Long John Silver, the one-legged pirate in *Treasure Island*."

"Good lord!" I said, and I meant it.

"It was one of the greatest moments in theatrical history. She still sometimes makes use of the battered wooden crutch she used so effectively in that role. She keeps it hidden in the depths of that ridiculous old bath chair, but pulls it out at dramatic moments. As I say, Poppy's a very great actress. But don't let her fool you. You'd be surprised what she's capable of."

No, I wouldn't, I thought, but I didn't say so.

I was thinking of the bruise on the back of Orlando's neck.

·TWENTY-TWO·

OUR RING AT THE rusting bellpull was answered by a surprisingly crisp young man in a blue cardigan and a yellow tie.

"Miss Mandrill is expecting you," he said, stepping aside to let us in.

"Thank you, Coatesworth," Claire replied, with a barely perceptible wink. "I hope we're not too early."

"Not at all, Miss Tetlock," he answered. "Miss Mandrill has made her preparations."

Preparations? What did he mean by that? Was the woman compounding poisons in her kitchen?

We'd better keep a sharp eye on the tea and biscuits.

Although her name had not appeared in Mr. Wanless's poison register, Poppy Mandrill did, after all, have indirect access to cyanide through Orlando, who worked occasionally at the chemist's shop. And Canon Whitbread's wasp killer would have been kept somewhere in the vicarage—probably the greenhouse—and any of the vicar's wardens, including Mrs. Palmer, would have had no trouble pinching enough of the stuff to do whatever nefarious deeds they had in mind.

"She'll see you in the second parlor," Coatesworth said as he led us past an open double door, through which I had a glimpse of a dusty parquet floor, high moldings, and a number of grim green hangings.

"Just in here," he said, showing us into an altogether smaller room.

I could see at a glance that sunlight was not welcome here. The windows were covered with blackout paper, sections of which were visible behind a set of heavy, dark curtains.

Three chairs had been arranged in a dead straight line at the edge of a threadbare Turkey carpet, upon which had been centered a small table, set with a vase of old-fashioned pinks and a large brass carriage clock. In the silence, I could hear its self-important ticking.

The spicy clove scent of the flowers overpowered even the moldy atmosphere of the parlor. I was reminded of a sickroom—or perhaps an undertaker's shop.

"Please be seated," Coatesworth said, fussing with a fully set tea trolley which stood parked on one corner of the carpet, as if on a stage set. "Miss Mandrill will be with you momentarily."

I raised an eyebrow at Dogger, who had once told me that the word meant "briefly," rather than "soon," and was best avoided if one didn't want to be mistaken for an

American. But Dogger was wearing his unreadable poker face, and I was left to feel superior all by myself.

"Thank you, Coatesworth," Claire said as we took our seats.

There was a feeling of expectancy in the room, as if even the wallpaper were listening to our every word. We sat in silence, hands folded, and we waited.

And waited.

Claire shot me a half smile before she returned to contemplating the carpet.

It seemed as if the lighting in the room was changing. Surely the shadows of the vase and clock were shifting slightly across the silk tablecloth?

How many shoe soles had that shabby old carpet seen in its day? I wondered. What famous feet had worn away its pile? Had murderers stood chatting upon its once-red nap?

There was a slight scurrying sound in the corner: the sound that a couple of mice might make when caught with the cheese, followed by a hollow groaning.

Poppy Mandrill's ornate wicker bath chair came sailing smoothly into the room like some ancient wooden ship under full sail, coming to anchor on the Turkey carpet between the table and the tea trolley.

Surely the lights were brighter at that spot than they had been when we came into the room; surely we were now sitting in a slightly greater darkness.

But it was the woman herself who commanded attention. I wouldn't have believed it if I hadn't seen it with my own eyes.

This was not the elderly invalid who had accosted me in the churchyard! Nor the same harpy who had hissed into my ear in the pews of St. Mildred's.

This was an Edwardian beauty in the full flush of high-colored womanhood. Her skin was like peaches and her eyes sparkled like happy diamonds.

Belladonna, I thought, but I pushed it out of my mind at once. It would be a sin to penetrate such artistry: an affront to decency. We were entranced, and I knew it.

Poppy Mandrill looked slowly and deliberately at each of us in turn: from Claire to Dogger, and then to me, her piercing eye relishing—no, not relishing, but positively *feasting upon*—our reactions.

She was coolly judging her effect upon our widening eyes, making us her mirror.

Her transformation was remarkable. From a frail and elderly invalid, this woman had summoned up a goddess.

I'm afraid I gasped.

"Welcome," Poppy Mandrill said in a voice like ancient honey, extending her arms, her palms upturned in a gesture of hospitality. "I bid you welcome to Alhambra House."

Now I wanted to applaud. I was in her grip already and I knew it; under her spell.

But I didn't care. It was as if the very nature of time itself had shifted and taken us with it: a slice of time in which we sat frozen in a pretty little tableau; living insects in amber.

Poppy was dressed in a classic white drapery, which I guessed was modeled on the Greek, overlaid with a large, dangling Art Deco necklace of shiny Bakelite lozenges, each of a different vivid color: a necklace for which the Duchess of Windsor would happily have sold herself— several times over—into slavery.

We sat suspended for several very long moments in this charmed state until Dogger broke the spell.

"Thank you for inviting us to visit, Miss Mandrill," he said. "It is most gracious of you to share your memories."

Already her eyes were glittering like a snake's. This woman's metabolism burned recognition in the same way that an automobile burns petrol.

She tittered slightly.

"You mustn't press me too much, Mr. Dogger, for I am of frail and tender years."

It was a joke, I suppose, and Dogger smiled dutifully.

"*Hypatia of Alexandria*," he said. "Act One, Scene One."

"You surprise me, Mr. Dogger," Poppy said.

I turned to stare at him but caught myself just in time. Dogger had surprised me, too. Just when I thought that I had got the measure of the man, he would reveal an entirely new and unsuspected side.

"As a student, I was fortunate enough to take up residence in a theatrical boardinghouse," Dogger said. "Complimentary tickets often served as the common currency."

Poppy Mandrill laughed a throaty laugh.

"In exchange for what, Mr. Dogger?"

"Favors," Dogger answered. "Friendship. Do you remember Frederick Linden-Smith?"

Poppy's face became a sunbeam. "Of course! He was Adagio in *Return of the Homing Angel*. Wonderful reviews. Wonderful. And Carlyle Quinn in *When the Sleeper Awakes*. Were you acquainted with him, Mr. Dogger?"

"I was," Dogger said quietly. "He died a prisoner of war in Burma."

Dogger did not mention his own captivity.

He was risking a great deal by opening this line of conversation, I realized, when even the slightest trigger—the most casual reference—could set him off on a nightmare journey of flashbacks to his own torture.

"Yes, I believe I heard something to that effect," Poppy remarked. "Poor chap, Freddie. He had a great future."

I bit my tongue, and from where I sat, it looked to me as if Dogger was doing the same.

"I believe he was once your protégé," Dogger said. "As was Orlando Whitbread."

Something glistened at the corner of one of Poppy Mandrill's eyes.

"You mustn't be too hard on me, Mr. Dogger," she said. "The flame must never be blamed for the death of the moth.

"Help yourselves to tea," she added, covering her own cup with an open hand when Claire offered to pour.

Dogger inclined his head, accepting the rebuke graciously. Was he trying to encourage her to talk?

"All the world envies a woman like me," she said, when we were settled. "They think it heaven to have been the quarry of every male, young or old, who ever laid eyes upon her. Let me tell you it is not. The bull's-eye on a target range has fewer holes than the heart of a woman on the stage. 'Oh!' you will say, 'but what about

the gifts: the flowers, the food, the jewels . . . the attention . . . the applause?' Well enough when you are young,
I suppose, and still blinded by your own beauty. But to
someone of my present age, it is quite frankly sickening.
One comes to fear the corpulent clergyman as the apple
fears the worm."

Aha! I thought. *The present vicar, Mr. Clemm, and his
loss of faith.*

How my heart was suddenly breaking for him—and for
her!

Claire, who had not spoken to this point, got up from
her chair and moved toward the woman in the wheelchair.

"No!" Poppy said, holding up a forbidding hand. "Sit
down. The priestess must never be approached upon the
altar.

"We must honor our traditions," she added.

Although she said this in rather a wry tone, almost half
joking, her meaning was unmistakable.

Claire returned to her seat. "Tell me about Orlando,"
she said softly. "I haven't yet been able to grasp—"

And in that instant I suddenly saw through her. She
and Dogger had planned this interview as precisely as a
pair of generals craft a battle plan. They had rehearsed
this conversation even before we set out for Alhambra
House! They had rehearsed this little scene as carefully as
any opening night in the West End.

I kept my mouth shut in admiration.

"Ah, Orlando." Poppy shook her head. "Dear Orlando.
He was too good to live. The world did not deserve him."

What was this? Was the woman confessing to murder?

"He was paying you a tribute, was he not?" Dogger asked. "I recognized the red ballet slippers and the blue silk costume at once as one of yours. *Pierrot in the Underworld.* One of your greatest roles. A record run at the Aldwych. I remember it with great pleasure."

Poppy's only response was to touch her upper lip with a startlingly long forefinger, and for a fleeting moment, her face was that of Pierrot—as if the character had been flashed upon her face by some cleverly concealed magic lantern.

"He was going to re-create my role . . . *we* were going to re-create my role. To astonish the world. There would be no denying his talent."

"You understood him," Dogger said. "Where others failed him."

Poppy nodded. It was easy to see how touched she was at even the mention of Orlando's name.

Which didn't mean that she hadn't killed him.

"Orlando's life was not an easy one," she said quietly. "His mother died before she could begin to love him. His father resented him in the beginning—hated him in the end."

"But why?" I couldn't resist.

"There are children," Poppy said, "whose lives are shaped by the minds of their elders. It matters not a jot what they are in actuality, but what they are *thought* to be. Orlando was such a child—and such a man."

"Sad," I said, because I knew exactly what she meant.

"Infinitely sad," Poppy said, "because Orlando had in

him, as I have said, the power to be the greatest actor of his generation. A gift from the gods."

"He must have been the envy of Volesthorpe," I said, putting it as gently as I knew how.

"Haw! Haw!" Poppy cried, her voice like that of an enraged hawk. "There were those who resented—"

"The Three Graces!" I blurted, as if I had just thought of it. I needed to flush this conversation out into the open to keep it from creeping back into the bushes.

In spite of that, I did not say what was actually on my mind.

"—his ease with women," Poppy went on.

Meaning what? I wondered. Was it possible for one woman to hate a man because of his ease with another? This was a question that was far beyond me. I tried to think of an equivalent problem in the world of organic chemistry, but I could not.

I would ask Daffy, who had read *Lady Chatterley's Lover* and accordingly knew everything there was to know about such things.

I turned my mind back to the Three Graces and their swift departure from the earth.

If not Canon Whitbread, who then had poisoned the chalice? Who, indeed, had dumped it in the river after the killings of the Three Graces?

"Look for the Invisible Ones," Dogger had told me.

And who could be more invisible in a parish than the minister's son? My heart fluttered at the thought. Was it possible that Orlando had poisoned the cup of the village gossips? He may well have had good reason to.

"Where was Orlando on the Sunday morning—the day of the three murders?" I asked.

Poppy was suddenly a hawk again, her wild eyes staring directly—perhaps too directly—into my mind.

"He was with me," she said.

I shot a glance at Claire. Hadn't she told me Orlando claimed to have taken the 7:02 up to London the previous evening? She gave me an eye shrug.

"Rehearsing," Poppy added unnecessarily. "And I testified to that fact at the time."

"What actually happened that morning, Miss Mandrill?" Dogger asked, with a little shake of his head. "One reads the papers, of course, but I have never quite been able to get it straight in my mind."

"You are a clever man, Mr. Dogger. And a very pretty trap you have laid. But obviously, since I was with Orlando, I could not possibly know what took place in the church."

"Quite right," Dogger agreed, not fazed in the least. "I thought it might have been spoken about in Volesthorpe."

"And so it was," Poppy answered. "It was also widely reported in all the newspapers, which you admit to having read—as did I—as did we all."

"May I help myself to more tea?" Claire asked brightly, getting to her feet and reaching for the silver pot.

How much of this conversation had she and Dogger anticipated? I wondered. How much of it was spontaneous?

"You've come to me under false pretenses, Mr. Dogger," Poppy said in a scolding tone, as if he were a naughty boy. I saw that the spark had returned to her eye. "I fear your interest in my theatrical experiences was merely a ruse. Your motives are not those of the theatrical historian, nor are they of the merely curious."

Dogger did not protest, as I might have done if I were him.

"I offer my apologies if I haven't made myself clear," he said. "But as a once-avid student of the stage, I couldn't help being struck by the remarkable similarities of the murders to your role in *Mildritha Kinbote*. The three poisonings from the common cup were particularly suggestive. There is also the coincidence of the name: St. Mildred's."

The silence that fell clotted the air of the drawing room. I hardly dared breathe.

And then there came an insistent "SSS-SSS-SSS." Poppy Mandrill was hissing like a kettle through her teeth.

"You must forgive me, Mr. Dogger," she rasped, pulling a handkerchief from her sleeve and wiping at her mouth. "Perhaps you won't believe me, but that similarity had never occurred to me. Not until this very moment. You are quite right, of course. Do you suspect some connection?"

"No," Dogger said. "I was merely pointing out the remarkable coincidence. In my experience, murderers in real life have neither the wit nor the ingenuity to plot and plan such literary crimes, let alone carry them out. Killers do not read books, nor do they frequent the theater. They are more often to be found in cinemas, or wrapped in the *Daily Mail*."

Poppy Mandrill let out a dry chuckle.

"Touché, Mr. Dogger," she said. "I am properly chastised. I should have known better than to bait you. Your point, of course, being that such fiendish killings occur only in the books of Mrs. Christie and her ilk?"

Dogger gave her a slowly beatific look. His face was suddenly that of a weary but understanding archangel.

"And, of course, in Volesthorpe," he said.

Although I could see that they were both taking a certain pleasure in the duel, it was time to remove Dogger from the line of fire. I knew the signs all too well.

I reached for my teacup and as I raised it to my lips, I let out the most appalling, gut-grinding belch.

It was an art that Daffy had taught me as a child, and one which I had perfected over the years in the privacy of my bedroom and my laboratory. My belches were not for the faint of heart.

"I'm sorry," I gasped, covering my mouth and holding my breath just enough to make my face go a convincing shade of red. "I suddenly don't feel well. The piggies-in-a-blanket at breakfast, perhaps."

I let out another train of injured air.

Dogger and Claire were on their feet at once, bustling me toward the door and making their apologies.

It was a performance worthy of Poppy Mandrill herself. *Had she spotted it as such?* I wondered.

I kept my shoulders hunched like a vulture and my hands over my mouth until we were in the Rolls and safely away from Alhambra House.

Only then did Claire and I burst into hysterical laughter.

Dogger smiled a tired smile and I realized that it really was time to get him home.

After dropping Claire off at Scull House ("Just leave me at the edge of the field," she had insisted), we drove back to the Oak and Pheasant in near-silence.

"Phew!" I said as we got out of the car. "It's been a long day already. I think I need a rest. You might as well have one, too, Dogger."

"Thank you, Miss Flavia," he said. "I believe I shall."

In my room, I stood on my head on the bed as I sometimes do when I need to concentrate my thoughts.

Why hadn't I asked Poppy Mandrill about Orlando's paraldehyde habit? I'd certainly had the opportunity. It was almost as if some powerful hand had held back my questioning—and perhaps for good reason.

"All's well that ends well," Shakespeare had said and, as usual, the wily old bard was right. It might not have done at all to let Poppy know how much I already knew about the characters in the case.

When I woke up, the shadows of late afternoon had subtly rearranged my room.

I got up, washed my face, and brushed my teeth. Daffy had become remarkably fussy about personal hygiene in the past several months, and I didn't want to give her an excuse to carp.

·TWENTY-THREE·

I TAPPED LIGHTLY AT Daffy's bedroom door with my fingernails. One long followed by two short: a Morse code letter *D* for Dickens, the password we had agreed upon during one of our rare truces.

After a moment, I heard the key turn in the lock.

"Well?" she demanded, peering out at me with one eye through the crack of the opening door.

"How are you getting on with the poems?" I whispered, keeping my voice down in case Mrs. Palmer was within earshot.

Daffy eased the door open wider—just enough to let me squeeze in—then closed it behind me.

"Listen, Nugs," she said, putting her hand on my shoulder, and my heart leapt up. She had not called me Nugs for years—not since we were children.

"Listen, Nugs, these are deep waters and dangerous. You'd be a fool to become involved."

I was too stupefied to speak. Daffy led me over to her bed, patting the quilt to indicate that I should sit.

Mrs. Palmer's book, *The Mussel Bed*, lay open face-down on the counterpane—which ought to have told me something in itself, since Daffy had raged more than once that anyone who left a book in that position ought to be flayed, hanged, drawn and quartered, and dragged by four black horses to the four corners of the globe, their tattered remains roasted and the ashes cursed and scattered to the winds.

Daffy snatched up the book and read.

"This one, for instance, about the copper mare and the brass stallion. Remember?

"The copper mare and
The brass stallion graze
In Flecker's Field.
He paws the turf,
While she the wind tastes.
And when he trots to her
She turns tail."

"Of course I do," I said. "It's about Leander, the ancient Greek chap who drowned trying to reach his lover, Hero, who was a nun."

"It's about horseplay," Daffy said. "And not the kind you're thinking. James Elroy Flecker died in bed, remember?"

"I don't know what you're talking about," I said, and I didn't. Daffy's mind and mine do not function in the same way.

"Do you remember *Madame Bovary?*" she asked. "Remember Rodolphe? The gentleman in the yellow gloves and the green velvet coat?"

"Holy moly!" I said. "You don't mean—?"

"Indeed I do!" Daffy said with a leer.

"Mrs. Palmer?" I asked. "I don't believe it!"

I still wasn't exactly sure what Daffy was referring to, but I didn't need the details.

"With whom?" I asked, managing to keep my head grammatically.

"With her Leander. The one who drowned."

"Hold on!" I protested. "She wrote this poem and published it ages before Orlando died."

"Which can mean only," Daffy said, "that she either foresaw his death or was herself the instrument of his demise.

"Ah!" she said. "Is there true love beyond the grave? Does the drowned hero await in some violet-scented afterlife? 'Fraid not, Flavia. Marvell said it best:

"The grave's a fine and private place,
But none, I think, do there embrace.

"Nope, you can count on it, little sister. The woman's either a psychic or a killer."

"Top drawer, Daff!" I shouted. "You ought to be in the detecting business yourself!"

I was amazed to recognize that there was no resent-
ment whatsoever attached to my words. My sister deserved all the praise and encouragement I could give her.

"Go on," I urged. "Is there more?"

"Tons more. Steaming cartloads of it."

That did it. I vowed there and then to take up the
study of poetry at the earliest possible convenience.

"I'm all ears," I said, putting my forefingers behind my
ears and pushing them forward until I looked like Dumbo.

"Well, this, for instance," Daffy said, turning to a new
page and striking a dramatic stance.

Her voice was different, I noticed, when she read poetry.

> *"'Tis not the hawk that frightens but the shadow of the
> lark—"*

"She is more afraid of the songbird than the raptor," I
interrupted. "I wonder why?"

"The Linnaean classification of the skylark is *Alauda
arvensis*, meaning 'field lark.' *Arvensa* is the Latin word
for 'field,' recalling both Flecker and the field in which
the copper mare and the brass stallion graze. And our
trusty landlord Palmer's Christian name is Arven. It's on
the hanging signboard out front."

Of course it was! Hadn't I seen it with my own two
eyes?

That did it. I resolved to take up the study of Latin as
soon as we were back home. I was already drooling at the
thought of those mountain torrents of leather-bound

texts in Buckshaw's overflowing library. What juicy secrets lay hidden in forgotten names!

"Sorry," I said. "Go on."

Daffy gave me an amused raised eyebrow and began
the poem again:

> "*'Tis not the hawk that frightens but the shadow of the lark.*
> *Most melancholy bird of all espies us in the dark.*"

"An owl!" I said. "Owls can see in the dark! Someone
has spied on them in Flecker's Field!"

"Partially correct," Daffy said. "Someone *has* spotted
them. But it's not an owl."

She closed the book, sniffing at its sandwiched pages as
if gratefully savoring the knowledge they had given up.

"'Most melancholy bird,'" she said, "is an allusion to a
poem by John Milton. Surely you've heard of *Paradise
Lost?*"

Heard of it? I had *lived* it! *Paradise Lost* was the story of
my life!

"Vaguely," I said.

"Excellent," Daffy said. "The reference to a melancholy bird, however, as every schoolboy knows, is from
one of his earlier poems, '*Il Penseroso,*' which, roughly
translated, means 'The Thinking Man.'"

"And what is the thinking man thinking about if he's
not referring to an owl?" I asked.

"It's a poem about his muse, and how she meets her
lover."

Daffy fell into her rich, dark reading voice:

"Oft in glimmering bow'rs and glades
He met her, and in secret shades
Of woody Ida's inmost grove . . .

"Quite frankly, Flavia, it's about an assignation."

Well! That put a whole new light on things. Had Mrs. Palmer's husband realized what was going on and killed the man who was meeting his wife "in secret shades," whatever that meant?

"And the bird?" I asked. I was not about to be thrown off the track by a lot of nauseous lovemaking.

"A nightingale," Daffy said. "The melancholy bird of which the poet speaks was a nightingale."

There are times when the breath is sucked out of your lungs as, in an instant, a forest fire consumes the living air.

Giddy and light-headed, I made my excuses (sudden fatigue) and fled the room.

"Wait!" she called after me. "There's more!"

But my head was spinning. I needed to be alone. Now.

When all else fails, there remains a single spot on earth where one can be alone: a place where teeming thoughts can be rounded up and organized; a place where one will never be imposed upon by the inhabitants.

And, as if of their own accord, my shoes were already making their way across the road to the graveyard. All I needed to do was to keep my feet in them.

Here I could collect my thoughts among the ancient stones.

Would I sit here with Fanny Greatorex, spinster of this parish, who departed this life on the third day of April, in the Year of Our Lord Nineteen Hundred and Six, or over there on that mossy bank with Thomas Button, Gent, whom "life abandoned" on November thirty-first (that's what it said) in the fifty-ninth year of the reign of our Sovereign King George III?

Since Fanny looked a little more welcoming, and somewhat less damp, I chose her. I settled myself among the lichens on her slab.

There is something mystical about sitting on a stone. It not only provides firm support for one's bottom, but also seems almost miraculously to stimulate the brain.

It was obvious that Orlando Whitbread was central to what I had already begun to think of as the Volesthorpe Mysteries: as tangled a knot of death as I had ever seen. The man himself was dead, as was his father, as well as the three village women who had perhaps gossiped too much about him for their own good.

The good canon had gone to the gallows for the deaths of the latter three ladies and now his son would be joining him—more or less—in the grave.

There was so little left to go on. Perhaps it was too late, anyway. Perhaps we should simply pack our picnic baskets in the Rolls, drive off into the sunset, and leave these dead to their own devices. Given enough time, it wouldn't matter anyway.

Or would it?

Would Flavia de Luce blot her heavenly copybook by overlooking a crime?

"*Four crimes!*" a little voice cried within me.

Would all the saints, when I arrived in Paradise, rub forefingers together at me as if starting a fire with sticks, and cry out to me "Tish! Tish! Tish!"? Would a choir of angels chant, to the tune of some grand and previously unknown melody by Bach or Handel, "Shame! Shame! Shame! Shame! Flavia's going down the drain!"?

With Heaven, you never knew. It was better not to take any chances.

A twig cracked and before I could even think someone seized me from behind and covered my mouth. I had only a flashing impression of rough red hands and a hot rasping breath at my ear.

"Keep quiet," hissed a voice.

My eyes must have been bugging out above the restraining fingers. I did the only thing I could think of. I bit them.

"Oww!" shrieked the voice as I was abruptly released. "You filthy little minx. You've bitten me! I'm going to lose a finger!"

I spun round to see Mrs. Palmer. She was staring at her bleeding hand, which had distinct teeth marks on the web between her thumb and forefinger.

My instinct was to make a break for it and run for my life, but her next words stopped me.

"Wait. I probably deserved it. I was simply trying to keep you from crying out and attracting attention. It's my fault entirely. I should never have followed you in the first place. I thought we could have a quiet talk."

She looked at her injured hand in a way which I believe is called rueful.

"Why didn't you simply walk up to me?" I asked, handing her the handkerchief Mr. Clemm had thrust upon me. "Why didn't you just hail me from a distance?"

"I thought you'd run away," she replied. "I thought you'd think I was going to kill you—just as I killed Orlando."

"*Did* you?" I asked. "Kill Orlando, I mean?"

"No," she said, wrapping her damaged hand in my now-ruined handkerchief. "I most certainly did not. But you *believe* I did."

"Do I?" I challenged.

The conversation was becoming like one of those absurd French dramas in which the characters stand about swapping nonsense dialogue while the audience pretend they know what's going on.

She did not reply to my question but dug deep into the pocket of her apron with her undamaged hand and pulled out a roll of banknotes.

"Here," she said, holding it out. "Take it. It's all I have. I can get more later if you insist."

I looked at her blankly.

"Just leave. Go away. Ask no more questions. Leave us in peace."

It took me several moments to see what she was getting at.

"Are you offering me a bribe?" I asked.

She shook the money in my face, then tried to press it

into my hands in what, because of her injured hand, was rather a gruesome gesture: all blood and banknotes.

I did not take them from her, but neither did I refuse. I needed to keep this conversation alive until I had what I needed.

"Who else is blackmailing you?" I asked. Because I had broken into her bedroom, it was probably not a good idea to bring up the brass stallion and the copper mare. I didn't want her to think me a snoop.

"Ah!" she said with a wry grin. "I see you've been talking to your sister Daphne. Serves me right. I ought to have known better than to trust anyone who reads Trollope."

There was a long, uneasy pause and then she reached with her good hand into her apron pocket and pulled out a packet of cigarettes and a book of matches. She made a clumsy effort to get one alight, but her fingers were shaking badly. I lit a match and held it for her in spite of my aversion to the habit.

There we were, inches apart, staring into each other's eyes.

"Orlando," I said, and I watched as her tears welled up instantly at the sound of his name. Surely this woman could not have—

"Orlando was a very special soul," Mrs. Palmer said. "He did not belong upon this earth."

"Who killed him?" I persisted, thinking of her husband.

She took a deep drag on her cigarette, sizing me up with tired eyes.

"You shouldn't listen to gossip," she said, exhaling a trumpet of smoke brutally. "Gossip kills."

"Sometimes there is no other choice," I insisted, "when you can't get at the facts."

I was quite pleased with myself for having thought of this.

She was already halfway through her cigarette, staring now at the horizon.

"Orlando, like many artists, was not strong-willed. He suffered from an abundance of addictions."

Which was rather a neat way of putting it, I thought: wine, women, and song, and paraldehyde—all without actually mentioning any of them: all swept under the carpet with all the efficiency of Mrs. Mullet on a Saturday morning and Aunt Felicity arriving unexpectedly from London.

"Talent is a terrible taskmistress," I remarked, picking this shockingly trite bit of rot out of thin air. I was ashamed of myself, but still rather proud.

"It is, indeed," Mrs. P said, dabbing at her eyes with her bandaged hand. "His father was so very, very proud of him, and yet—"

"It must have been very difficult for Canon Whitbread," I said. It is often best to lead with a general remark and leave the other person to release a flood of details. But in this instance, it didn't work.

"Yes, it was," she said, and left it at that.

I detected some awkwardness developing. I needed to be more personal.

"Mrs. Palmer—" I said.

"Greta," she blurted. "Please call me Greta."

She was as anxious to be chummy as I was. Chummi-
ness invariably leads to confidences being exchanged,
which, when you get right down to it, is what the art of
detection is all about. Sleuths learn nothing by being
aloof. It was the one thing that the great Holmes got
wrong.

"Greta," I said. "I'm curious about just one point. Perhaps you can set my mind at ease."

*Brilliant, Flavia. Make it sound as if I'm the one who is
discommoded (which doesn't mean what you probably think it
does).*

Before she could even think about it, I fired away.

"Where was Orlando on the morning the Three Graces
died?"

I already had two answers to this question. Poppy
Mandrill claimed he had been with her. Canon Whitbread's prosecutor insisted he had gone up to London.

"Presumably at home at Scull Cottage," Greta said.
"He had just come down from London the day before."

"Hold on," I said. "Gone *up* to London, you mean. Saturday. The night before the murders."

That's what Claire had told me.

Greta laughed.

"You see how stories get muddled in a time of murder?
He had, as I say, come *down*. I know because I picked him
up at the station."

"From Dollylands," I said. "He had just been released
from the private clinic."

"Yes," she agreed.

"Then this is my question," I persisted. "Was his treatment successful? Or was he still under the influence of paraldehyde?"

"What would you know about that?" she demanded. If she'd had feathers, they'd have been ruffling.

I shrugged. I needed to find out if Orlando, at the time of the poisonings, was shot full of paraldehyde, and in the grip of the delusions and hallucinations that sometimes accompany its use.

I could feel the resistance. She did not want to reply.

"It all came out at the time of his father's conviction," she said bitterly. "You can read about it in *Great Trials*."

"I don't have a copy of *Great Trials*," I said gently. "And besides, I'd rather hear it from you."

"Why are you doing this, Flavia?" she asked, fumbling for another cigarette.

"Because I trust you," I rejoined, suddenly inspired.

That did it. Greta began to talk.

"Orlando had been in and out of several institutions and private hospitals, all of them promising, but none, in the end, providing a cure. Dollylands was the end of the line. They admitted only the most badly addicted patients. He came down on the Saturday evening train, went straight home to Scull Cottage, and, as far as I know, injected himself with the stuff immediately. He came into the Oak and Pheasant an hour later and I bustled him out the back door into the garden. You could smell him from across the room. He was extremely agitated. Went on and on about his reputation ruined, his good name grabbed from him by gossips. He was receiving vile letters. Said he had no choice but to involve the police. I told him to go home and sleep it off. It was dreadful. He cried. And so did I, but not until later."

"And did you see him on Sunday?"

"No. Apparently no one did. He claimed to have been lying in Scull Cottage in a stupor until the Monday morning after the murders."

"Thank you, Greta," I said. "You've been a great help."

And I meant it.

"I'm glad of that," she said. "And now I want you to drop the whole thing. Orlando is dead but there are still many secrets in Volesthorpe. Some of them will come out and some will not. None of us need the trouble. Take this, go home, and forget about us."

Again she held out the roll of banknotes.

"Keep the money," I said. "I don't take bribes. I'm not that kind of person."

"What kind of person are you?" she asked, and I could see that she was offended.

"I'm the kind of person who is going to make a difference in the world," I told her. "As soon as I get rid of my braces."

Greta began to laugh a low, slithery laugh, like a snake in the grass. But the laugh died in her throat like a shot pheasant.

A man's voice, nearby, was calling out "Greta?"

She seized me by the arm and pulled me roughly down behind a weathered tombstone.

"It's Arven!" she hissed. "My husband. He's come after me. He's going to kill me!"

"Why would he want to kill you?" I whispered.

"You don't want to know," she whispered back, clutching my elbow to her chest as if it were a life jacket.

I did not bother telling her that I already did.

I peered round the edge of the tombstone. Arven Palmer was standing about thirty yards away, looking round, scratching his head.

"Can you see him?" she whispered.

I nodded yes.

"Just keep still," she pleaded. "Arven has no patience. He'll give up and go away before he'll search the churchyard."

"You know him very well," I said.

She shot me a grim grin.

"Too well," she said. "He may have no patience but he never forgets a wrong . . .

"*Ever!*" she added.

We sat for perhaps ten minutes in silence, our backs against the tombstone, before Mrs. P scrambled to her feet.

"I'm leaving now," she said, brushing off her skirt. "I'll go the long way round. But promise me this, Flavia . . ."

She waited until I met her eye.

"When Constable Otter gets round to questioning you, don't mention my name. Please. I beg you. I thank you. Goodbye."

She touched my hand and then she was gone. I lost sight of her before she reached the river.

·TWENTY-FOUR·

I HAD HOPED THAT Hob would be at his father's shop. It would have made things so much easier.

As things turned out, it was probably as well he wasn't.

I stood in the street gawking for a few minutes, as I always do when I want to be taken for a tourist. There were no funeral notices in the window of the Nightingale shop, which came as no surprise; a set of faded and threadbare purple curtains hid whatever lay behind the plate glass. I cupped my hands against the window and peered through them, hoping to somehow see what lay inside.

Nothing but a brace of dead flies.

I tried the door, but it was locked. No point in going round the back, then. I didn't want to be seen trespassing upon private premises.

What was I to do?

As so often happens when you are a girl of intelligence, the answer was already right there in my head, ready for immediate use, like a celestial screwdriver.

I remembered sitting once, only half attentive, through one of Denwyn Richardson's lazy summer sermons on the Book of Matthew. Perhaps it was because Denwyn often recirculated his winter preachings that they were sometimes so memorable. In any case, it was a message I had heard more than once:

Ask, and it shall be given you; seek, and ye shall find; knock, and it shall be opened unto you: For every one that asketh receiveth; and he that seeketh findeth; and to him that knocketh it shall be opened.

What a wonderful text it was—and how appropriate. I closed my eyes, folded my hands, and asked.

It was in that instant that I remembered the wool shop just down the street. I turned away and strolled casually toward it.

The bell over the door rang, and I stepped into the shop.

"Good day to you," said the woman behind the counter. She was sitting in a chair, knitting. I couldn't help thinking that she was vaguely familiar until I realized that she looked uncannily like a sheep herself.

I pretended to interest myself in her balls of wool.

"Do you knit?" she asked.

"Not myself, no," I said. "But my aunt Felicity does. She's a wizard knitter. She's promised to knit me a Fair Isle pullover if I can find some wool of my favorite color."

"Which is?" the woman asked.

"Peacock," I said.

The woman put down her knitting and began to haul herself out of her chair.

"Peacock?" she asked.

"Yes," I said enthusiastically, "it's one of my school colors."

"And your school is?" she asked skeptically.

"Miss Bodycote's," I said.

"It's Canadian," I added, as if that explained everything.

Without another word, she shuffled off toward a little back room, as I had desperately hoped she would.

In a flash, I had seized a couple of crochet hooks from a display on the counter and rammed them into my pocket.

I could have paid for them, of course, but I didn't want to leave such an easy trail of evidence, should I happen to be caught. I would balance the books later.

The woman—blast her—was back in a jiff. She dumped half a dozen balls of wool on the counter.

"Peacock," she said proudly. "It's on sale. I can let you have the lot for six shillings."

I picked up a ball and fingered the wool.

"Oh, dear," I said. "I'm afraid this is Indian peacock. Miss Bodycote's is Javanese peacock. Miss Bodycote herself, you see, was brought up in Batavia. The Javanese peacock is said to have derived its unique green color from the volcanic nature of the soil there."

I gave her my most horrid, know-it-all leer, as if to confirm this mixture of fact and fiction. At the same time— although I could hardly believe I was doing so—I offered up silent thanks to my obnoxious cousin, Undine, for her endless prattling about wildlife in Singapore and the former Malaya.

"That's fine, then," the sheep-woman said in that voice which means that it isn't, really. She stuffed the wool under the counter and resumed her knitting.

"Thank you," I called loudly and cheerily as I walked out the door. "Lovely shop."

I took my time walking back along the street to the Nightingale establishment.

Pausing again to look at nothing in the window, I stood with one hand idly in my pocket, bending one of the crochet hooks into a letter *L*.

When it seemed about right, I took it out and applied it to the lock, using the other hook as if the two of them formed the jaws of a pair of pliers.

Dogger had given me extensive training in the art of picking locks. This was just one of the many accomplishments he had picked up in his earlier life. I would have loved to ask where, and how, and why, but of course one doesn't do that sort of thing. One merely listens and observes.

As if by magic, there was a deeply satisfying *click* and the knob turned easily. After a quick glance up the street and down, I stepped inside the shop.

This was not the first time in my life I had reconnoitered an undertaker's shop. The trick of it was, of course, to find out what I needed to know without being caught. Although it might seem like a good idea at the time, meddling with corpses is difficult to explain in the cold light of day.

First thing, then, was to determine if Orlando's body was actually here.

An arched doorway to the right led to a small chapel in which several rows of straight-backed chairs faced an empty wall.

Nothing here. To the left were a pair of double doors which caused my heart to beat a little faster: double doors are made for the wheeling in and out of things that cannot walk themselves.

I tapped lightly on the paneling just in case someone was inside. I could still explain my way out of this. I was looking for Hob. I had found the front door ajar, and so forth . . .

I pushed the door open and peered inside. This was more like it! The inner sanctum: the control room for the Empire of Death.

Two tilted slabs of porcelain with drains stood side by side, both of them, unfortunately, empty. Glass reservoirs of what I knew to be embalming fluid were close at hand, their contents tinted the shade of candy floss to restore in the subject what was believed to be a healthy complexion.

On a wall, stainless steel surgical instruments—one of them a colossal syringe with a snout like some prehistoric mosquito—stood ready to extract stomach contents, and so forth.

I gave a thought to the dead Orlando, and to the contents Dogger and I had analyzed from his stomach. What were they called? Diatoms! Yes, that was it, diatoms: those microscopic creatures whose sandy skeletons had told us whether Orlando had been dumped dead or alive into the river.

In any case, he wasn't here, as I had half expected he wouldn't be. I was beginning to get that familiar feeling at the back of my neck: not out of fear, but out of a sense that your hunches are more than hunches.

I backed out of the room and turned to face the remaining door which must lead, I knew, to the workshop, which I had already seen on my previous visit.

Again I knocked out of courtesy, as I make it a point never to startle a man with a hammer in his hand.

The same dark and beautifully polished coffin stood as it had before, on trestles in the middle of the workshop. I flicked the finish with my fingernail. Mr. Nightingale had certainly put a lot of work into this masterpiece of the carpenter's art. Again, I wondered who it had been made for.

In a far corner of the room was a desk, bulging with papers and letters, which spilled out of its many pigeonholes in a most haphazard manner.

As I took a step toward it, I brushed against a chisel which had been left lying atop a wooden trestle. It went clattering to the floor—and I froze.

The Nightingales' living quarters were probably upstairs over the shop.

Had I been heard?

I stood listening for several endless moments, but all I could hear was the pounding of my heart.

I tiptoed my way to the desk.

By their dry, faded paper, I could see that these documents stretched back over many years. It appeared as if Mr. Nightingale had begun filling the top left pigeon-holes in the early days of his business and moved on from side to side, over the years, and down.

The freshest-seeming envelopes were in the bottom right compartment, spilling over onto the desktop. I pulled the drawers out, one by one. These, too, were jammed with bills and invoices.

I pulled one out at random. It was three years old.

The next drawer down was a complete surprise. It was filled—almost to overflowing—with loose race cards: cheaply printed greyhound racing programs from Wimbledon, Harringay Arena, Southend Stadium, and the White City—certain dogs in each race checked off in pencil, presumably to win, and every one of these, I realized, purchased with the wages of death.

With races on weekdays and at weekends, afternoons and evenings, and the sheer amount of travel involved, his commitment in time must have been colossal, to say nothing of the money wagered.

And suddenly I knew. Mr. Nightingale was no angel. He was also in deep trouble.

It was just then that something caught my eye: a fat, solemn-looking ledger that lay flat on the top shelf.

I reached for it and took it down, my hands trembling.

Inside the front cover, on the flyleaf, in a remarkably ornate hand, was written in businesslike black ink (oak gall, I thought) *F. T. Nightingale.*

The first entry in the book was dated thirteenth September, 1922, and had to do with the funeral of an infant named Margaret Rose Cawfee.

In meticulous copperplate script were written the details of the transaction:

Attendance at The Laurels, 10/, pine coffin, £8, shroud 7/, ribbon, 2/, motor hearse and driver, £2, opening grave, bearers & sexton, £2, undertaking, £1.

All of it coming to about £14.

Poor little Margaret Rose Cawfee. Had anybody loved her? They surely must have: The ribbon told the tale.

I turned toward the back of the ledger which was not quite filled. There were only a few blank pages left.

The last entry had been made two years ago.

I whistled.

Canon G. L. O. Whitbread!

The bill had been paid in full by H. M. Prisons. The cost had been five hundred and sixty pounds.

There were no details.

And there hadn't been a single entry since.

With fingers flying, I leafed back to the previous page, and there they were—the Three Graces: Miss Willoughby, Miss Harcourt, and Miss Cray.

All on the same day.

It must have been a bumper season for Mr. Nightingale. But why, then, had his business so suddenly failed? Why had he only carried out four funerals in the past two years?

I needed to dig deeper into his personal papers. If only I could find his checkbook, or perhaps his diary. Even the mail that he had received might well shed some light on his most peculiar business.

I was trying to decide where to begin on this mountain of papers when I spotted something on the floor: something which had been flung carelessly toward the wastebasket but had fallen short, almost hidden behind the leg of the desk.

I picked it up with my fingernails.

Unfortunately, it was blank. Just a piece of blue-lined paper from which a portion had been torn.

Sometimes, out of the heavens, the Great Gods will drop something unexpectedly into our laps. It's their way, I suppose, of saying "Thank you for your custom. Thank you for believing in us." It is their way of throwing us a bone.

The only word that can adequately describe our feelings when this happens is "thrill," which ought to be spelled with a couple of Z's instead of L's, since it has the same effect as sticking your finger into an electrical receptacle.

I put the scrap on the desk and reached into my pocket, smoothing as I pulled out the piece of paper I had found in Orlando's pocket.

54 6 7 8 9, I read.

Same ink, same written numerals as those in Mr. Nightingale's ledger.

I pushed the two torn edges of the papers together. It was a perfect fit. I pocketed both pieces.

Well done, Flavia! I thought.

There was a step and a stir behind me, and as I whirled, something rough was clapped over my face, covering my nose, my mouth, my nostrils. I was filled instantly with a sickeningly sweet, stinging, and pervasive odor which I recognized at once as diethyl ether. Oddly enough, I even managed to remember the chemical formula of the stuff—$(C_2H_5)_2O$—and the fact that it could be obtained by distilling a mixture of ethanol—common drinking alcohol—and sulfuric acid.

I struggled to break free, but it was no use. Whoever had seized me was stronger than I was.

I clawed at the wrists that were pressing against both sides of my neck, realizing even as I did so that it was a lost cause. Carried by the breath, diethyl ether, like those poisonous clouds in a cheap thriller film, swirls up the nose and goes directly for the brain. There is nothing subtle about the stuff. Its smell is so powerful that the odor of a single drop can fill a room, and I remembered reading somewhere that a cat would refuse to eat the flesh of an etherized rabbit, even after it had been boiled.

I knew that there were just a few seconds left before I lost consciousness. The telltale buzzing in my ears—like a swarm of invisible insects—had already begun.

Half in a haze, I felt myself being lifted bodily in someone's arms, lugged across a crazily spinning room, and dumped heavily like a bag of bones into what looked, to my burning bulging eyes, like a large wooden box.

That—and then something that seemed to sound like coffin screws biting into wood.

On the one hand, it was the most terrifying thing that had ever happened to me in my entire life and yet, on the other, the most strangely satisfying.

Here I am at last, I thought. *Now I know what it is actually like.*

It was, in one sense, as if I had crossed some mystic finish line and had come home at last in a blaze of great glory, but yet in another, as if I were back at the beginning, tensed, waiting for the starter's pistol: about to die, yet about to be born again.

What would I be, I wondered, *if it turned out there really was such a thing as incarnation: a dweller in a grass hut, perhaps, like one of those carefree tribal beauties I had seen in the cinema travel films, whose only desire in life was to pull the most frightening faces for the white man's camera?*

Or a slave, perhaps, in ancient Egypt, milling corn on a slab for the flatbread which would feed the hordes of sweating slaves who were hauling stones to build the pyramids?

But perhaps not. The world was changing and I, whatever I was, was changing with it. By the time I came around again I might well be a famous scientist—a chemist, of course—calibrating the controls of some new and, as yet, undreamt-of device, which would permit me to peer into the most secret heart of the universe.

But first I had to suppress the feeling of panic that was rising in my chest. I fought frantically to swim to the surface of my senses. The first of these to return was memory.

It is a fact that oxygen deprivation begins damaging the brain after less than five minutes. I had learned this by studying the notebooks of my late uncle Tarquin, who had participated in several experiments with John Scott Haldane, the renowned Scottish physiologist. Haldane had famously sealed himself inside specially constructed glass chambers in order to observe, firsthand, the effects of certain gases—including ether—upon his own brain.

Haldane had come to the conclusion that lack of oxygen does not stop the machinery—meaning the brain—but destroys the whole apparatus.

I also remembered, although rather vaguely, that Haldane had analyzed the air in the sewers beneath the House of Commons.

It was not easy, though, to think. The ether was making it difficult to distinguish between thought and reality. Was Haldane a thought, or was he one of the faces that was now rushing toward me through a swirling tunnel at the speed of the Flying Scotsman?

Because my body failed to respond, I couldn't leap out of the way. Was I moving sideways or merely thinking about moving sideways? There was no way of knowing.

I felt oddly like Alice, falling endlessly . . . endlessly falling, floating, rocking from side to side like an autumn leaf, down the rabbit hole, but with nothing to grab: no cupboards or bookshelves, no jars of marmalade to seize.

Now I was becoming aware of a stinging tingle around my mouth and nose, as if the middle of my face had been held too close to a campfire.

Diethyl ether does that, I found myself thinking idly, as if someone else were thinking my thoughts. *It irritates the skin.*

I forced open my burning eyes, but could see nothing. Nothing but total darkness.

Have I been struck blind? I remember wondering idly, as if it didn't matter.

Consciousness must have been returning by then, although I didn't think that at the time.

I am in a box, is what I thought in actuality. *A coffin.*

For an instant, the odor of pine overwhelmed the chemical smell of ether.

But what are its dimensions? How much air is available—and how long will it last?

The standard coffin, I remembered, measured about five and a half feet by two by one and a half, which made a little over sixteen cubic feet, if my woozy mind was any judge.

Minus, of course, the volume of my own body, which was roughly half that of the coffin. I didn't actually work this out in my misfiring brain, but it made sense that the size of any container is proportional in some way to its intended contents, except in the case of breakfast cereal, of course.

If the average person breathes, say, seven liters of air per minute, that would work out to about half an hour's oxygen remaining.

I must not panic.

I must breathe slowly . . . shallowly . . . evenly . . . regularly. I must feed my brain without wasting oxygen on useless muscle movement.

This is easier said than done when the mind is already flying ahead to vivid images of a black and desiccated corpse being dug up in some remote forest, its features frozen in horror, its fingers worn to stubs by frantic, fruitless clawing at the lid.

No point in pounding at the wood, or screaming out my burning lungs. My attacker, whoever he or she might be, was still in the room, and would be the only person on earth who could possibly hear my cries for help.

Besides, I thought, if I made too much noise, they might well decide to take certain other steps to speed my death. Although I didn't want to dwell on this idea, I have to admit that fire—or water—crossed my mind.

A person locked in a wooden box is a sitting duck, so to speak, to flame and flood.

Better to keep quiet. Better to play dead.

I winced as the inevitable ether headache wrapped a rope around my temples. I had read about this effect, of course, but this was the first time I had ever experienced it.

How fortunate I was not to be suffering that other complaint which ether often causes: gut-wrenching vomiting. At the moment, in spite of the danger of the situation, I could think of nothing worse than to be locked in an airless box filled with my own stomach contents.

I reached up slowly, tentatively, with my fingertips. As

I had known it would be—feared it would be—the lid was right there, inches above my face.

"Don't dwell on claustrophobia," a voice said quite clearly from somewhere close by—or was it in my head?

My wits were beginning to return. Although there was still the stink of ether inside the coffin, it was not nearly so noticeable—or so I thought—as it had been.

As a scientist, I knew that things must be dealt with in logical order: A helter-skelter chain of thoughts would result in my death. It was as simple as that.

The first requirement was oxygen. Without it, there would be no second requirement. I focused upon oxygen and how to get it.

A breathing hole would solve the problem: Even a tiny one could be breathed through in a pinch. All that was needed was some small metallic tool to work through the wood.

Unfortunately, I had refused to wear my braces on this summer holiday.

"Put them in your pocket, dear," Mrs. Mullet had insisted. "You can wear 'em at night in bed when no one's lookin'."

But I had sauced her dreadfully, and how I regretted it now!

I wiped away a tear which, I realized, hadn't been caused by the ether.

I took silent inventory: no braces, no hairpins, no pens. Even my little silver crucifix with its concealed magnifying glass and switchblade knife had been left at home through my own stupid fault.

If ever I escaped this predicament, I decided, I was going to acquire a ladies handbag with a tool kit that would cause any burglar to drool with envy. I would never, in future, go anywhere without it. Not even to the WC.

No wonder women lugged all that stuff around on their shoulders! It was necessity—not vanity—that determined what you carried in your kit.

But wait!

What about the crochet hooks in my pocket? I had almost forgotten them.

Taking care not to exert myself—*keep calm, Flavia!*—I worked one hand slowly into my pocket. My fingers touched the L-shaped hook.

Slowly . . . gingerly . . . I extracted it and, anchoring its business end against the side of the coffin, began a twisting motion.

After only a few minutes my fingertips were throbbing. The awkwardly shaped hook was going nowhere. The varnish was too hard, the coffin wood too thick.

As I had noticed earlier, this was a well-made coffin. Too well made for my liking.

I mentally cursed Mr. Nightingale for various reasons, and as I did so, the crochet hook snapped in half.

Son of a sea-cook!

Although each half now had a sharper end than before, they were both too short to get a decent grip on.

I reached for the second hook. Perhaps the sides of the coffin were thinner. Lids and bottoms would be the thickest because, well, we wouldn't want any unpleasant accidents during funerals, would we?

I shifted myself to one side and resumed my drilling motion, but I soon realized it was in vain. The hook was slipping in my sweating hands.

I was breathing too rapidly.

How stifling it was in the coffin, and how heavy my lungs had suddenly become.

No point in using up whatever remained of the oxygen. How much time remained?

Twenty minutes? Less, perhaps, because of my exertions.

Time to face reality. It was now quite clear that if rescue were to come, it would come from the outside. I had exhausted my resources.

I shifted my head slightly, first to the right and then to the left, pressing my ear softly against one side of the coffin, and then the other.

As I knew from years of listening at doors, an ear to a wooden panel amplifies the slightest sound remarkably. If anyone else was in the room, I would certainly hear them.

Thank heavens, I thought, that my attacker had chosen a coffin which had not yet been lined with decorative padding of muffling silk or satin. Even a single layer of fabric, such as curtains, for example, can be frustrating to an eavesdropper.

But outside the coffin, the room sounded as silent as the tomb.

A breath caught in my throat as I tried to ration the air.

All right, I admit it: I wanted to weep for myself. I wanted to explode with fury.

Surely, I was entitled to that? A little display of fire-works to celebrate my entry into the afterlife?

Even a condemned killer was entitled to a last supper, as pointless as it may seem. To the best of my knowledge, no one had ever died from going hungry to the gallows.

Which turned my mind back to Canon Whitbread. What had *his* last meal consisted of?

Had he ordered up a banquet of roast beef with all the trimmings or had he humbly settled for Holy Commu-nion, and gone to the grave with the taste of sacramental wine on his lips, as had his victims, the Three Graces?

Suddenly, everything began to fall into place. I re-membered Daffy once reading aloud from Boswell's life of Dr. Samuel Johnson, in which that ancient bore had said, *"Depend upon it, Sir, when a man knows he is to be hanged in a fortnight, it concentrates his mind wonderfully."*

Although I had at the time thought this the most awful load of rubbish, it turned out to be true after all. The prospect of my own immediate death washed win-dows in my mind which must have become clouded over with the scum of my own accumulated pigheadedness. At that very instant, I made a solemn vow. Should I survive this day, I would never, ever scoff at anything or anyone again.

And—by all that's holy—it worked!

Suddenly—just as the good Dr. Johnson had said it would—the darkness had lifted and my mind was spar-kling with remarkable clarity. It could not possibly be due to the ether, which is known, in fact, to have quite the opposite effect.

My spirits rose. I would go out in a blaze of glory.

Hang the exhausted air in the coffin. I might be dying, but I would die a de Luce. I would die defiant!

How proud of me my mother, Harriet, would have been. How proud my father, also.

In a very few moments now I would be rejoining them.

Farewell chemistry, I thought. Besides my parents, I would also be greeted by some of the greatest chemical minds of all time: Humphry Davy, Henry Cavendish, Edward Frankland, Ernest Rutherford. How proud I was of my country.

Die I might—but I would die British.

How exhilarating that decision was! I lay rigidly at attention, my arms straight down at my sides, and began to sing:

> *"God save our gracious King!*
> *Long live our noble King!*
> *God save the King!"*

Although King George VI, my dear and beloved old friend, had died four months ago, his daughter, Princess Elizabeth, had not yet been crowned queen.

But she would be. Oh, yes, she would be! Before my bleached bones had settled into the English soil, Queen Elizabeth II would be seated on the throne and the world would be fresh again.

And now I was bellowing the words, the tears springing hot to my eyes:

"Send her victorious,
Happy and glorious,
Long to reign over us,
God save the Queen."

Now only darkness and death remained.

I awaited them, my head held as high as I could manage.

Someone was hammering ... hammering ... hammering. I wished they would put an end to it and leave me in peace.

"Go away!" I wanted to shout, but my tongue was dry and swollen in my mouth.

Then came the nauseating grinding sound of protesting wood. I tried to wet my lips but there was no moisture left.

In the darkness, I was being jerked and jolted, like shot game in a hunter's bag.

Stop it! I thought, since I couldn't form the words.

A sudden blaze of light caused me, in spite of my weakness, to throw up my boneless hands defensively in front of my face.

Someone was wrapping their arms around me. I struggled to fight them off, but it was no use. My entire body was an unpleasant, reeking jelly.

"Flavia?" said a voice, and I tried with all my strength to force one eye open against the stabbing pain of the light.

Again: "Flavia!"—more insistent this time.

As things swam into focus, I saw a face looming above me: a huge, round face, its features grossly distorted as if viewed through a fishbowl.

It couldn't be! It was impossible!

"Flavia," Dieter said as I threw up on his cashmere jumper. *Pity*, was my only thought. *It was such a beautiful robin's-egg blue.*

"Sorry," I mumbled, as he lowered me gently to the floor and propped me against the wall. I looked wobbly-eyed round the room in amazement.

Feely was bending over the prostrate Mr. Nightingale with a rubber mallet clutched like a cricket bat in her hands and, from the rising red welt on the back of the undertaker's neck, I knew that she had recently used it.

The poor man wouldn't have stood a chance against Feely's anger.

"How dare you manhandle my sister?" she shouted, seizing the man by the collar and giving him a shake that would have loosened a monkey in a tree. "How dare you attack my fiancé?"

Nightingale seemed not to be hearing her.

"How . . . ?" I asked weakly, waving one of my flippers at the open coffin. "Did Dogger send you?"

"We were outside in the courtyard," Dieter said, coloring slightly, highlighting the fresh abrasion on his chin. "Feely and I. Behind the coffin cases. We wished to—you know—to be alone. We thought no one would ever—"

"Dieter!" Feely snapped, her cheeks like Mary Poppins's. "That's enough!"

In spite of the risk to his life, Dieter shot me a secret wink. I wiped off my mouth and did my best to grin.

"Ring up Dogger and have him bring the Rolls around," Feely said, pointing to the telephone on the desk. "Then call the police. They'll know what to do with him."

"Don't count on it," I managed to say.

The rest of that evening is best left to the imagination, except to say that mops and buckets played a prominent part. Who would have believed that a girl could sleep so much in June?

·TWENTY-FIVE·

I HAD BEEN UP since long before the sun. The sickly sweet effects of the ether had still not worn off completely and my stomach felt like a seagoing barge.

We were going home today, but before we left, I had several things to do, one of which was to telephone Inspector Hewitt. I agonized about how best to manage this.

I had covered a sheet of paper with scrawled notes, with headings such as "Opening Pleasantries," through "Topics for Discussion," all the way down to "Thanks and Closing Remarks."

But what if the inspector didn't want to talk to me? What if he decided that unsolved murders were not a permissible topic for discussion with a member of the public?

I would simply have to take my chances. The worst the inspector could do, I suppose, would be to tear a strip off me and hang up in my ear. I'd have to prepare myself for that.

The hours seemed to drag by, as if they, too, had been soaked with ether. Dawn took forever.

When I told her I needed to make a personal call, Greta Palmer had kindly offered the use of the telephone in the private cubicle tucked away beneath the stairs, where I would be free from prying ears.

"It's on the house," she had said. "After all, we're sisters under the skin."

She must have seen my puzzled look.

"'The Colonel's Lady an' Judy O'Grady are sisters under their skins,'" she said. "Rudyard Kipling. The sly old bird knew more about women than he's been given credit for.

"I'll leave you to it," she said as she closed the door. "I don't fancy a lot of embarrassing gush so early in the morning."

I grinned, even though she was already gone.

Just after sunrise, I put through a call to Bishop's Lacey.

"Hello? Mrs. Mullet? It's Flavia. I hope I didn't get you out of bed."

"Lord, no, ducks! I was peelin' parsnips for Alf's soup before I go out. Where are you? Is everything all right?"

Poor Alf! I thought. His life was measured in parsnips.

"Yes, thank you, Mrs. M. We're still at Volesthorpe, but we're coming home today. I thought we'd better let you know."

I didn't tell her that I desperately needed to hear her voice.

"It's good of you to think of me, dear. I shall peel some extra parsnips. Did you 'ave a nice holiday?"

"Quite pleasant," I said. "We viewed the church, and so forth."

"I missed you," she said suddenly, almost reluctantly. "Missed 'avin you underfoot and stickin' your fingers in my custard mix. I shall be glad when you're home."

"Thank you, Mrs. Mullet," I managed. "So shall I. I trust you're keeping well?"

"Same as always. But I have to go now, dear. My friend Mrs. Waller 'as a prolapsed eucharist and I promised I'd bring 'er round some water biscuits for breakfast. 'Er doctor says she needs to stay off 'er feet."

I expressed my sympathies, we said our goodbyes, and I rang off.

I waited until I could no longer stand the tension. Was there the slightest chance that Inspector Hewitt had come in early to work? There was only one way to find out.

I wiped my sweating hands on my jumper and reached for the phone.

"I'd like to speak with the Hinley Constabulary," I said. "Inspector Hewitt."

There were various electrical clicks, hums, buzzes, and disconnects before a powerful, weary voice which could only belong to a police sergeant answered.

"Who shall I say is calling?" he asked.

"Flavia de Luce," I told him, and there was—at least I *think* there was—a fleeting silence.

After what seemed like an eternity but which must have been, in reality, no more than twenty seconds, the phone was picked up.

"Hewitt," said that familiar voice: that voice of which I realized I had been far too long deprived.

"Inspector Hewitt," I said, "this is Flavia de Luce speaking."

"Oh, yes, Flavia. How are you?"

At least he hadn't forgotten me!

"Quite well, thank you," I replied. "I should like to report a murder. No—four murders."

Curses! I'd forgotten to ask about his wife, Antigone, and their baby.

"Where are you?" he asked.

"Volesthorpe," I told him. "At the Oak and Pheasant."

"I'm afraid that's rather off my turf, Flavia," he said. "Perhaps you should get in touch with the station there?"

"I'm afraid I can't do that." I lowered my voice. "You see, I have reason to believe that the police themselves may be involved."

Did I actually think that? Or was my mind doing acrobatics?

"I see," the inspector said. "Tell me a bit more."

"Do you remember the Canon Whitbread affair several years ago?"

"Yes."

He was being noncommittal.

"He was hanged for the murder of three of his parishioners. Cyanide," I said.

"Yes?" he asked.

"He was innocent," I said. "He didn't do it."

"He confessed, as I recall," Inspector Hewitt pointed out. "They had no choice but to hang him, did they?"

I laughed, perhaps a little too loudly. The inspector was pulling my leg—making a joke—and I wanted to show him it hadn't gone over my head.

This little witticism was a remarkably good sign. Police inspectors do not make jokes with those they do not view as equals. At least, I hope they don't.

"Begin at the beginning and go on until you come to the end, Flavia. Then stop."

And so I did. I told the inspector how I had entangled my hand with Orlando's dead body in the river; of how Dogger and I had fished him out and laid him on the bank.

I even confessed to finding the rumpled piece of paper in the dead man's pocket.

"Interfering with a dead body at the scene of a crime can be a criminal offense, Flavia," he said, not in an accusing way, but matter-of-factly, as if he were examining his fingernails.

"I thought he might still be alive," I protested, rather lamely.

"And you'd bring him back to life by rifling his pockets?" Inspector Hewitt asked. "A most novel method of artificial respiration, and one I've not heard mentioned before."

I did not tell him about my interviews with Claire Tetlock and Greta Palmer. It was not necessary. They had told me things in confidence, and I mustn't violate their trust. He would find out all he needed to know about Orlando during his own investigation.

"The point is," I continued, "Canon Whitbread didn't

poison those three old ladies. His son, Orlando, did. They had been gossiping about him. He was a paraldehyde addict. I could still smell it on his body."

"I see," Inspector Hewitt said. I pictured him making notes.

"And who killed Orlando?" he asked, as I had hoped and prayed he would.

"Nightingale, the undertaker. He tried to kill me, too. He overcame me with ether and sealed me in a coffin to die."

"Good lord," Inspector Hewitt said, and my heart soared. "Are you all right now?"

I realized, even as I spoke, that the tears were welling up. I hadn't realized until now how close I'd come. I began to shake like a December leaf.

I could hear the legs of the inspector's chair grating on his office floor.

"Stay where you are," he said. "Don't talk to anyone. Don't go outside. I shall be there as soon as I can manage."

"Thank you," I whispered.

"Oh, and Flavia . . ."

"Yes?" I barely managed to whisper.

"Well done," he said.

Precisely eighty-nine minutes later—I had Dogger time it with his watch—Inspector Hewitt's blue Vauxhall pulled up and parked beside the Rolls in the forecourt of the Oak and Pheasant. Two minutes later, the three of us, with me wrapped in a blanket and sipping a cup of hot Oxo, faced one another across a table in the privacy of the saloon bar.

"You must tell me everything," the inspector said. "Even those things you might not wish to."

I looked at Dogger. Dogger nodded solemnly, and I began to speak.

It all came pouring out. Our chemical experiment with the diatoms, our visit to Scull Cottage, Poppy Mandrill, all of it. Even Constable Otter.

"Constable Otter is very ambitious," I said. "He keeps insisting Orlando's death was a drowning accident. I think he's covering up: protecting someone—or himself.

"The constable was involved in the arrest and trial of Canon Whitbread, who's buried under the altar, by the way, in spite of being a convicted murderer. I don't have the means of finding out why, which is partly why I rang you up, Inspector."

"I see," he said. "But, if such *should* prove to be the case, I must place both of you under a pledge of secrecy. This could have grave implications at the highest levels. Very grave implications."

"I promise," I said, and Dogger nodded assent.

"You see, Inspector, Canon Whitbread was . . . *framed,* I believe, is the word you use. A number of people knowingly gave false evidence against him. One of these was Constable Otter. A great many falsehoods were put about and allowed to spread. Orlando's train trip to London, for instance. Why? I can't begin to understand it all, but I have good reason to believe that blackmail was involved—as well as a certain amount of hanky-panky. Orlando had threatened to involve the police in certain letters he had received—which can be interpreted in more ways than one. But I must leave such delicate matters to you, Inspector."

Greta chose that moment to come bustling into the room and my heart almost stopped. I simply didn't have it in me to tell the inspector that she herself had met Orlando's train. She would need to make that—and other equine matters—part of her own confession.

"Would anyone like a bite to eat?" she asked, putting her hand on my shoulder. "This little girl's looking peaky."

I could have killed her!

"No, thank you, Mrs. Palmer," Dogger replied. "A quiet place to talk is all we require."

Good old Dogger.

"Very well, then," she said, seemingly reluctant to let go of me. She drew in a great deep breath as if coming to some decision, then said: "But when you're finished here, Inspector, I should like to have a word with you myself. In private."

I gave her an encouraging smile, in spite of her recent remark. I was grateful that it would be she who would explain to him that business of the brass stallion and the copper mare. When it comes to poetry, I'm way out of my depth.

The inspector watched her leave, and then said, "Tell me more about Orlando Whitbread. I assume you've compiled quite an impressive dossier on him."

Now here was a man who knew how to give credit

where credit's due. I tried, by lowering my eyes, to look properly humble.

I took the crumpled bit of paper and its matching mate from my jumper and placed them on the table.

"This was in Orlando's pocket," I said. "The numbers refer to the book of Timothy: 'But they that will be rich, fall into temptation, and a snare—'"

"'—and into many foolish and hurtful lusts which drown men in destruction and perdition,'" Inspector Hewitt finished for me.

With no more than a quick inspection of the paper scraps themselves, he extracted a glassine envelope from an inner pocket and slid them neatly into it.

"As you have suggested," the inspector said, "he was being blackmailed."

"Yes," I replied. "I believe he murdered the Three Graces in revenge and to silence their gossip, although I suspect his fears were greatly magnified by his use of paraldehyde."

"What makes you think that?" the inspector asked.

"Hob Nightingale saw him talking to himself on the riverbank. People assumed he was rehearsing some theatrical role, but to my mind, Inspector, he was having hallucinations. Paraldehyde, especially in large quantities, has strange effects upon the human brain, of which religious visions and hallucinations are an excellent example. He might even have fancied himself to be some heavenly avenger."

The inspector looked me in the eye and hauled out his Biro.

"Go on," he said.

"Paraldehyde addiction may result in delirium tremens and delusions. In severe cases, it may result in complete moral deterioration."

I let my words hang in the air.

"I see," Inspector Hewitt said.

"It's in *Medical Jurisprudence*. I can show it to you, if you wish."

"Thank you, Flavia," he said. "I take your point.

"Back to your dossier," he added, almost absentmindedly.

"Well, Orlando was an extraordinarily gifted actor," I said. "He was planning to re-create one of Poppy Mandrill's greatest stage successes, with himself in the starring role."

One of Inspector Hewitt's eyebrows went slowly up, like a hawk rising on the wind.

"I see," he said.

"In some ways," I went on, "he was like a child. Wanted to run away with the circus. Which is why his father was so protective of him."

"To the extent of going to the gallows in his place?"

"The canon was a martyr," I said. "Someone will have to make amends."

As the inspector made another note, I glanced over at Dogger. If eyes alone could signal approval, that was the message he was sending.

"In spite of his addiction, Orlando had many friends. Everybody loved Orlando."

Inspector Hewitt made a note. "Just so," he said. "But he obviously also had several enemies."

"The Three Graces?" I asked. "Well, yes."

"I recall the case," he said. "Something of a landmark. So you believe it was Orlando who poisoned the Communion wine?"

"Yes. Dogger told me that we must keep an eye out for the Invisible Ones. And who is more invisible than the rector's son at a vicarage? Especially one who lives scarcely a mile away in a tumbledown boathouse."

Dogger was sitting with his hands folded, listening. He was leaving things to me.

"Orlando allowed his own father to be hanged for the crime. It was all too fatally easy. He was supposed to have been in London at the time."

"Hmmm," Inspector Hewitt said.

"Since then he'd been enormously wracked by guilt. So much so recently that, several nights ago, he returned to the very spot where he had ditched the poisoned chalice, and swallowed cyanide. It was to be an act of repentance. Very dramatic. In keeping with his talents."

I saw a certain light come into the inspector's eyes.

"Unfortunately, he was spotted," I went on. "Someone saw him and clubbed him, not realizing the poor creature had already poisoned himself."

"And so," Inspector Hewitt said, "we come to Mr. Nightingale."

This was the moment I had been waiting for, and I meant to relish it.

"Well, you see, Inspector," I said, "when I saw that highly polished coffin in his workshop, I knew that he

was in trouble. The finish was too hard. He had not conducted a funeral for a very long time—two years, in fact.

"As you know, the French polished finishes involving
shellac and methylated spirits take a remarkably long
time to dry, which is why they are so seldom used. Coffins
tend to be required on short notice, and there's no time
for fine finishes. That coffin, Inspector, had been in his
workshop for simply ages. I wondered why."

"Whoa! Let's back up a little," Inspector Hewitt said.
"But I see what you're getting at. You believe that it was
Nightingale who killed Orlando Whitbread."

"Yes," I said.

"And his motive?"

"Money. Undertakers are the only ones who profit
from every death. Mr. Nightingale has had no income
since the deaths of the Three Graces two years ago. Except, of course, for Canon Whitbread's burial, which was
paid for by His Majesty's Prisons—which seems suggestive in itself, don't you think?"

"That's quite a leap, Flavia," he pointed out.

"Yes," I agreed, "—but I'm quite a leaper."

"I can vouch for that, Inspector." Dogger's face gave
away nothing.

"Of course, the undertaker is another of the Invisible
Ones," I said. "No one thinks anything of it to find them
in the church or the churchyard. Oh, dear, what's going
to become of poor little Hob?"

"We shall cross that bridge when we come to it," Inspector Hewitt said. "But tell me this: Did Nightingale

say anything to you before his attack? Before he overcame you and put you in the coffin?"

"Nothing," I told him. "I didn't even see him. He came at me out of nowhere."

"For no particular reason?" the inspector pressed. "Entirely unprovoked?"

"Except that he must have known I was on to him."

"Yes, there might be something in that," Inspector Hewitt said, closing his notebook.

How maddening this man could be!

"Well, then," he said, getting to his feet. "I shall have to leave you now. I have certain—ah—inquiries to make."

Which meant arranging with the local authorities to have Nightingale—and possibly Constable Otter—clapped in irons.

"Crikey!" I exclaimed, clapping my hand to my head. "Where *is* Mr. Nightingale?"

"I should be surprised if he's not having a nice cup of tea with Mr. Dieter and Miss Ophelia," Dogger answered. "They offered to keep an eye on him until Inspector Hewitt arrived. I don't expect he'll give them any trouble."

When the inspector had gone, Dogger and I sat for a time in silence at the table. As an old clock ticked slowly and companionably on the mantel, I suddenly understood—*really* understood—the meaning of time.

"Dogger," I said, "I want to go home."

"As you wish, Miss Flavia," he said. "Buckshaw is at its most convivial in the summer months."

I nodded in agreement as I allowed the dear old place to come flooding back into my consciousness for the first time in ages. The estate was now entirely mine to do with as I pleased: I could keep it, or sell it, or give it away. Aunt Felicity be blowed!

There had been recent indications that all the long years of legal wrangling would soon be coming to an end. The fortunes of Buckshaw would be entering into a new age.

The last pieces of the puzzle had suddenly fallen into place while I was lying only partly conscious in Nightingale's abominable coffin. Were they the remnants of a dream? A fantasy? A vision of the future?

I would probably never know how inspiration came to me, but it was no less real for all that.

"Dogger," I said. "We're going to have a brass plate made and mounted on the gates. Very discreet, of course. Very tasteful."

With Feely soon to be married, it made perfect sense. Of course it did! And hadn't Daffy just demonstrated her unsuspected genius at solving difficult puzzles?

My heart began to hum like a spinning top as I added names to the register: Aunt Felicity, of course; Mildred Bannerman, the once-convicted murderess and former teacher at Miss Bodycote's Female Academy; my old friend and would-be associate Adam Tradescant Sowerby, the florarchaeologist; and, yes, even my obnoxious little cousin Undine, whose weird enthusiasms and uncanny persistence could, in time and in the right hands, be put to good use.

"A brass plate, Miss Flavia?" Dogger asked.

"Yes," I said, drawing a rainbow in the air with my spread fingers. "And on it we shall have these words: *Arthur W. Dogger & Associates—Discreet Investigations*."

"Hmmm," Dogger said. "It does roll off the tongue, doesn't it, Miss Flavia? *Discreet* is such an elegant touch."

ACKNOWLEDGMENTS

AT THE END OF any long journey, the traveler cannot help but look back and remember with great affection all those who, somewhere along the way, have helped to lighten the load. Quite often—and quite surprisingly—these kindred souls do not realize either the timeliness or the importance of their assistance. Although they have sometimes even forgotten their contributions, the grateful author has not: They have become as much a part of the finished book as its pages and binding.

All thanks, then, to Eileen Roberts, of St. Hilda's College, Oxford, for her friendship, and for the many stimulating conversations about the rivers in our midst, and the role they play in detective fiction. Eileen's delight about everything from residential trapezes to toxicity has so often been the necessary tinder to my flame.

And to Doug Bell, whose generosity and patient companionship is embedded invisibly throughout this book.

To friends Doreen and Geoff Dixon, for putting into my hands so many rare and fascinating books—and always at precisely the moment when they were most needed. It's beyond synchronicity: It's downright spooky! Doreen and Geoff have also very kindly, and so frequently, taken me places I needed to go. Driving with them in the rain to discover junk shops and overgrown churchyards is simply delicious: like wine to the wicked.

Special thanks to Marie-Andrée Lamontagne of the Montréal International Blue Metropolis Festival, and grateful acknowledgments to the Canada Council for the Arts, the Embassy of Canada in Rome, and the Délégation du Québec à Rome for making it possible for me to meet so many Flavia fans in Italy.

To Beatrice Orlandini for being herself: a beautiful and most charming shepherd.

And to Marella Paramatti, of the Festivaletteratura di Mantova, and interviewer Chiara Codecà; and to Laura Grandi and Luisa Rovetti, of Grandi & Associati, in Milan: a thousand thank-yous would never be enough.

To the memory of my cousin, the late Bill Bryson, and his wife, Barb, for providing important photographs and documents, and for bringing me home again through time to my childhood.

To Denise Bukowski and Stacy Small, of the Bukowski Agency, Toronto, for handling all the really important matters with such efficient grace and good humor.

Once again, to Roger K. Bunting, Professor Emeritus,

Department of Chemistry, Illinois State University, whose wise counsel has saved me from excessive chemical mischief.

My chemically inclined readers will have spotted at once that I have taken certain liberties with the Levine-Bodansky method, by which the presence of paraldehyde is detected in biological fluids. I can plead only that great simplification is sometimes necessary, even with the most fascinating procedures.

And finally, as always, to my wife, Shirley, who has allowed Flavia to occupy our days, our nights, and our home for nearly ten years. If anyone deserves a medal, it is Shirley, and so I hereby award her the first and only Companion of Valor, First Class, for love and patience and tolerance far, far beyond the vows of marriage.

Isle of Man

Maundy Thursday, 2017

ALAN BRADLEY is the internationally best-selling author of many short stories, children's stories, newspaper columns, and the memoir *The Shoebox Bible*. His first Flavia de Luce novel, *The Sweetness at the Bottom of the Pie*, received the Crime Writers' Association Debut Dagger Award, the Dilys Award, the Arthur Ellis Award, the Agatha Award, the Macavity Award, and the Barry Award, and was nominated for the Anthony Award.

alanbradleyauthor.com
Facebook.com/alanbradleyauthor